THE BODY IN THE SWIMMING POOL

An earsplitting shriek made me nearly jump out of my skin.

"My gown! It's gone!" Becca pointed to an empty, crumpled silver garment bag lying in a ball on the floor in the kitchen.

"Someone stole the Scarlett O'Hara wedding dress?" I looked wildly around the room, but no gown could be found.

"First my grandmother, now me!" Becca pulled her hands through her hair and sat down, stunned. Then she stood up like a rocket and began ripping apart the room, searching in vain for the dress.

I helped her look until I heard a loud expletive uttered from the back of the house. Becca raced to the glass doors and slid them open with such force they jounced in their tracks. Keith stood rooted to the spot, his mouth open in a little round *o* as he took in the pool. Becca and I spilled out onto the sleek redwood porch, the obsidian rock garden calm and still.

As was the body in the pool. She floated face up in the gently bobbing waves, her gaze forever frozen on the brilliant sun above. She was clad in the famed wedding gown, the creamy silk and embroidered gauze now heavy and waterlogged. The voluminous dress fanned out around the body, appearing slightly blue-tinted from the pool's waters. . . .

Books by Stephanie Blackmoore

ENGAGED IN DEATH

MURDER WEARS WHITE

MURDER BORROWED, MURDER BLUE

GOWN WITH THE WIND

Published by Kensington Publishing Corporation

Gown with the Wind

Stephanie Blackmoore

KENSINGTON BOOKS
www.kensingtonbooks.com

KENSINGTON BOOKS are published by

Kensington Publishing Corp.
119 West 40th Street
New York, NY 10018

All Kensington titles, imprints, and distributed lines are available at special quantity discounts for bulk purchases for sales promotion, premiums, fund-raising, educational, or institutional use.

Special book excerpts or customized printings can also be created to fit specific needs. For details, write or phone the office of the Kensington Sales Manager: Attn.: Sales Department. Kensington Publishing Corp., 119 West 40th Street, New York, NY 10018. Phone: 1-800-221-2647.

Kensington and the K logo Reg. U.S. Pat. & TM Off.

First Printing: January 2019
ISBN-13: 978-1-4967-1751-1
ISBN-10: 1-4967-1751-1

ISBN-13: 978-1-4967-1752-8 (ebook)
ISBN-10: 1-4967-1752-X (ebook)

10 9 8 7 6 5 4 3 2 1

Printed in the United States of America

CHAPTER ONE

"You're either a saint or completely crazy." My sister Rachel put down her wand of electric-blue mascara and tried to catch my eye in the rear-view mirror. "You can still back out, you know."

I kept my eyes on the road, a slalomlike dip of pavement retreating from our Italianate mansion B and B, toward the other side of the town I'd come to call home. Port Quincy, Pennsylvania, rose up before us at the top of another steep hill. Pretty Painted Lady Victorians flanked both sides of the brick street in shades of lilac, butter yellow, and petal pink, like little girls in Easter dresses. The turreted and gingerbread buildings gave way to wide Craftsman bungalows and squat Cape Cods. Ruby geraniums, winking black-eyed Susans, and lush magenta impatiens bloomed in profusion in front yard flowerbeds. The sky was an overturned bowl of rich robin's egg blue, with a scrape of cirrus clouds scattered like feathers. I rolled down the window of my ancient tan Volvo station wagon, a vehicle I'd christened the Butterscotch Monster. The air was sweet and warm, carrying the scent of a recent rain. It was a gorgeous mid-May afternoon. Summer would soon be upon us, but spring still held sway, the world around me dewy and fresh and new.

"I think I'm a little bit of both." My heart rate accelerated as I turned to follow the road next to the roiling Monongahela River, away from Port Quincy and toward the countryside. "I can't just leave Becca hanging. What I would have given to have some help standing up to Helene last summer." I shivered despite the warmth of the late-day sun and recalled when I'd been in Becca's position. When I'd been engaged to Keith Pierce, Port Quincy's favorite son, about to go through with my inflated albatross of a wedding. Back when I was an attorney. Before I'd found out about Keith's cheating, called off the wedding, and inherited his grandmother's mansion, Thistle Park.

So much had changed. I was now a wedding planner and B and B purveyor, working with my sister to make brides and grooms' dreams come true. I loved my new career and my life in Port Quincy. I felt like I'd found my true calling, and had the good fortune to stumble upon a place I could call home. The only glitch was occasionally running into my ex-fiancé, Keith, his mother, Helene, and his new fiancée, Becca Cunningham.

"Well, I know *I* wouldn't even give Becca the time of day, much less plan her wedding to Keith." Rachel had moved on to the lipstick portion of her car face-painting routine, and carefully applied a swath of rose gloss to her lips.

"She extracted a promise in a moment of weakness." I'd tried to help the man I'd once thought I'd marry, and the woman he'd been cheating with, elope just this past February. But a blizzard stymied their plans to jet off to St. Kitts. Becca had acquiesced to Helene's demands for a big Port Quincy society wedding, and I'd taken pity on the bride. I was once in her position, fulfilling Helene's every wish for my wedding, against all my own wants and desires. I'd felt sorry for Becca, and though she was once the other woman, no one should have to stand up to Helene without reinforcements. I squared my shoulders behind the seatbelt and glanced at my sister. "We're lucky in a way that the Norris party canceled their big day. We can get Keith and Becca's wedding out of the way, and in two weeks, this will all be behind us."

The bride and groom were on a waiting list to be married at my B and B, and had accepted the slot from the last-minute cancellation. Their nuptials were to be the first week of June, and then I'd be done with them for good.

Rachel rolled her eyes in apparent disbelief at my proclamation as we reached the housing development of mega McMansions nestled in the rolling green countryside. I reached the cul-de-sac Keith and Becca called home and stifled a giggle. I parked the Butterscotch Monster behind Keith's familiar navy BMW in the circular driveway and cut the engine.

"Holy heck." Rachel dropped a compact of bronzer in her lap and yelped as a spray of tan talc covered the worn leather bench seat.

"I warned you." I couldn't tamp down the grin I

felt spreading across my face as Keith and Becca's hulking colossus of architectural wonder stood before us. The bride had designed the house, a busy collection of cubes and rectangles jutting out at improbable angles. The house was a dark red-brick edifice that would rival any creative toddler's LEGO construction. Floor-to-ceiling glass block windows glimmered in long, unpredictable slices peeking out from under a shiny copper roof. Severe and precise topiary huddled next to the structure in random groups.

"If this is a clue to Becca's wedding style, we may be in trouble." Rachel dusted off the last bit of bronzer from her berry-colored leather miniskirt and craned her head to take in every inch of the modernist structure.

"It gets better. Wait'll you see the inside." I advanced up the wide brick path to the double-lacquered front doors and took a deep breath before I rang the bell. It was flung open a nanosecond later, and I found myself face-to-face with a woman I'd never met before.

"You must be Mallory. I'm so glad to meet you." I found myself being gathered up in an impetuous hug on the threshold of the house, and I smiled as the woman next embraced my sister.

"I'm Becca's mother, Jacqueline Cunningham. Her father and I are so thrilled you're able to accommodate Becca and Keith so much earlier than we were expecting." I tried to listen to Becca's mother and take in my sister's reaction to the interior of the house at the same time. Rachel's pretty green eyes grew round as she did a double take.

The inside of the house was a study in nineteen

eighties' boudoir finery, with yards of white, cream, and ecru chintz and silk. Gold and seafoam green accents were scattered throughout the cavernous open floor plan, and everywhere the eye landed, there was peach. Peach tile, peach ceilings, and peach pillars. Even the kitchen cabinets were a shade of apricot. It took my eyes a few seconds to adjust to the glow of the room. A room that had my nemesis, Helene, written all over it. I wondered how Becca liked living in this split-personality house, where she'd designed the outside but had to acquiesce to her fiancé's mother with regard to the inside decor.

But I wouldn't be dealing with Helene today. Becca and Keith were keeping it a secret from the reigning queen bee of Port Quincy that they were to be married in two weeks' time. She would never consent to having the wedding at Thistle Park, and they were going to reveal their plans to marry the day of the wedding. I wasn't sure how I was going to keep their ceremony under wraps, but I would try. I didn't want to face the wrath of Hurricane Helene.

Rachel and I followed Jacqueline through a maze of white and peach furniture to the sleek black deck at the back of the house. I shielded my eyes as we stepped outside, briefly noting the spare obsidian rock garden beyond the low, rectangular pool. It was before Memorial Day, but the wide expanse of blue water looked to be up and running and ready for swimmers.

"You're finally here." Becca leaned down to give the side of my face a cool air-kiss, and I stifled a wince as she pulled away. We weren't friends, if not exactly enemies either, but I didn't need to exchange pretend pleasantries.

"I'm glad we were able to move your wedding up," I said in a neutral voice.

Becca gave Rachel a curt nod. The bride-to-be had donned a pretty pink sundress for the occasion, her large princess-cut diamond front and center as she folded her left hand over her right. She wore her ubiquitous flats, the better to attempt to match Keith in stature now that she was engaged. Her hair was its usual fall of shiny flaxen tresses, her trademark stripe of dark roots standing out at her part.

"You must have a lot of cancellations if you were able to accommodate us so quickly," Keith Pierce stated with a glint in his eye. My once fiancé was clad in his best prepster wear for this wedding planning meeting. He wore a navy blazer with gold buttons, a pink check dress shirt to complement Becca's sundress, and he completed the outfit with khakis and boating shoes. A bead of sweat dripped down from the bald spot forming atop his head and landed on his shoulder with a plop.

"This is the first cancellation this year," I responded, trying and failing to remove the frosty tone in my voice.

"And we're glad that luck was on our side to move up the wedding." A sprightly woman of an indeterminate age, somewhere between eighty and ninety, clutched my arm with warm, gnarled hands. She had a slight stoop, bringing her height under five feet, but her grip was firm. A full, fluffy corona of shocking white hair graced her head, and her blue eyes twinkled merrily like those of a young woman.

"I'm Alma Cunningham, Becca's grandmother," the woman gushed. "And this is my son, Rhett."

A short, portly man shuffled forward to grip my hand in a surprisingly hard shake.

"Pleased to meet you, Mallory." Becca's father had a little button nose, an amused smirk, and the same twinkling eyes as his mother. His hair was a longish iron gray, the ends nearly brushing his shoulders. He reminded me a bit of the Quaker Oats man. I couldn't help but swivel my head from Rhett Cunningham to his wife, Jacqueline. Becca definitely favored her mother. Jacqueline Cunningham and Becca towered over Rhett by an easy foot. Both mother and daughter had a sophisticated, if brittle kind of grace. Jacqueline wore a coral shift dress, her frame willowy and tanned and toned.

"And I'm Samantha, Becca's sister." A slight, short woman seemed to emerge from the shadows, dressed simply in a black tea dress and strappy sandals. "Pleased to meet you." Her lips parted and she gave a bright smile, and it was then that I saw her resemblance to Becca. Samantha favored her father and grandmother, with her short frame and twinkling blue eyes. But her hair was dark, the color of Becca's roots.

"My twin sister, actually." Becca slung an arm around Samantha and bestowed her with a winning smile.

"Twins?" Rachel squinted at the sisters.

"Fraternal," Samantha qualified. "I've been overseas in Colombia, working as a human rights attorney," she added. "I couldn't make it back for my cousin Whitney's wedding last October. It's so good to be home for Becca's." I found myself warming quickly to the sweet woman, who obviously loved her twin sister.

"Shall we get started?" Keith's droll voice cut through the air, and he glanced officiously at his Rolex.

"Of course."

I accepted the chair Rhett pulled out for me and opened the book of ideas I'd fashioned for Becca and Keith.

"You wanted a Japanese cherry blossom–inspired wedding, to mirror your backyard, but also to take advantage of the grounds at Thistle Park." I pulled out a photograph of the gazebo at the back of my property. It was festooned with cherry blossoms and stands of orchids, lit from within by red-lacquered lanterns.

"Oooh . . ." Becca shimmied in her chair as I slid the book toward her. Keith continued to look unimpressed, but I felt all my misgivings melt away. Becca seemed pleased with my vision, and I relaxed by degrees. I was going to give Keith and Becca a beautiful day, and maybe earn some karma points.

"The wedding will be a joint catering effort between our cook and the restaurant Fusion. For appetizers, we'll have sushi." Rachel took over the food portion of our planning reveal. "Dinner will feature ginger beef short ribs, coconut curry risotto, and Thai chili mint chicken."

"And the cake will be a five-tiered cherry and almond vision in pink."

The doorbell chimed somewhere deep within the house, solemn and gonglike.

"We've arranged for a small replica of the meal from Fusion for you to taste."

Rhett licked his lips appreciatively as Rachel and I emerged several minutes later with trays of food bearing appetizer-size bites of the wedding menu.

"And what about the dance floor?" Becca set down a half-eaten spring roll and delicately touched the sides of her mouth with a cherry-blossom-patterned napkin. "I don't just want a boring white tent."

Ah, that's more normal.

Becca's usual imperious tone had returned. I knew it was only a matter of time.

"We'll rent tents with a bamboo-thatched roof, and the sides will be mosquito netting," I smoothly promised. I pulled out the brochure of the company in New York that had agreed to let us rent the tents at extremely short notice. "They'll be translucent and will look lovely with the torches we'll place around the grounds."

Becca seemed to love the idea despite herself.

"And what about—"

"Well, well, what do we have here?"

Becca went silent as all our heads swiveled in unison to take in Helene Pierce, standing in the doorway of the deck in her trademark Chanel bouclé jacket. Her face was a mask of barely controlled rage, her pageboy fanned out above her ears like a king cobra.

"I see you opened the pool before Memorial Day," she tsked as she made her way to the table. "A savage move, but not unexpected."

"Mother—" Keith rose to greet Helene, carefully stepping in front of a seated Becca, as if to shield her. Becca frantically grabbed at the idea book of her wedding and shoved the large tome under the table.

"And what is this?" Helene quickly retrieved the book and did a cursory flip-through, her papery cheeks growing red and mottled under her peach blush.

"This looks like Thistle Park." Her voice was quiet and quaking, the volcano about to erupt. "And just when were you planning on carrying out these clandestine plans to wed?"

"In two weeks," Samantha answered brightly. She seemed to have misunderstood Helene's hot face for excitement, not barely controlled anger.

"Not on my watch!" Helene tossed the idea book into the pool, where it broke the smooth expanse of blue and sent up a splash. "And at Thistle Park no less? You," she turned to me, her index finger a mere inch from my nose. "You are behind this, once again?"

"Calm down, Helene." I took a step back from my once-mother-in-law-to-be and bumped into Rachel, who sent Helene a powerful glower. "Perhaps if you had been a bit more understanding, Becca and Keith would have included you in their plans." Helene was a pistol, but I didn't think she'd ever resort to fisticuffs, no matter how mad she got.

"Why, you little—" Helene lunged for me. I'd miscalculated.

A flash of white materialized at my elbow, and I barely comprehended the wooden cane that nimbly tapped Helene behind the knees, setting her off-balance. Helene grabbed at my elbow as she went down, and nicked the edge of the large silver tray laden with appetizers instead.

The beautiful plated pyramid of elaborate sushi returned to its marine beginnings and toppled into the pool with a satisfying splash. Edamame and a rainbow of sushi rolls bobbed upon the waves like a mini school of fish come to the surface. The contents from upended bowls of wasabi drifted around in the water like green algae.

And above it all was the frantic caterwauling of the woman I'd almost once called mother-in-law. She continued to carry on, splashing and screaming, channeling the melting witch in *The Wizard of Oz.*

"I can't swim! Help me!" She bobbed under the water again and resurfaced, gasping and gulping in huge breaths of air. Her signature gray pageboy finally succumbed to the effects of the water despite a prodigious amount of hair spray. Wet clumps of hair hung limply on either side of her face.

"You're in the shallow end. Just stand up." Becca's voice was spasmodic and high-pitched. I wondered if she was all right, then I realized she was trying to hold back gales of laughter. She finally gave up and began to hysterically giggle, tears rolling down her face, leaving inky trails of mascara.

Keith looked at his bride in disgust and shrugged off his navy sports coat. "I'll fish you out, Mother." He leaned over the edge of the pool and meekly offered his hand to Helene. She grasped it like a drowning woman and nearly pulled her son into the pool. He hoisted her up and out of the water, careful not to get himself too wet. Helene stood quaking with rage, a puddle of cold water forming below her now-ruined pale blue suede kitten heels. Rivulets streamed down the sleeves of her sodden wool bouclé Chanel jacket, and her plaid skirt clung to her frame.

"This is all your fault, Mallory Shepard." She crooked her index finger in my direction, the large sapphire wobbling. I took a step back and bumped into Rachel. It was our cue to leave.

"Let's get out of here."

CHAPTER TWO

Helene's retribution worked fast. By the next morning, she was firmly in charge of Keith and Becca's wedding plans. As Helene gave her marching orders over the phone, a sickening wave of déjà vu crested and crashed over my shoulders like an icy bath. I recalled my own once-to-be wedding to Keith. I had been no shrinking violet, but over a period of months, Helene had managed to wear me down in a weary war of attrition waged with veiled barbs and less-veiled threats.

I'd wanted a small affair, an intimate reception for thirty people after a short ceremony at the courthouse in downtown Pittsburgh. I'd mentally picked out a sleek sheath of a wedding dress, and planned on dinner and dancing at a restaurant on Mount Washington overlooking the glittering chasm of city below. But after Helene's interference, my plans had morphed into a bloated albatross of a pageant relocated to Port Quincy. The new plans had included a voluminous tulle ball gown and yards of pink, white, and peach frippery. A fine wedding, just not for me. Unbeknownst to myself at the time, I'd inadvertently taken on my first gig as a wedding planner. I'd planned a wedding for Helene, not myself and Keith.

And this go-around, Helene had gotten to Becca and Keith and made them fall in line in less than twenty-four hours. I rubbed my bleary eyes, thinking of the work I'd put in the night before, whipping up a new wedding plan to go off in two weeks, all according to Helene's specifications. She'd decreed that we have a new tasting a mere day after the poolside debacle, and I'd had no choice but to acquiesce.

"I'll have more ideas for you later today at the tasting," Helene imperiously intoned through my cell phone. Her commanding voice ricocheted around the room via speakerphone, and her pronouncement jostled me from my trip down memory lane. "Did you write all that down?"

"Yes. But I have to say, Helene, you really need to consult with your son and his fiancée before you make each and every choice. While I'm sure they appreciate your input," I tried to tamp down a wry smile even though Helene couldn't see me, "it is ultimately their big day."

"You listen to me, missy. I just saved their wedding from becoming an absolute abomination! They'll be thanking me when it's all said and done." And with that, the phone went silent.

"Yup, you're definitely crazy for taking this on." My sister materialized at my elbow and crisply swiped the cell phone from my hand. She flung it onto the couch, where it bounced under a cushion.

I threw up my hands and sat down with a huff. "It's too late to get out of it. Keith and Becca signed their contract and paid triple our going rate to move their wedding up so fast."

"At least it'll be over in two weeks," Rachel soothed, smoothing down the front of her magenta jumpsuit. She'd paired her daring getup with gold, strappy stilettos, shoulder-skimming gold hoops, and a jaunty genie ponytail atop her head. Her sun-kissed caramel tresses bobbed as she shook her head at the memory of Helene's conversation.

I loved my sister's outrageous style, though I'd never attempt to carry off a similar look. I'd dressed for today's tasting in a lavender dress with subtle, small polka dots, a white cardigan, and low-heeled wedges, the better to navigate the porch when I later set down samples of food and drink. My unruly sandy hair was scraped into a bun, and I'd gamely tried to cover the dark circles under my eyes with a touch of makeup.

"If we survive that long," I countered. My tiny calico cat, Whiskey, seemed to sense my consternation, and materialized on my lap for a cuddle. "But I think this is the worst of it. We'll take orders from Helene for the next week or so, and never have to work with Keith and Becca again." Whiskey purred in approval, as Rachel gave me a skeptical look. She raised one artfully arched brow and blinked with her heavily mascaraed eyes.

"We're booked most weekends of the month with weddings, each and every Saturday. And now some Fridays, too. We don't have to take on the likes of Becca and Keith next time; we can be choosier."

"True, but technically we're only moving their

wedding up. This just comes at a busy time, what with Whitney's baby shower and the Mother's Day tea." I ticked off the multiple events we would be hosting on my fingers and stood to pace around our third-floor apartment living room, carefully placing the purring Whiskey back on the couch.

I loved the living space I shared with my sister. We resided in the top portion of the mansion I'd inherited from Keith's grandmother and turned into a bed and breakfast. Our apartment was a pretty canvas designed by my decorator mother, a pleasing blend of cozy accoutrements and cheery, bright Emerald Coast décor. My mother Carole had furnished the space with a mixture of plump couches and funky rattan and cane chairs, with comforting fabrics and wall hues that were a study in turquoise, soft yellow, lime, coral, and cream. I loved returning to the soothing space after a day tending to my guests in the B and B portion of the house, Thistle Park, and managing weddings. It was a welcome cocoon of calm and light, and Helene had managed to break up the equanimity with her commanding call.

"C'mon, let's head downstairs and finish setting up." I headed toward the back stairs and down two flights to the B and B's kitchen. We'd renovated the house last October, and the kitchen space was a seamless blend of late 1800s' architecture and modern, sleek appliances carefully concealed behind period-appropriate wooden facades. I slid a tray of food for the tasting into the oven to warm and turned to face my sister.

"Speaking of non-wedding parties, we need to do more general event planning if we want to be bigger and better." Rachel leaned down to touch up a rose on the miniature, three-tiered cake she'd baked and decorated for Becca and Keith into the wee hours of the morning. She looked up, her pretty green eyes gleaming. "We should host more retirement parties, baby showers, and anniversary soirees."

"Whoa, whoa. We can expand, but we have to do it right." I placed some crusty rolls in a floral napkin-lined basket and tried to bring my sister back to earth. "It takes careful planning to make each wedding go off well, and we need to make sure things are running smoothly before we put more on our plates." It was a debate we'd been having for the last few weeks. My sister wanted to expand our business at a dizzying rate, and while I shared her enthusiasm, she had no interest in the books and figures end of things. I favored a more measured expansion, as we were humming along but barely in the black. It took a lot of funds to run a business anchored by a gorgeous but aging Gilded Age mansion, no matter how carefully it had been lovingly restored. I was all for bigger and better, but a few missteps along the way would be costly.

"We'll just hire more staff." Rachel stood from touching up the icing and flicked away my concerns with a movement of her hands, her long nails sparkly with glitter polish. "Easy-peasy." But her slightly downturned mouth gave away her concerns.

"Not easy-peasy. Our last few hires haven't worked out." I wanted to temper Rachel's pie-in-the sky ideas and reel her in. But I didn't want to be the stick-in-the-mud, just a smart business-woman. "Thank goodness we've found a reliable and talented cook." I tried to stamp out the grin slowly spreading across my face as I pictured Miles, the man we'd hired to help us prepare for each wedding, a man who, like most single men in Port Quincy, was utterly besotted with my sister. He trailed around her like a little lost puppy dog every free moment, when he wasn't whipping up delicious dishes.

"Yes, we've had a few duds, but I'm sure there are some diamonds in the rough, like Miles." Rachel conceded the point behind a pout. "And I'm working to get credentials that will help us! Remember the Foster wedding?"

"How can I forget?" The couple's officiant had come down with a stomach bug the day of the wedding. We'd held the ceremony with the bride's un-ordained father officiating, and they'd had to wait to officially tie the knot until the courthouse opened on Monday. While it had been a lovely day, the bride was a bit miffed to be celebrating the event without having truly been married.

"Well, I'm taking an online course to become an official officiant under Pennsylvania law. The next time we have an absent minister, priest, or judge, I can save the day!" Rachel beamed and executed a little twirl. I had to grin at her enthusiasm.

"She's right, you know."

My sister and I swiveled around to take in my boyfriend, Garrett, as he entered the kitchen via the door from the porch. He carried two steaming carryout cups of coffee, and carefully proffered one each to my sister and me.

"Why, hello there." I tilted up my face to receive a swift kiss under the watchful eyes of my sister. Garrett leaned back with a grin as I reveled in the familiar scent of him, a pleasing echo of spearmint and oranges.

"I'm right about what?" Rachel grinned and took a swig of her coffee. "Mmm, caramel and chocolate!"

"Both of you are correct." Garrett offered my sister and me a smile in turn, deferential to the core. Though we'd been dating for nearly a year, I never tired of taking in his tall and steady frame, today ensconced in a navy three-piece suit. He ran a hand through his dark hair and pressed on. "You can expand in a smart way," he said, giving a nod to my beaming sister, "but you don't need to move too fast. And I'd personally be thrilled if you hired more help." He traced the line of my chin, and I blinked up at him. "Then I could see more of your beautiful face."

I wished we were alone, instead of in the audience of my sister, about to serve a second wedding tasting to my ex and his commanding mother. But my heart soared at Garrett's words.

"I'll think about it," I promised, finally taking a sip of the lavender latte he'd brought over. "Maybe it is time to get some more help."

"I've got to get going. I have a trial underway this week, and hopefully things will be wrapped up before Summer gets back." Garrett leaned away from the counter and readied himself to leave. His fourteen-year-old daughter was visiting her mother, the director of a reality show in Los Angeles. It had been the longest Summer had been away from him, and I knew he was itching for her return.

"Summer will be here for the Mother's Day tea, right?" I couldn't wait to see her myself. A small smile played at the corners of my lips. I looked forward to her tales of being on set of her mother's show and getting to meet various celebrities.

"It can't come soon enough." Garrett leaned down for another fleeting kiss, and then he was gone.

"He's the perfect boyfriend." Rachel sighed and sank into a kitchen chair. "You've managed to scoop up the most eligible bachelor in Port Quincy, Pennsylvania." Her keen green eyes narrowed as she studied me. "And now you just need to seal the deal."

I sputtered and spit out a spray of lavender latte, which thankfully didn't land on my cardigan or dress. "I need to do what, now?"

Since when has Rachel morphed into our mother, hinting at marriage at every turn?

I'd been dodging not-so-subtle hints from my mother, Carole, that an engagement might be on the horizon. I was comfortable with things just as they were with Garrett, and too fresh from my broken engagement with Keith. It was as if my sister had a special kind of familial ESP and could read each thought in my panicked brain.

"Just because it didn't work out with Keith doesn't mean it's not time to take the plunge again." Rachel popped out of her chair to turn off the oven timer as it clanged out that the food was done. "I bet Garrett will pop the question soon. It's been almost a year since you started dating. You'll finally be married, and a stepmom to boot!" She grabbed my hands impulsively in hers, still clad in oven mitts, and attempted to twirl me around in a circle.

"What do you mean, *finally* married? I was almost *finally* married to Keith last year, and we saw how that went." I broke from her mad spinning, still holding on to the now-empty oven mitts. I felt my eyes narrow and cocked my head. "Did Mom put you up to this?"

"Don't be silly. I'm just saying it's time. You're thirty now, almost over the hill. You need to tie the knot before you get stale."

This time I was prepared, and had refrained from draining my latte. "I'm not a loaf of bread, Rachel Marie Shepard. I can't go stale." I drew myself up to my full height of five feet two inches, no match for Rachel's five-foot-nine stature, compounded by her gold stilettos. "And what are you getting at? Do you know something I don't know?"

My heart began to beat a staccato rhythm as I imagined an impending engagement. One that Rachel may even be in on.

I'm not ready.

The thought skittered through my head unbidden, but I instantly knew it was true. I was comfortable. Comfortable in my burgeoning business, in my cozy yet grand B and B, and with my delicious boyfriend. But I wasn't ready to take the next step.

Rachel gave me a maddeningly enigmatic *Mona*

Lisa smile and refused to answer my query. Deep from within the bowels of the mansion, a bell clanged, announcing our guests for the tasting.

"Saved by the bell," I muttered as we headed off to greet Becca, Keith, and their families.

The tasting was going better than I'd hoped, though the seating arrangements were puzzling. Becca and her family occupied one side of a round table anchored on the deep back porch overlooking the garden, with the bride flanked by her mother, Jacqueline, and twin, Samantha. Becca's father, Rhett, rounded out the Cunninghams, while Keith sat in solidarity next to his mother, Helene. I'd thought the arrangement odd when the families chose seats, that the bride and groom weren't sitting together. If I hadn't watched so carefully, I would have missed Helene commandeering Keith to sit with her rather than beside his bride with a firm yank of his elbow.

"Divide and conquer," I muttered under my breath.

"What was that, dear?" Jacqueline set down her fork and craned her head in my direction.

"I was going to explain how the reception will be set up," I recovered. I motioned to the wide expanse of grass, and the angel statues and fountain located at the entrance to the intricate flower garden. "We'll no longer be having bamboo and net tents," I began, taking in Becca's wince, "but I've arranged for traditional white tents and cane chairs circling round tables. Dinner will consist of wedge

salad, wedding soup, prime rib, and chicken piccata with roasted potatoes."

The new menu was fashioned after the very
same fare served by the Port Quincy Country
Club, a staid and fusty institution that had provided the duplicate menu for my own jettisoned
wedding to Keith. I'd recreated their boring classics to Helene's exacting and rather bland tastes.

Everyone ate the sample-size portions of the
meal with appreciative murmurs. Everyone but
Becca, who couldn't seem to muster up the will to
try a single dish.

"Excuse me." Becca stood so fast from her chair
that it caromed backward and hit the wooden
porch with a thunk. "I need to powder my nose." I
caught a glimpse of a tear blossoming in the corner of her eye and moved to follow her.

*This is going exactly the way it did when I was going
to marry Keith.*

"I'll go," Samantha murmured as she stood to
follow her sister.

An overwhelming shower of empathy doused
my nerves as I watched the sisters retreat to the
kitchen.

"This isn't right," I hissed to Rachel as we rounded
the corner of the porch. "Becca is no friend of mine,
but I can't let Helene walk all over her."

Rachel threw up her lacquered nails in defeat.
"But what can we do?" She tilted her head toward
the back door, where a more-composed Becca and
her sister were returning to the tasting.

"I'm not sure, but I'll make this right. I'll be
damned if Helene tries to ruin two women's weddings."

I wished I'd stood up to Helene a year ago, even though I'd thankfully not wed her son. I'd have to come up with a plan to give Becca the day she wanted.

"I'm sorry I got emotional," Becca said, her voice low and raw. "I was just thinking of how much Grandpa Glenn would like to be here to see me get married."

I drew up my head sharply at her pronouncement. Maybe Becca wasn't as upset about Helene riding roughshod over her plans, and instead was missing her grandfather, a man I'd not heard mentioned until now.

Keith reached across the table and gave Becca's hand a squeeze, then jumped up to trade seats with Samantha, rightfully by his bride's side. I found myself warming to him by a degree. He'd stood up for Becca, even if it was just a small step. Helene glowered at her son's change in seating arrangements and tossed down her napkin in disgust.

"May Glenn's soul rest in peace." Jacqueline quickly crossed herself and grasped Becca's other hand.

"Let's discuss happier tidings," Helene admonished, eyeing the cream-colored cake Rachel wheeled out, "and not be mired in scandal."

"Are you calling my father's death a scandal?" Rhett stood from his chair so fast it followed the fate of Becca's, and fell back onto the porch with a clatter. His formerly merry eyes were indignant and alight with anger. He brushed back a lock of gray hair and placed both meaty hands on the table, leaning toward Helene. "If anything, Glenn's death is a tragedy. I will not have the likes of you, Helene Pierce, besmirching his name."

Helene flinched and pushed back from the table by a degree.

"Almond white wedding cake!" Rachel's falsely cheery voice fell on the scene like a discordant wind chime.

"I'm sorry about your grandfather," I murmured as Rachel and I cut healthy slices of the ultra-traditional cake.

"He was murdered last year," Samantha slowly began.

"I don't think this is the time or place, Samantha dear," Rhett volleyed, a note of warning in his voice.

"Sorry, Dad." Samantha's pale cheeks colored and she studied the napkin in her lap.

"It's okay, sweetie pie. We all miss him." Rhett gave his daughter a fond glance, then seemed to snap to attention.

"Jacqueline and I have discussed the wedding, and we'd be willing to contribute a larger amount to defray costs, provided our Becca is able to make some last-minute changes."

I had to admire Rhett's attempt to try to wrest some control back for his daughter. It hadn't worked for me when I'd footed the bill for my entire would-be wedding to Keith, and I had a hunch it wouldn't work now.

"That won't be necessary," Helene nearly snarled. "It will be my pleasure to fund the wedding." Her countenance didn't match her ingratiating words. Her icy-dagger eyes clearly said, *Back off, buddy. Or else.*

Last night, Helene had directed me to wire back the funds paid by Keith and Becca in exchange for her funding the wedding. I'd demurred and checked with Keith, who had regrettably agreed to the plan. I took in Becca's staid black sheath and Keith's somber matching sports coat, and compared today's tasting with the happy affair of yesterday. That is, before Helene had shown up. Yesterday's poolside tasting had been an affair of celebration and praise, while today felt like a funeral march. I wished Alma had been here today too to set Helene in her place, although we didn't have a pool to push Helene into.

"Alma is late, even more so than usual." Samantha seemed to pick up on my thoughts and glanced at a sturdy nautical watch on her tiny wrist. "Should I call her?"

"I've been texting her," Rhett admitted, sheepishly placing his cell phone on the tabletop. "But I've gotten no response."

Jacqueline stared at her husband with narrowed, jealous eyes, and slid them carefully over to the phone. But Rhett was too quick for her, and pocketed the device before she could get a glance at its contents.

"I'm worried." Becca grasped Keith's hand tighter and pulled her black sweater closer as if to ward off a shiver. "Maybe we should check up on her."

"We can make up a plate to bring to her because she missed the tasting," I offered, moving to assemble the food. I cleared several platters and moved toward the kitchen, Becca hot on my heels.

"Mallory. You've got to help me." She latched onto my arm like a drowning woman, and it was all I could do to keep from removing her talonlike nails from my flesh before she toppled the trays of food I was carrying.

"I'm so sorry, Becca. She was just like this for—" I stopped myself in time, before bringing up my own defunct wedding to Keith.

Becca flinched, and dropped my arm like a live coal.

Oops. Never remind the bride that you were once engaged to be married to her fiancé.

"Yes, well, you do have the unique position of understanding *exactly* what I'm going through right now." Becca's face twisted into a frown as I used my now-free hands to assemble a plate of food to take to Alma.

"Time to go, dear." Jacqueline bustled into the kitchen and accepted the wrapped plate of food.

"Come with me? Please." Becca turned and grasped my arm anew. "I need to formulate a plan to take back this wedding, and I need to do it now. Before it's too late."

I stared into Becca's beseeching blue eyes and gulped. The wedding was in a mere fortnight. It probably was too late. But I nodded. "We'll make this right."

I left Rachel to disassemble the tasting and headed off to Alma's house. Becca brushed off my attempts to drive myself and deposited me in the back of Keith's navy BMW. I squirmed in the leather seat, imagining the pictures I'd once anonymously received of this very backseat. Taken by a private detective, they'd shown incontrovertible evidence of Keith's cheating on me with Becca in his car, in all the gory details. And now I was trapped in the same vehicle. There wasn't enough brain bleach in the universe to make me comfortable in the seat in which I sat.

"She's got to be okay," Becca worried, peering down the street. "We lost Grandpa Glenn last year, and I don't know what I'd do if we lost Alma."

"She's fine," Keith stated with authority. "She's ninety. She probably just took a nap or something."

We pulled into the long driveway of a stately home, one that looked vaguely familiar. The facade was white, with dark, hunter-green floor-to-ceiling shutters, the high roof anchored by two chimneys. Before the house gathered a cluster of grand oak trees. I followed Keith and Becca up the red-brick walkway to an impressive set of thick, square white pillars, holding up a wide roof over a red-brick porch. An echo of something itched in my brain, but I couldn't place it.

Jacqueline and Rhett bustled up the brick walkway, Rhett hustling to keep up with the long strides of his wife. Samantha followed more slowly, her eyes glued to her phone. She was the only one not behaving as if this were a fire drill.

"Allow me." Rhett inserted a key into the door and pushed it open with an ominous squeak. "Mother? It's Rhett and the gang. Mother? You missed the tasting!"

We all poured into the cavernous hallway, complete with chandelier and curving staircase. Busy, intricate green wallpaper covered the walls, and lurid red carpet stretched out as far as the eye could see. Gilt mirrors hung from the walls, and delicate gold lattice patterns graced the vaulted ceilings. I felt as if I'd stepped back in time. The grandeur and opulence could have given my own Thistle Park a run for its money. But something felt a bit off. It was as if I were on set in a period piece movie, rather than in a real house.

"Grandma?" Becca pushed through us and began to run up the palatial red staircase. "Grandma?" We all followed behind, Samantha bringing up the rear, the silence in the house more ominous.

"Oh, Alma!" Becca's voice rang down the hall and we raced to catch up to her. "Help her! Help her!"

Alma lay on the floor beside her bed. A series of rough, red marks marred her papery neck. She was unmoving. A gorgeous Irish setter paced around her body, keening and whimpering.

Not again.

I'd seen my fair share of immobile bodies over the last year, as serendipity would have it. I wasn't trying to involve myself in any cases or trouble, but some strange occurrences had happened. And seemed to be happening again.

"She's still breathing, but just barely." Samantha materialized at Becca's side and gingerly removed her hands from Alma's wrist. The beautiful dog moved out of the way and sat down, staring like a sentinel.

Alma's eyes briefly fluttered open, no longer merry and bright. She seemed to be searching for something, or someone. Then they rolled back in her head, and Becca screamed.

"Call 911." Rhett knelt next to his mother and placed his hands on her wrist. He took in a deep, rattled breath. "I think we've lost her."

CHAPTER THREE

The next day dawned serene and still. It was another gorgeous May morning, the sun a round orb slowly crawling across the sky. A slight breeze was warm and caressing. Fat bumblebees danced a minuet among the fragrant blossoms in Thistle Park's lush garden, and birds chirped merrily on branches. The world seemed bright and calm. The lovely day was almost an affront after what had happened to Alma the afternoon before. I wandered through the garden with a set of shears in my hand. I carefully selected an array of delicate pink roses, sunny yellow daylilies, and fragrant lavender to make a bouquet. Back in the kitchen, I closed my eyes as I placed the blooms in a vase and inhaled their heady fumes. But the lovely flowers did no good. I couldn't erase the image of Alma lying on the floor from my mind.

Yesterday, the ambulance had arrived as Samantha performed CPR. The paramedics had lifted the seemingly lifeless Alma onto a stretcher and carried her away, her son Rhett and her daughter-in-law Jacqueline riding in the ambulance down the long driveway. I'd been relieved to receive a text from Becca a few hours later, stating Alma was going to make it. And perplexed when I received a text the next morning, just a half hour ago, summoning me to Alma's bedside in the hospital.

"I wonder what Alma wants." Rachel materialized at my side and helped to rearrange some of the delicate lavender stalks. "And why it can't wait until after she's discharged from the hospital."

"I'm just happy she's alive. I'll help in whatever way I can, though I can't really see why the family would need me there." It seemed like a miracle Alma was even still with us, after Rhett's announcement he couldn't find a pulse. I wondered what was more pressing than focusing on making a recovery.

I left my sister to hold down the fort at the B and B and drove to the McGavitt Pierce Memorial Hospital. The vast health complex was named after the family that built Thistle Park, the McGavitts, and after Keith's father's family, the Pierces. No wonder Keith acted like he was all that and then some, when his family's names were plastered on all the important buildings and foundations in town. It was enough to give even the most humble person a complex. And let's just say Keith wasn't the most humble person to begin with.

I texted Becca for Alma's room number, and paused before I tentatively peeked my head into the antiseptic-scented space. I wasn't sure what to expect. I did know one thing. I prayed Alma was fine, as fine as she could be under the circumstances. She reminded me of Keith's Grandma

Sylvia, who had bequeathed me Thistle Park. Both were feisty, lively women who made being in their nineties seem like they were having the time of their lives. I wanted the best for Alma, not just as a force to stand up to Helene.

Becca's family was arrayed around Alma's hospital bed. The once-spry woman was propped up by a host of fat, fluffy pillows, no doubt smuggled in from her own home. A flat, anemic hospital pillow lay cast aside against the wall. A small photograph of the pretty Irish setter who had stood sentinel over Alma when we'd found her rested on a movable bedside table. And the woman herself seemed to be on the mend, though tired and meek. Her family appeared to be hanging on to her every word.

"You came!" Alma announced my arrival as her family's heads swiveled in the direction of the doorway. Becca's grandmother sported a jaunty Kelly-green-striped scarf atop her hospital gown, which gamely tried yet failed to hide the now-deep bruises on her neck. The scarf clashed magnificently with her pale floral robe, and seemed to be an afterthought to hide her injury. Alma had tried to sound cheery, but her voice was hoarse.

"I'm so glad you're okay." I moved toward the bed and gave Alma's thin, papery hand a squeeze. She gripped my fingers with encouraging force.

She's going to be just fine.

A spout of relief welled up in my chest, and I took a step back. Rhett fluttered around his mother. He fixed the angle of her pillows and refilled her water glass with nervous movements. The short man was surprisingly light on his feet for being so portly, and he seemed eager to make his mother feel at ease. Alma gazed at her son with loving eyes.

"Mallory, please take a seat, dear." Alma gestured weakly toward a chair flanking her bed, and I sat next to Jacqueline. "I was just telling my family what happened."

Ah, so that's why her family had seemed so preternaturally attentive when I'd arrived. I gulped as she began her tale.

"I let Wilkes out to do his business after lunch, just like I always do. That dog is on military time, I swear." Alma chuckled and gave a fond glance toward the picture of the Irish setter. I detected a slight southern accent in her tones. She seemed to enjoy having all eyes on her as she recounted yesterday's incident.

"I settled in for my nap around noon. All of the doors were locked, I'm sure of it." She sniffed. "My would-be killer must have had a key."

Becca stifled a cry and dabbed at her eyes with a tissue.

"But you didn't turn on the security system." Rhett's tone was even and devoid of accusation, but his eyes were undeniably narrowed.

"I didn't think I needed it!" Alma's hands fluttered weakly in her lap. "It took me months to work out how to use that darn smartphone, I'm not about to take lessons on how to work that digital alarm thingamajig." She stared down her button nose at her son, daring him to argue with her. Rhett just crossed his arms and sighed, settling back into his chair, muttering under his breath something about a collection.

"Now. As I was saying, I'd just tucked myself in for my nap. Wilkes fell asleep beside the bed per usual. I had an awful dream." Alma paused, and twin beads of moisture gathered at the corners of her eyes. "I dreamed someone was strangling me!"

"Oh, Grandma." Samantha leaped up to hand Alma a tissue.

"And to make matters worse," Alma paused to feebly blow her nose, "it wasn't a dream. I awoke, and felt the hands around my neck. The person was wearing a ski mask! Wilkes was crying, poor dear, and I couldn't breathe."

Rhett shook his head in disgust. "That's some guard dog."

Alma sat up in bed like a rocket, her weepiness gone. "He's an Irish setter, not a Rottweiler. And we all know Wilkes is a big baby. He's my confidante now that Glenn is gone, and I won't have you blaming him." She turned with kind eyes toward the photograph of the auburn pup, and gave the frame a small pat.

"Grandma, who would have done such a thing?" Becca chewed on her lower lip, removing the swath of pink lipstick that she'd no doubt carefully applied earlier that day.

"I can think of a few people." Alma sat back with a weary sigh, not able to conceal the wry tone of her pronouncement. "For starters—"

"That's enough, Mother." Rhett shook his head, his longish gray hair hitting the sides of his face. "You don't need to excite yourself with matters you should only be telling the police."

Alma opened and closed her mouth like a fish, her gray brows knitted together. She appeared annoyed at being shushed, and opened her mouth a final time. Then she threw up her hands and sighed, an exhalation that belied her weariness. "You're right, Son. No use getting all worked up now." She closed her eyes for a full minute, and I squirmed in my uncomfortable chair. I wasn't sure why she'd summoned me and contemplated slipping out. Just as I gathered my bag in my lap, Alma's eyes flew open.

"This does put some perspective on the collection." She paused and glanced at her family, who hung on her every word. Samantha sat up straighter, and Becca leaned her chin on her hand. I could practically see Jacqueline's ears perking up, and Rhett's intake of breath was audible in the now hushed room.

What is she talking about?

"I'm not going to live forever." Alma paused and picked at a piece of lint on her snowy hospital blanket. She seemed to enjoy teasing out the information. "And what with Becca's wedding just around the corner, it dawned on me. Now would be the perfect time to decide what to do with the collection. And I've come to a decision." She turned her face toward her granddaughters, all the feebleness gone. "Rebecca Scarlett Cunningham, I've decided to gift you my *Gone with the Wind* collection in its entirety."

The room was silent for a mere moment more. Then Becca let out a squeal of delight and bounded from her chair.

"Grandma, that's wonderful!" She showered Alma with kisses, and the older woman laughed in delight. "I'd be honored to receive it." Becca pulled away and returned to her chair, an earsplitting grin lighting up her face.

I panned around the room, taking in the reactions of the other family members. Samantha sat stunned, her muted, pretty face a poorly concealed mask of shock. Her blue eyes blinked double-time, and she fussed with her purse's contents to hide the act of brushing away a tear. She composed herself pretty well as she looked up and adorned her face with a shaky smile. But her eyes still held a wounded look. A fleeting flitter of alarm seemed to mar Jacqueline's face, and Rhett was downright mad.

"That's your plan for the collection?" He snorted and stared defiantly at his mother. "News to me."

Alma looked triumphant, if not also weak. She seemed to melt back into her pillow. A stray thought danced through my brain, pulling me back to yesterday. I recalled the impressive white house where Alma lived, the fussy period interior, and the feeling I'd been on a movie set.

"Your house is Tara!" I clapped my hand over my mouth, silently castigating myself for my outburst.

"Yes, dear," Alma confirmed, seeming to finally remember I was still there, crashing one weird family get-together. "I have one of, if not *the* greatest, collections of *Gone with the Wind* memorabilia in the world." The corners of her mouth turned up in an undeniably cunning smile, and she bestowed it on one of her granddaughters. "Although I should say, you, Becca, now have the greatest collection."

Rhett rubbed his hands on his knees with such

force that I feared they would catch fire. His once-serene blue eyes nearly bugged out of his head. He opened his mouth to say something when a nurse broke his train of thought.

"Time for your medicine, Mrs. Cunningham." The young woman placed a small, clear cup containing two red pills on Alma's bedside tray, along with a second cup of water. Alma dutifully took the medicine and blinked up at the woman.

"When can I get out of this godforsaken place?" She'd laid on the Southern charm for this request, the warm, honeyed tones sweetening her plea. Alma's query brought out a group round of laughter, and the high tension over her collection was finally broken.

"You'll have to talk to the doctor, Mrs. Cunningham. I bet it won't be long." The kind young woman bestowed Alma with a smile and walked out of the room, leaving the old woman to fret in her wake.

"I'll need to bust out of here soon if I'm going to finish planning the theater reopening."

"You own a theater?" I figured I might as well ask because I was still there.

"The Duchess," Alma said with no small amount of pride. "I won't let a little altercation like this stop me from realizing my dream, even if it has been decades in the making."

I racked my brain and recalled the snippet of an article I'd read online last week that had mentioned the return of a once-celebrated small theater to downtown Port Quincy. There was a big, modern movie theater at the edge of town, in the same shopping center as the mall. But so far, there wasn't anywhere to see indie films, or nostalgia pieces like some of the smaller theaters in Pittsburgh. The Duchess, according to the paper, would fill that niche. Garrett and I had been excited about the prospect of a small theater right in the heart of town. I hadn't realized this was Alma's project.

"There, there, Alma. You don't have to worry. I've been with you every step of the way for the theater relaunch, and I'm prepared to see it through now that you're in the hospital." Jacqueline reached out to touch her mother-in-law's hand, but Alma snatched it away as if Jacqueline were a snapping turtle.

"I beg your pardon, Jacqueline, but I've been making the big decisions for the theater. I'll continue to shepherd my dream to fruition if I have to sneak out of this hospital to do it. I don't really need your help." Alma neatly dismissed her daughter-in-law with a shrug of her shoulders, followed by a wince of pain.

"Like hell you don't need my help," Jacqueline muttered under her breath as she leaned away from Alma. Samantha gave her mother's hand a squeeze, and Becca's eyes cooled toward her grandmother.

"Besides, I'll have Mallory to see the details through." Alma beamed at me and crossed her hands in her lap, the blue veins standing out against the translucent, papery skin.

Say what?

"Um, excuse me?" I sat up straighter in the firm hospital chair and gulped down a flitter of trepidation. What had I walked in to?

"You do plan events, correct?" Alma arched one gray brow and peered at me expectantly.

"Well, yes. Weddings mostly, and a few showers and parties here and there. But the opening is in less than two weeks, right?" There was no way I was taking on another project. Thanks to my sister's nudging, our plate was more than full with a Mother's Day tea, a baby shower, and Becca and Keith's moved-up wedding. Not to mention the other weddings we'd booked.

"The details are almost all finalized," Alma soothed, while Jacqueline seethed. "You could whip this up in your sleep." Alma leaned back into her pillow with a sigh that I wasn't sure wasn't just a bit calculated to drum up some pity. I took in the Kelly-green scarf as it slid down her neck, exposing the now-angry mottled black and green bruises. A wave of pathos welled up in my chest. The poor old woman had nearly perished in her bedroom the day before. Who was I to refuse her?

"Of course I'll help you." The words flew out of my mouth before I could think of a way to let Alma down. I just hoped I wouldn't regret taking on one more project.

"And I can help too," Jacqueline muttered under her breath. Alma shot her a sharp look.

I only had a second to consider the relationship between Alma and her daughter-in-law, when the chief of police made an appearance.

"Good afternoon, Alma." Truman took up the doorway, his six-foot-four frame skimming the trim, his uniform sharp and imposing. "Your doctor told me this would be a good time to begin some questioning."

Alma gathered her floral robe tighter around herself and seemed to draw up some inner reserve of steel. "If I must."

Truman seemed to let out a sigh of relief, and I stared in puzzlement at the chief. He wasn't intimidated by anyone, and I couldn't see what beef Alma would have with him.

"But I do have one question before we begin." Alma seemed to relish making Truman pause in midstep as he crossed the hospital room. "How will you manage to find out who did this to me, when my husband's killer is still on the loose? It's been one year, and you and your department aren't any closer to a resolution." Alma's old spitfire demeanor had returned in full force, but the show she'd put on seemed to finally catch up with her. She leaned back into her pile of pillows and seemed to satisfy herself with simply giving Truman a steely glare.

"We're still on the lookout for your husband's murderer, Alma." Truman's voice was professional and sincere, if not a little curt. "You know I personally will not rest until I figure out who did that to Glenn."

I made a mental note to poke around the online newspaper archives to find out what had happened to Alma's husband. I could've just asked Truman, because he was my boyfriend's father. But the case was obviously unsolved, and I didn't want to rub salt in the wound.

Alma made a snuffling sound of dismissal. "Finding my late husband's killer is more important than what happened to me. We all know why I was strangled." The ninety-year-old sent Truman a look that clearly read, *duh.*

"And why is that?" Truman raised one bushy eyebrow, his gaze sweeping toward the last empty chair. No one made a move to invite him to sit.

"My collection, of course!" Alma rolled her blue eyes heavenward and threw up her hands. Truman blinked impassively at her consternation, his poker face out in full force.

"It's known in all *Gone with the Wind* circles as *the* premier collection. Someone obviously trespassed on my beloved Tara and attempted to strangle me to get their dirty mitts on my memorabilia." Alma stopped and cocked her head as if just realizing something, her fluffy white hair somewhat matted from her stay in the hospital. "My lovely things are still intact, I presume?"

Truman seemed to study the growing cloud of agitation gathering in Alma's eyes. He turned to the other members of the Cunningham family. "I'd like to talk to Mrs. Cunningham without an audience. If you all wouldn't mind, you can visit with Alma again soon." Truman was professionally evasive, neatly sidestepping Alma's pointed question.

"Anything you say to her you can say to me." Rhett stood and puffed out his barrel chest, attempting to stand eye to eye with Truman and failing by about a foot.

"Oh, just go, child." Alma waved off her son with a feeble gesture of her gnarled hand and crossed her hands in her lap. "Let's get this over with."

A discordant trill echoed from the direction of

Rhett's pants pocket, and he pulled out his cell phone. "I have to take this," he muttered. He leaned down to give Alma a brief kiss, then made a hasty retreat from the room. I followed him out, hoping to buy enough time to make it back to Thistle Park before heading to the dress shop with Becca. That is, if she still wanted to keep the appointment. Her wedding was in less than two weeks, but perhaps staying with Alma today would take precedence.

Truman paused in the doorway before shutting us out. He flicked his hazel eyes over Rhett and turned to go.

"Wait." Rhett jabbed at the screen of his cell phone to silence it and grasped the sleeve of Truman's uniform. Truman raised one bushy eyebrow and carefully extracted Rhett's pudgy fingers from his arm. He cast him a slightly reproachful look.

"Yes?"

"What's really going on with my mother's collection?" Rhett rocked forward on his toes and crossed his arms in anticipation.

Truman glanced in the doorway of Alma's room and took a step back. His hooded eyes bore no emotion. "We can talk about this later. I didn't want to upset Alma needlessly in her condition." He was professionally evasive and moved to sidestep Becca's father.

"The collection is a family affair, and I am due to inherit the items in question. I need to know the status of my mother's things."

What? Didn't Alma just gift the entire shebang to Becca?

Truman didn't know Alma had just announced

the collection was now Becca's. I squirmed and plotted my exit from the hospital, debating whether to let Truman know that tidbit later.

Truman ran a hand over his chin and glanced back to the hospital room. Samantha and Becca were fussing over their grandmother, and Jacqueline was staring out the window, shielding her eyes from the sun as she gazed over the parking lot.

"Between you and me," Truman began, leaning in to deliver his message to Rhett, "the collection has definitely been tampered with. I'll need a list from your mother and from insurance to match up to the remaining items."

"*Remaining* items?" Rhett spluttered out. "Things have been stolen?"

"What was that you said?" Alma's voice carried across her room and out to us in the hall. She must have had excellent hearing for her age. I recalled the small buds of white plastic protruding from her ears and wondered if they were hearing aids. "You tell me right now what's going on with my precious things!" I could see from the doorway that Alma had lurched forward in her bed and attempted to swing her legs over the side. "That collection is my baby!"

"I thought I was your baby," Rhett muttered a bit disgustedly.

"Now you've done it." Truman ran a hand uneasily through his thick salt-and-pepper hair and shook his head at Alma. A sincere and pained look graced his face. A loud clang rang from Alma's room as some kind of monitor went off.

"Excuse me, you'll all have to leave." A nurse

pushed past us and quickly bustled into the room, taking in Alma, who was struggling to stand.

"I need to know right now!" The caterwauling of Alma's cries rose above the noise of the alarm.

"Mrs. Cunningham, what you need to do is lie back." The nurse pressed an oxygen mask to Alma's face and the cacophony of the alarm ceased.

"Mother, calm down." Rhett strode back into Alma's room and knelt by her side. He spoke to her in calming tones for a brief minute, then dropped a kiss on her cheek and stole from the room. He pushed open a door in the hallway labeled Stairs, while Jacqueline continued soothing her mother-in-law. I took the commotion as my cue to leave and slipped from the scene.

I made my way to the elevator with a heavy heart. Someone had tried to strangle poor Alma. And I'd just taken on another task, planning The Duchess theater opening. A rueful smile did turn up the corners of my mouth. Rachel would be pleased that we had another gig on our plates, though I knew she'd agree it was an unfortunate turn of events that made it so. I jumped when a slender hand thrust itself between the swiftly closing doors and stopped the elevator. Becca bounded into the tiny space and let out a weary sigh.

"Grandma Alma just got a little excited. She's all right now." She twisted her massive rock of an engagement ring around and around on her ring finger. "She knows we have a dress fitting, and she sent me off to make sure I kept the appointment." Becca wore a mask of reluctance on her pretty face and swallowed as the elevator resumed its downward course. I felt myself softening toward Becca. She obviously cared deeply about Alma, and I was finding that I did too. The elevator stopped with a soft thud as we reached the lobby, and I motioned Becca out ahead of me.

"I'll be right back." Becca gestured at the twin streaks of mascara marring her cheekbones. She rushed off to the restroom.

And not a moment too soon.

There was Rhett, in all his glory, smooching a woman in the parking lot, not far from the lobby exit. A woman who was most definitely not his wife. Jacqueline was a willowy blonde, and this woman was considerably shorter. She wore a pair of black leggings and a hoodie, so I guessed she was younger than her paramour. But you could never tell these days. It didn't matter. Jacqueline was upstairs with her mother-in-law, while her husband was canoodling with a mystery woman. I craned on tippy-toes to get a better look as the couple pulled apart to get some air. I couldn't see the woman's face, but I did catch a swath of dark brown hair peeking out from a baseball cap, now that the hood of her sweatshirt had fallen down. She wore large sunglasses, the better to conceal her face. The woman broke into a dazzling grin, then set off across the parking lot at a bit of a jog. Rhett sighed contently, and a dreamy smile crossed his countenance. His Quaker-Oats-man equanimity was back. A cheating scoundrel Quaker Oats man, at that.

Does Becca know?

It was possible the bride knew about her father's

dalliance. And if she didn't, she had a right to know. Then again, the inner workings of the Cunningham family were none of my business. Meddling had gotten me into some sticky situations in the past, and I wasn't about to dive into this quagmire. It wasn't my intel to spill, especially on the eve of what should have been a happy day and a momentous occasion, the marriage of Becca, even if it was to my ex-fiancé. A trill of a shiver danced down my back. All was not right with the Cunningham family.

"Are you ready?"

I nearly jumped out of my skin as Becca surprised me by appearing just over my shoulder. I quickly scanned the parking lot before swiveling around to meet her now-composed gaze. Rhett was just returning, his eyes seemingly laden with suspicion.

"Of course. Bev is expecting us, and she's set aside some gowns you might like." I gulped as Rhett made a beeline for us. He searched my face, perhaps trying to determine if I'd witnessed his snogfest in the parking lot. I blinked and tried to project a neutral visage, all while I felt my heart jouncing around in my rib cage under the glare of his questing gaze. I must have passed his test because he relaxed and turned to his daughter.

"You'll look beautiful in whatever you pick out, darling. I'm so thrilled you were able to move the wedding up." Rhett deposited a kiss on Becca's forehead, and I couldn't help but grimace. Samantha took in the scene with narrowed eyes from a chair in the corner of the lobby and rose to meet us. I wondered how long she'd been there, and if she'd seen her father with the other woman. From the murderous glare she sent Rhett, I assumed she had.

"Mom is staying with Alma," Becca's twin announced. She linked arms with her sister and pulled her away from Rhett. "C'mon, Becca. You don't want to be late."

Becca cast a wistful look at Rhett as she allowed Samantha to pull her through the automatic lobby doors. Her face was laden with sadness, and she looked nothing like a happy bride-to-be. I felt a rush of empathy for her, and then steeled myself.

Buck up. You have a job to do.

CHAPTER FOUR

"**S**hould I really go on with the wedding?" Becca's blue eyes clouded with concern as they met mine in the rearview mirror. We headed north from the hospital complex, passing fields dotted with black-and-white cows. Soon we passed a bluff overlooking the Monongahela, the river water winking as it reflected the rays of the midday sun.

"It's what Grandma wants," Samantha broke in from her seat in the back of my station wagon. "I'd want to postpone too, but Alma wouldn't want you to delay your wedding now that you have a chance to move it up."

Becca nodded after her sister's reassurance and seemed to compose herself. "If anything, getting married in two weeks will inspire Alma to make a quick recovery." A slight cloud marred Becca's face. "I wish Alma were well. I could use her help standing up to Helene."

I kept my hands on the giant steering wheel and sent Becca a brief look of commiseration. "I know just how you feel. Helene bulldozed me too, and I wasn't even sure how it happened. She's a force of nature." I knew it might not be kosher to discuss my own experience planning a wedding to Keith, but the elephant in the room had to be addressed.

Becca let out a false laugh and peered down her perfect nose to give me a pitying gaze. "Our situations are hardly alike, Mallory. We both may have been engaged to Keith, but you couldn't seal the deal. In two weeks' time, I will be Mrs. Keith Pierce." Becca sighed a deep breath of contentment, with a healthy side of gloat, and settled back into the worn, tan leather.

Okay, forget trying to empathize.

I offered her a gentle smile instead of a piece of my mind, and mumbled under my breath as I rolled down my window to get some air. "And you can have him."

Samantha stifled a giggle from the backseat that came out like a strangled sneeze. The woman's concern over her father's embrace with the mystery woman seemed to have evaporated, and I began to question whether she'd actually seen it happen.

I slid my giant car into a tight parallel parking spot and cut the engine. As we approached the bridal shop, Silver Bells, I took in Samantha's ooh of delight. My friend, Bev Mitchell, owned Silver Bells, and her window display artistry never ceased to amaze me. For the month of May, Bev had crafted a spring scene both sophisticated and cheerful. A garden path fashioned from silver bells in a nod to the store's name wended its way beneath a blue silk sky with tissue-paper clouds. A garden of silk, tulle, and taffeta flowers in shades of buttercup, lavender, and blush flanked the path. And a dress form stood under a wicker trellis, awaiting its groom. The dress form wore a creamy lace explosion of a dress, a sunny yellow scarf draped over its shoulders. A pink parasol lay in repose on the ground, and several butterflies danced, suspended from the ceiling from invisible wires. The display was jaunty and fresh, and the serene scene calmed my nerves.

"Hello, my dear!" Bev fluttered around Becca at once after the jingling bells on the glass door announced our arrival. Becca allowed a fuss to be made over her, and Samantha stood beaming at her sister.

"And how is your dear grandmother?" Bev held out Becca at arm's length before letting go of her shoulders.

"We were worried we'd lost her," Becca said in a small voice. "But Alma is now on the mend. She's strong, and she won't let this get her down." Becca raised her chin a degree. "It's important to Alma that I follow through with my wedding." There was a tiny thread of defense in her last pronouncement.

"Of course it is." Bev paused hungrily to let Becca go on, but Becca wisely went silent. Much as I loved Bev, it was well known that she was the most inveterate gossip this side of the Mason-Dixon line. If something happened in Port Quincy, Bev would find out in an alarmingly short amount of time, and spread the story far and wide in an even more shockingly short amount of time. No doubt the notorious gossip had already heard all about Alma.

"But I do worry if Alma will be well enough to attend." Becca's pretty, pert lips turned down in a frown. "The doctor hasn't even said when she can leave the hospital. I wish I could do more for her."

"There, there. Alma will work hard on recuperating, and today we'll work hard to find you a magnificent gown that will help bring a smile to your grandmother's face." Bev smoothly changed the subject, and brought out a small smile of its own to Becca's face.

"Okay." Becca quietly agreed and sat on a plump purple chair, accepting a flute of champagne proffered by Bev's assistant.

"Here's one I think you'll adore." Bev returned with a rolling rack of gowns, each one prettier than the next. "It's an Oscar de la Renta, in ecru silk, with a mermaid hem."

Becca shook her head and pinched her mouth, as if she'd just taken a bite of something sour. "It's too trendy."

"Or this one? A Vera Wang ball gown in taffeta. This beading—"

"Oh, no, no, no." Becca shook her head, her flaxen hair momentarily fanning out, then settling down and exposing her trademark stripe of dark roots. "It's too . . . fussy."

Again and again the show and tell continued, with Becca turning down gowns with alarming alacrity.

"Why don't you just try one on, Bec?" Samantha gave her sister's arm a squeeze.

Thank you, Samantha.

I didn't want to butt in, but I thought Samantha's suggestion a sound one. Many of the dresses would look different once Becca tried them on, and she wouldn't get a feel for what style she preferred if she refused to don a single dress.

"How about a sleek sheath?" Bev wearily pulled out a slim silhouette of a dress, all slippery silk and silver thread woven through.

"Ugh, *absolutely* not!" Becca was the worst incarnation of a Goldilocks bride I'd yet encountered in my almost one year of planning, and I was about to give her a gentle but tough love talk.

"Hm . . ." Bev rapped her plump finger on her chin, and a slow smile graced her face. "Yes, maybe. Hold on a sec, ladies. I did get a delivery this morning that I think will pique your interest." She shuffled off to the back of the store and left us in her wake.

"That's it." Becca slammed down her flute of champagne on the ottoman in front of her so hard I feared the stem would snap off. "Mallory, we're catching a red eye to Manhattan. You need to get me an appointment at Kleinfeld's immediately."

"Whoa, whoa, whoa!" I stood from my chair and grabbed my own flute of untouched champagne before it caromed from the armrest. "Kleinfeld's has a waiting list several miles long. And I have other business here in Port Quincy to attend to. I can't just leave—"

I stopped short as Becca's hand reached out to grab my arm. Bev wheeled out a dress form clad in a striking gown.

"This is a Delilah French creation." Bev grinned proudly and fussed over the dress. "I'll need to fluff it out a bit, it's been sitting in the shipping box all morning. This gown was inspired by—"

"*Gone with the Wind*!" Becca squealed and jumped up and down.

Phew.

At the end of the day, I wanted my brides to be happy, even if they were being a bit unreasonable. Planning weddings seemed to bring out crazy, exacting standards in everyone, and Becca was no different. But this gown seemed to have potential, and we were finally getting somewhere.

"Grandma will be tickled pink." Samantha made a slow circle around the gown, nodding and appearing a bit wistful. The dress was worthy of a hoop, it was so round and voluminous. It was poufy, with a set of intricate ruffles descending into a deep V neckline, complete with a velvet green sash and a delicate smattering of barely perceptible green flowers embroidered over the skirt. Bev rustled the built-in petticoats and beamed with pride.

"Yes, it's a gown with the wind, if you will," Bev joked, her merry blue eyes twinkling at her pun. I let out a giggle, and Samantha laughed, a surprisingly healthy sound from such a small woman. But Becca remained unmoved, her pretty pink lips turned down in a pout.

"This isn't a joke," she whined. "This is my wedding, and I need to look fabulous."

Samantha made a face behind her sister. This time I couldn't help letting out a genuine laugh, one I tried to cover unsuccessfully with a small yelp.

"What matters," Becca said, allowing herself a

slow smile and seemingly ignoring my outburst, "is that this gown is absolutely gorgeous!"

Bev nodded vigorously, her butterfly earrings clanging and jangling with enthusiasm. "It's meant to be, honey. I haven't even placed it on the rack yet. You'll be the first person to try it on."

Becca simply glowed, two rosy spots of pink gracing her delicate cheekbones. I found myself warming to her and smiled despite myself.

"And it looks like the sample size zero will fit you perfectly, too." Bev quickly circled Becca's minuscule waist with a tape measure and nodded, her rhinestone glasses slipping down her button nose. She unzipped the dress from the dress form and held it out to Becca.

"Grandma will be ecstatic!" Becca held the gown up to her body and executed an excited spin in front of the three-way mirror.

"Then it's all settled. Let's try on the gown; it already looks like it'll be perfect." I opened the door to the dressing room and Becca gathered up the dress to try it on. I should have known I'd counted my chickens before they'd hatched.

"This will certainly honor your grandmother Alma," Bev mused, chewing on the end of her glasses. "And because she has suffered so much as of late, you could take the gesture so much further."

My ears practically pricked up as Becca stopped before the dressing room door. "What do you mean?"

"Well," Bev began excitedly, seeming to warm to her idea, "you could have a *Gone with the Wind*–themed wedding as a way to venerate Alma!"

No, no, no!

The original plans for the Japanese-cherry-blossom-inspired wedding flashed before my eyes, muddled with Helene's peach plans, and I considered for one moment changing up the wedding again to accommodate this new idea.

"Um, Bev?" I pleaded with the dress store owner, but she didn't seem to hear.

"And," Bev continued, placing the glasses back on her nose, "I know your grandmother is reopening The Duchess theater soon, too. A *Gone with the Wind* wedding later this year would dovetail so nicely with that."

She doesn't know the wedding is in two weeks.

My heart rate accelerated. I wondered if it would have made the monitors in Alma's hospital room clang out. I gestured wildly to Bev from behind Becca's back to stop suggesting ideas. Becca took that moment to turn around and offer me a quizzical, and pitying, look. I must have appeared to have been doing some kind of interpretive dance, what with shaking my head vehemently, my hands held up in front, and waving. Bev and Samantha started giggling.

"A *Gone with the Wind*–themed wedding will be *perfect*," Becca intoned. "Mallory, why didn't you think of it?"

I blinked back at Becca, willing myself to be calm.

"Don't look so alarmed." Bev materialized at my side. "You'll be able to whip up a lovely, Southern-themed wedding to emulate *Gone with the Wind*. When's the wedding?"

"In less than two weeks," I mumbled, my miserable voice barely above a whisper.

"Two *weeks*?" Bev dropped her tape measure and her cheeks colored. "Oh, dear," she spluttered. "Perhaps, Becca dear, the Scarlett O'Hara–inspired gown will be enough in and of itself to honor your grandmother Alma. You could stick with your original wedding theme for the rest of the nuptials." Bev furiously backpedaled, but I knew it was no use. The cat was already out of the bag.

"We'll just scrap all our current plans," Becca said crisply. She undid all my carefully, if not hastily, drawn-up elaborate plans for the two weddings we'd already contemplated.

Maybe the third time's the charm.

I'm so sorry, Bev mouthed behind Becca's back. I gave my friend a weak smile and shrugged.

"It's probably for the best," I admitted as Becca disappeared into the dressing room to try on the gown. "Helene has taken over Becca's latest iteration of her wedding, and Becca wasn't happy about any part of the plan. She's actually excited about this. And even Helene won't be able to take this new wedding plan off the table, because it's honoring Alma in her current state."

I sank into a velvet love seat, ideas swirling around in my head. A *Gone with the Wind* wedding would be traditional, if not exactly Southern couture, and Helene wouldn't be able to quibble about it too much. But she would try to get her way in the end. I closed my eyes and thought of the dizzying jumble of contracts and contacts I'd amassed to quickly pull off the scrapped cherry blossom theme, Helene's peach pageant, and what I'd have to rustle up to plan this new wedding. I worried in the end that I would make no one happy. And I also wondered if the logistics would work out at this late date. There was the reality of florists and table linen rentals, tents and dance floors. Helene or Keith would no doubt attempt to throw money at the problem to make a wedding materialize in such a short time, and I hoped it would work.

"I'm sorry about my sister." Samantha sat next to me and offered me a rueful smile. "She's hard to please, but I think this really is the last change in plans. Let me know what I can do to help this wedding go off."

I grinned at Samantha, and turned to see a radiant Becca emerge from the dressing room. The white gown with green accents fit her as if it had been tailored precisely for her tiny frame. The voluminous bell skirt floated across the floor as Becca made her way to a platform with a triptych mirror. She brushed tears from her eyes as she fluffed the delicate ruffles of the dress's neckline, her shining hair brushing her shoulders. I had to admit she looked lovely.

"This is the one." Becca quickly composed herself, and dabbed at her eyes to quell a run of mascara. Samantha quietly studied her sister, her smile falling. I couldn't help but compare the twins, who seemed so different in appearance and demeanor. It couldn't have been easy sharing the spotlight with Becca. I had some inside knowledge of the situation, growing up with Rachel. We were opposites in so many respects, and it might have been even harder if we had been the same exact age. Still, I shared a strong and irreplaceable bond with my sister, and I would do anything for her, and I knew she would for me too. And there seemed to be just as strong a bond between Becca and Samantha.

"You were meant for this gown, sweetie." Bev helped Becca step down from the platform and hustled her off to the dressing room. "We'll barely have to alter it. We'll just let out an inch of the hem if you're planning to wear heels, because you're so tall. I'll work double-time to get this dress ready in time."

"Thank you, Bev," I gushed to the seamstress.

Becca sniffed. "Of course you'll alter the dress," she whined, squinting at the price tag. "I'm paying a fortune for this gown!"

I felt my eyebrows shoot up in shock at her pettiness, but before I could come back with a measured reply, an altercation grabbed everyone's attention. Two increasingly heated voices drifted over from a dressing room across the store. I caught snippets of a piqued conversation between two women, something about money and time and leaving.

A pretty brunette spilled out of the dressing room in question. She smoothed her silver robe embroidered with the Silver Bells logo and attempted to compose herself. She scanned the store with large brown eyes, and did a double take when her gaze alighted on Becca.

"Becca Cunningham, is that you?" A wily smile graced the woman's face as she advanced across the store to greet us.

* * *

Becca emerged from her dressing room clad in a silver robe matching the brunette's. She adopted a haughty look and sat down on a plush purple chair where she sipped the dregs of her champagne. She took her time in answering the woman.

"Felicity. So interesting to see you here." Becca, now composed, smiled serenely and identified the brunette by name. I had to give Becca credit. Felicity had originally seemed to rattle her, but now Becca was calm and in control.

"So you're finally sealing the deal with Keith?" Felicity flipped a lustrous lock of chestnut hair over her shoulder, where it slithered down the back of her robe.

Becca smiled, but it didn't reach her eyes. "I'll be wed in two weeks. Mallory," she gestured toward me with a regal flip of her hand, "had an opening to accommodate us early. Keith and I are so in love, we can't wait."

"And I hear your grandmother has suffered a mishap. How is dear Alma?" Felicity's sharp beauty was piqued as her mouth curved up into a cunning smile.

Becca's own fake smile dissolved into an ice-hard line. "My grandmother is recuperating in the hospital. Someone attacked her and tried to steal her *Gone with the Wind* collection."

Felicity's deep-set brown eyes went wide. "That shouldn't have been able to happen. Alma has a duty to protect one of the greatest *Gone with the Wind* collections." A wry smile lifted up the corners of Felicity's lips. "Maybe she'll finally sell all her items now that it's proven she can't adequately protect the memorabilia. I made her an offer myself just last week, but Alma wouldn't hear of it."

Samantha took a closer look at Felicity after this last admission. The attorney's eyes flicked carefully over Felicity, studying her with keen interest.

Becca rolled her eyes heavenward and more firmly tied her robe's sash. "You've asked my grandma several times to sell, and each time she's had the same answer. Absolutely not! Here's a clue, Felicity, since you seem especially dense when it comes to this matter. Alma's not selling today, or tomorrow. Not ever! Especially now that she's given me—"

Bev chose that moment to bustle back in, her entrance stopping Becca from revealing that Alma had given the collection to her as an early wedding present. Bev wheeled the Scarlett O'Hara–inspired gown on a dress form, a garment bag slung over her arm. "I'll just ring you up, Becca, dear." Bev seemed to want to get us the heck out of her store, and I didn't blame her. The tension was unbearable between Becca and Felicity.

"Oh. My. Goodness." Felicity materialized next to the gown and stood in rapture before the dress form. She took in the wide expanse of white with the barely perceptible overlay of the most delicate spray of green flowers, and the off-the-shoulder sleeves with the neckline's riot of frothy ruffles.

"A *Gone with the Wind* gown," Felicity nearly whispered in her reverence. "I *must* have it!" I realized who Felicity reminded me of. With her lustrous dark locks and delicate looks, she'd be a close double of a young Vivien Leigh. The dress would look fabulous on her, just as it had on Becca.

"You're too late." Becca nimbly sprang up from her chair and positioned herself between Felicity and the dress, as if the dress form were a human being she was trying to protect from intimidation. "This dress is mine."

Felicity let out a joyless laugh. "Don't be silly. You haven't purchased it yet. And you don't even care about *Gone with the Wind.*"

It was a fair point. Felicity obviously had a vested interest in the gown if she had been pursuing purchase of Alma's collection. But, Becca had tried on the dress first.

Felicity stretched out a hand to lovingly caress the gown. Becca, in a flash, rapped on Felicity's fingers and pulled the dress form back a foot.

"You struck me! How *dare* you! That's assault." A stung look marred Felicity's pretty face.

"I barely touched you. And I had to get you to stop soiling my gown!" Becca stuck out her lower lip like a chastised toddler and crossed her arms over her robe. Samantha slung an arm around her twin, seemingly as much to curtail her from resorting to getting physical as to protect her.

"Besides," Becca continued, "the last time I checked, Felicity, an engagement usually precedes a wedding. And because you aren't engaged, and I am, I take precedence for the dress. You can find another *Gone with the Wind* dress to fuel your obsession. This dress was meant for me, and for my wedding." Becca presented her case as if she were the attorney she'd trained to be and was delivering a triumphant closing argument.

But a smug smile graced Felicity's face. She dangled an impossibly large diamond in Becca's face, her left ring finger weighed down by the intricate Edwardian design of hundreds of tiny diamonds flanking one seriously colossal center stone.

Becca blanched at the beacon of a ring shoved in her face, and I watched a kaleidoscope of emotions cycle over her. She seemed to rest on jealousy, and bit her lip. "You finally got Tanner to pop the question, Felicity? What has it been, five years?"

Felicity snorted as she polished the gleaming bauble with the sleeve of her silver robe. "Hardly. We got engaged last night. We did our engagement photos this morning. Look for an official announcement in the newspaper. Tanner and I will be wed by the end of summer."

Becca seemed to fixate and salivate on Felicity's ring. "Did your father design this?" Her voice was a thinly suppressed strain of jealousy.

Felicity's father.

That was it. The woman looked familiar, in addition to bearing a passable resemblance to Vivien Leigh. I could see an echo of the town jeweler, Roger Fournier, in her features.

"Daddy and Tanner designed it together," Felicity confirmed. "Good things come to those who wait, Becca. I'm not rushing through my wedding and marriage. It makes me wonder why you are. What do you have to hide? I mean, come on! Getting married in two weeks because there's been a cancellation?"

Becca's hands curled into fists, her own massive engagement ring making a painful-looking kind of brass knuckle.

"Easy there, bruiser." I squeezed Becca's shoulder and mentally begged her to remember she was in a place of business, not a boxing ring.

"I'm sure we can settle this amicably," Samantha chimed in, her lawyer hat still on. Samantha's voice of reason seemed to soothe her twin.

"I suppose," Becca grumbled.

"And since Bev was just ringing us up, when she returns, we'll finish our transaction and go," I finished.

And it would have been a sensible plan. Except Felicity appeared to have lost her mind and lunged for the dress.

"Get your mitts off of it!" Becca pushed Felicity away and attempted to wheel the heavy dress form behind a counter displaying twinkling, delicate bridal jewelry. Felicity jammed one long leg into the opening behind the counter and cut Becca off.

"This dress belongs with me!" Felicity grabbed one sleeve and gave a sharp tug. Becca grabbed the voluminous skirt and pulled the dress toward her. A rough tug-of-war with the delicate gown as a rope ensued. The poor gown didn't stand a chance.

The sickening rip of fabric made time stand still. Both women dropped their holds on the dress, and the heavy dress form toppled over. The back of the dress was utterly destroyed. The poufy skirt displayed its innards, the layers of sewed-in petticoats and stiff netting that created the bell skirt spilling out of the gaping maw of torn fabric.

Felicity began to hyperventilate. "You. You *ruined* it! You ruin everything, Becca Cunningham." Her eyes wildly tore around the room, and settled on a half-drunk flute of champagne. Felicity picked up the vessel and threw the contents all over Becca. It was a hideous reincarnation of *Girls Gone Wild* come to Port Quincy, Pennsylvania. The elegant setting of the Silver Bells dress shop didn't make it any classier. The champagne landed in Becca's face in a bubbly jet.

Becca stood still, the sticky wine trailing down her checks. She brushed champagne from her eyes and calmly retrieved a tissue from the counter. "Now we're talking assault charges, Felicity."

Bev returned, and all the color drained from her face. "What in heaven's name is going on in my store?" She swiveled and pointed a finger at Felicity. "You. And you." This time Becca got the finger point of censure. "I want to know right now."

We all sheepishly studied the smooth expanse of dark wood floor. For once I was at a loss for words. Normally, I would be advocating for my bride, but I couldn't find the will to do so today. And Bev now seemed silenced too. She appeared appalled by the shenanigans in her store, usually a place for joyful celebration and nervous but good-willed energy. Oh, I'd witnessed the occasional spat between competing bridezillas and momzillas. But things never resorted to knock-down, drag-out fights.

Bev wrung her plump, bejeweled hands. The butterflies in her beehive shook with apparent consternation. I had to reflect on the irony. Bev loved drama and a good story as she claimed her title as Port Quincy's resident queen of gossip. But she wasn't enjoying this crazy tale as it unfolded in her own store.

"All right, girls, we'll settle this before you manage to tear my store apart." Bev took a deep breath and clucked over Becca and Felicity like a mother hen. "Maybe neither of you should wear this dress," she chastised.

"But—" Becca began to argue.

"I did offer it to you first," Bev cut her off, "but in light of what has happened to this poor gown, I feel a bit of fairness needs to be injected into the situation. We'll flip a coin," she dramatically announced, the judge and jury of final decision-making in her store.

"Here." I dug around the contents of my purse and retrieved my wallet, selecting a single tarnished penny.

"I call heads." Felicity seethed as Bev placed the penny on her thumbnail. Felicity's eyes were aglow with hunger and anger, and I knew I never wanted to cross her.

Bev flipped the coin, and it soared through the air in a dramatic arc.

"Let me see!" Becca shoved Felicity out of the way and made for the penny as it rolled around on the sleek hardwood floor like a demented top and finally came to rest.

"Tails!" Bev swooped in to pluck the coin and turned to Becca. "The dress is yours."

Dark clouds gathered in the irises of Felicity's eyes, and she swept from the shop, still wearing a Silver Bells robe. She clutched her clothes in a ball to her chest, and tore down the street wearing flip-flops.

Bev rung Becca up and accepted her debit card before carefully packing up the ruined Scarlett O'Hara gown in its garment bag. Bev tsked one final time over the large rip down the back of the dress, and gave the gown a little pat, as if to console it. I swear, I saw the bead of a tear in the corner of her eye.

"I'll just place this in the back for safekeeping," Bev announced. "I'll mend the back as soon as possible, since time is of the essence for your wedding." Bev had been an accomplished seamstress before she'd opened Silver Bells, and I knew if anyone could fix the ruined gown, Bev could.

"The gown isn't safe here," Becca savagely intoned. "I'll take it home with me, and you can mend it there."

Bev's blond eyebrows shot up to her forehead at Becca's impudence. She opened her mouth as if to rejoin, then thought better of it. But her normally merry blue eyes were crackling with barely suppressed ire.

"I'll come to your house to do the personalized fittings; in light of this . . . altercation here today," Bev acquiesced. "Though such on-site seamstress work seems to be reserved for the likes of the British royal family," she muttered under her breath.

"Perfect." Becca disappeared into a dressing room, and emerged mere minutes later in her clothes. She swanned out of Silver Bells, and Samantha and I scurried after her in her wake.

If this little trip was indicative of how planning Becca's wedding was going to go, I was in for one heck of a ride.

CHAPTER FIVE

"**S**he did what?" Rachel stared at me with incredulous eyes after I gave her the capsule synopsis of Becca's altercation with Felicity at Silver Bells.

"It was an actual physical fight," I said in wonderment. "All over a Scarlett O'Hara–replica gown. And while I do agree that switching the theme to a *Gone with the Wind* wedding to honor Alma is a lovely idea, we really don't have time to make a new menu, order food from our suppliers, and switch up our other vendors."

Rachel dished out a heaping helping of mapo tofu from our favorite takeout joint and handed me a plate. "This is all my fault! I pushed you to accept all these other events this May, and it's come back to bite us in the rear end."

I offered my sister a rueful smile and took a vicious bite of a spring roll. "Business is booming. It could be worse. We'll make it work. We have to."

I tossed and turned after retiring to bed that

night. My calico cat, Whiskey, sensed my unease and opened one ocher eye, which glowed in the moonlight. Her daughter, Soda, a tiny orange cat, slept on at the foot of my bed, blissfully unaware. It was soon morning, and I was greeted with a text from Alma herself, beckoning me to meet her later at her house for her homecoming.

"She must be doing well to have only spent a few days in the hospital," I mused to Rachel over waffles in the big kitchen downstairs. We were free of guests this week because there would be no wedding this weekend, and our guests were usually affiliated with the weddings we held here. Instead, we'd be hosting a baby shower, and later the Mother's Day tea over the weekend. It felt strange to whip up a breakfast for just the two of us instead of a group of guests. I dressed the waffles in a simple fashion with a pat of butter and a pour of maple syrup and deposited one plate in front of my sister.

"Maybe well enough to take back planning of her theater opening," Rachel said hopefully as she spooned some strawberry preserves atop her waffle.

"I'd almost forgotten." A gulp of hot coffee went down the wrong pipe, and I coughed and spluttered. "Will you go with me?" I wanted some reinforcements when meeting with Alma. Becca and her family were turning out to be on another level of cray cray than even I had initially suspected, and I wanted someone there on my side.

"Of course! Let's go."

Ten minutes later, and Rachel and I were headed

west through Port Quincy, out to the suburbs ringing the town.

Rachel let out a giggle as we slowly drove up Alma's driveway. "This lady doesn't mess around."

I could see now that the house was obviously a perfect copy of the movie version of Tara. I hadn't noticed when we arrived the first time, as I was worried we hadn't heard from Alma. But now I could appreciate the hulking white house for what it was meant to be. I peered carefully at the house's skyline to try to determine if it had been built from the ground up as an homage to Tara, or if Alma had redone an existing house to mimic the mansion from the book and movie. It was a perfect replica; the only thing missing would be true Southern foliage, like some magnolia trees or live oaks.

"Hasn't she taken things a bit far?" Rachel giggled, then rapped sharply on the heavy dark green door.

"Wait'll you get a load of the inside. Then tell me if she's gone too far."

"What are you doing here?" Becca stood with a guarded look masking her features as she opened the door a tiny crack.

"Your grandmother asked me to come." I raised one brow and waited for Becca to invite us in.

"Very well. But shouldn't you be working on some task for my wedding?"

"I'll get back to your wedding as soon as possible, Becca. That is, after I've tended to whatever matter your ailing grandmother has requested to see me about."

Becca's face softened, and she let us in. We followed her through the vast, busily patterned and chandeliered entry hall to a sitting room off to the left. Rachel craned back her head and took it all in, not succeeding in suppressing a little gasp.

Alma made convalescing look good. She was propped up on a chaise in a new floral robe, this time with Wilkes the Irish setter by her side. I took in creepy, life-size portraits of Vivien Leigh as Scarlett O'Hara and Clark Gable as Rhett Butler. The oil paintings presided over the room with arresting stature. The Vivien Leigh portrait bore a striking resemblance to Felicity from the dress shop, although Rhett Cunningham looked nothing like his character namesake.

"I was just telling Grandma about my altercation in Silver Bells," Becca gushed. "Felicity called heads, but she guessed wrong! And that's how I ended up with the dress. It was totally worth it, even if I did have a glass of champagne thrown in my face."

"Oh Becca, it sounds simply dreadful." Jacqueline laid a hand on her chest and looked near tears.

"Bravo, Becca!" Alma nearly cackled and leaned forward to touch Becca's hand. "You get your spirit from me, my dear." I could tell it was Alma's opinion that Becca courted the most. She seemed proud of her descent into fisticuffs. Becca blushed, twin spots of genuine color showing up a fraction lower than the rouge she'd artfully applied.

"Yes, I am proud of you for claiming dibs on

that dress!" Alma's eyes twinkled merrily, and I almost forgot the terrible ordeal she'd recently been through.

"I had to have the Scarlett dress," Becca gushed. "It was meant to be."

All the while, Rhett gazed at his daughter in abject and barely muffled horror. "Rebecca Scarlett Cunningham, your mother and I raised you to be a lady, not a barroom brawler." Rhett drew himself up in his chair to his full height, still not matching that of his daughter Becca.

"Do stop." Alma laid on her Southern accent with full effect, and reached for a delicate lavender-colored atomizer. She spritzed herself several times, an effort, I suppose, to literally clear the air. A pleasant, citrusy scent filled the room. "It's lemon verbena," Alma explained. "Ellen O'Hara's scent."

I racked my brain to recall the Margaret Mitchell novel and famed movie.

"Scarlett O'Hara's mother was Ellen, right?" I took a seat near the window because none of the Cunninghams had bothered to offer me a place to sit. Rachel followed suit.

"Yes!" Alma beamed at me. "You've read the book!"

"Not recently," I murmured. "But I do recall bits and pieces."

"I have a signed first edition of the novel." Alma grinned, barely able to contain herself. "And dozens of other editions as well. I'll lend you a copy, so you can enjoy the novel again."

"That would be lovely." I offered the older woman

a smile, but I had no intention of reading what I recalled was a rather hefty tome anytime soon.

"Felicity mentioned she'd made another offer on your collection." Becca sniffed in disdain and took a delicate sip of sparkling water.

"That's what I need to talk to the police about." Alma drew her robe closely around her with a shiver. "I've been racking my brain as to who could have done this to me—" she gestured limply toward her bruised and mottled neck "and I keep coming back to Felicity Fournier." She'd abandoned the scarf she'd worn in the hospital, and her injuries were on full and lurid display.

"That poor lady," Rachel whispered to me, taking in Alma's neck.

"And who are you?" Alma seemed to notice my sister for the first time, her keen eyes sliding over Rachel's short silver miniskirt and the strip of midriff exposed below her white sweater.

"I'm Mallory's sister, Rachel."

Jacqueline seemed to remember her manners and got Rachel and me cups of coffee.

"As I was saying," Alma continued, "I'm not sure she has it in her to literally strangle me, but Felicity has been badgering me about purchasing every major piece of memorabilia I have."

"And it sounds like she made you another handsome offer," Rhett grumbled from the corner. "Would that girl really try to kill you, Mother?" He snorted, and Jacqueline dispensed a sharp look.

"She got engaged two nights ago," Becca said in wonderment. "Though I wonder what Tanner sees in her."

"She was your rival in everything growing up," Samantha offered. "And apparently she still is. If there's anyone who's a bigger *Gone with the Wind* nut than you are, Grandma, it's Felicity Fournier." Samantha spoke her words with love and affection, but they still agitated Alma.

"That's blasphemy! Felicity Fournier is nothing but a two-bit hobbyist, while I have made *Gone with the Wind* my life."

"Now, now," Rhett counseled. "Enough talk of Felicity; Becca and Samantha, you're upsetting your grandmother!" Judging from the jowls working up and down on his face, Rhett was even more bothered by the talk than his mother. "And many other people know of your collection. It's world-famous, and there are lots of people who would kill for even a small portion of the things you own."

A shiver danced up my back. Someone had been in this very house two nights ago, intent on killing Alma, ostensibly for items in her collection.

"Didn't you tell me that Alma gave her collection to Becca?" Rachel whispered into my ear.

"Good point," I whispered back. One that Rhett conveniently kept forgetting.

"The collection that belongs to you now, my dear," Alma said, bestowing Becca with a munificent smile.

"Be that as it may, the collection will remain here for now." Rhett wasn't questioning, but ordering. Becca shrugged at her father, not seeming to especially care. "And because you won't consent to giving up this house to move in with me and Jacqueline, or for an apartment in Whispering

Brook, I've taken it upon myself to get you some protection." Rhett had mentioned the same nursing home where Keith's grandmother had lived out her life.

"A bodyguard?" Alma looked tickled pink, and actually peered through the doorway, as if a security person would instantly appear.

"No, even better." Rhett knelt down next to the couch and retrieved a package wrapped in plain brown paper. He gently placed the box in his mother's lap. "Open it!"

Alma licked her dry lips and tore open the paper as if she were a young child on Christmas morning. She lifted the box and stared within, then gingerly picked up a gun. A dawning sense of recognition stole over her, and her lined face broke into an infectious grin. She turned over the gun in her gnarled hands, marveling at its craftsmanship. It appeared larger than the guns I'd seen on television, and the one I'd unfortunately once been around during a high-stakes situation.

"A Remington 1858 revolver!" Alma raised the gun and took practice aim at a large red vase.

Everyone stiffened as she closed one eye to get better focus. I felt like I should hit the deck.

"Is this old bat playing with a full deck of cards?" Rachel gripped my arm with her talonlike gel nails and leaned back, out of Alma's line of fire.

"I'd shoot Felicity if I ever caught her here, just like Scarlett shot that Union solider!" Alma moved her imaginary target to something outside the window, and Rhett blanched as the gun's path swept over him.

Jacqueline whispered to Rhett, loud enough for all to hear, "What were you thinking? Are you sure you want her to have that gun?"

"Wait . . . Is that a *Gone with the Wind* gun?" Rachel couldn't tamp down her smirk as she posed her question. "Let me guess: that's an exact replica."

"Why, yes," Alma cooed, bestowing Rachel with a warm smile and placing the gun in her lap. The heavy weapon made an interesting contrast to her English rose–patterned robe. "I've wanted one for ages but couldn't justify the purchase. Thank you, Son." Alma beamed at Rhett and lovingly stroked the cold metal of the gun's barrel.

A wheeze racked through Rachel, and I felt the small couch we were sitting on start to shake.

Oh no.

Rachel was almost unsuccessfully holding back a gale of laughter. She could staunch it no more, and a thin giggle escaped her lips. Alma shot her a dirty look that could scorch earth. I dove for my purse, hanging from the arm of the couch, and made a show of searching for a tissue. My ribs ached as my sister's infectious laughter spread, and it took me a quarter of a minute to compose myself. Thankfully, Alma didn't seem to notice.

"Control yourself," I whispered to Rachel.

"I for one am not a fan of guns," Jacqueline said primly. "I know what they can do, especially around those who don't know how to use them."

Alma shot her daughter-in-law a withering glare. "I've been around guns my whole life, Jacqueline. Plus, perhaps if Glenn had consented to have a gun last year, he would still be with us." A sad look stole over Alma, and she began to place the gun back in its case.

"You can't have guns in most school buildings here in Pennsylvania, Grandma," Samantha counseled.

That's interesting.

From Samantha's remark, Glenn must have worked at a school. I filed that tidbit away and tried to figure out a way to politely ask Alma why in the heck she'd summoned me again. I needed to get cracking on helping her with her theater relaunch; there wasn't a minute to spare. And while the coffee was delicious, and her replica Tara mansion was interesting, if not a bit kooky, Rachel and I had better things to do with our time.

"Maybe now that you've gotten home you'll consider postponing plans for reopening The Duchess theater," Jacqueline carefully suggested, her face an impassive mask. "You could just wait until after Becca's wedding, for instance, and then you'll be more fully healed." Jacqueline's voice slipped into a pleading range, and she stared beseechingly at Alma.

"Nonsense." Alma snapped the gun case together with a crisp clatter and set the sleek wooden box on a polished teak end table. "As God is my witness, I will be well enough to relaunch that theater."

"Then at least let me help you." Gone was Jacqueline's cool, willowy demeanor. She was practically begging.

"Just focus on your daughter's wedding." Alma dismissed Jacqueline, who deflated like a week-old balloon, and turned to me. "Mallory, that's why you're here. I have my binder of ideas and contracts and vendors all ready for you to take over. You'll barely have to lift a finger," the older woman promised. "Just tie up some loose ends." Alma imperiously motioned for Samantha to hand me the binder, a huge three-ring monstrosity of a tome that weighed at least half a pound.

"This looks very . . . thorough," I announced. It would take at least a day just to go through the thing. I recalled the beautiful yet crumbling building on the corner of Main and Spruce that had been under construction for the past year, a lattice of scaffolding crisscrossing the edifice. Was it even near completion?

What have I gotten myself into?

Rachel squirmed on her cushion next to me. She'd wanted to expand our business, but I was willing to bet this series of last-minute affairs, beginning with Keith and Becca's wedding, and now this theater opening, weren't what my sister had in mind. Jacqueline looked longingly at the binder. I made a mental note to ask Jacqueline for her help later, and decided I didn't need to let Alma know. It would be my and Jacqueline's little secret.

Rhett let out a sigh from across the room, and began to roll a small wooden stone through his fingers. He pocketed the item and glanced at his watch.

"You'll soon be rid of me," Alma noted drily, taking in her son's boredom. "But before you go, Rhett, I'd like to see my most-prized items. Be a dear and get me my cane, I'd like to take a trip to the vault."

Rhett colored and rubbed his meaty hands together. "Why don't you have another cup of tea, Mother?"

"Rhett Cunningham, are you hiding something from me?" Alma sat up in her chair so fast she startled the sleeping Wilkes, who had been lying in repose next to her. The pretty Irish setter raised his regal head and peered at all of us before yawning and resuming his nap.

"I just think it's best we wait for the police to arrive." Rhett wouldn't meet Alma's eyes. A knock at the door caused all of us to jump, all except Wilkes, who slept on. The dog truly must have been hard of hearing.

"Speak of the devil," Alma muttered.

Samantha returned from the hallway with Truman dogging her heels. I adored my boyfriend's father and couldn't get past Alma's displeasure with him. I was certain Truman had done everything he could to catch and bring Alma's husband's killer to justice.

"Good morning, Alma. I'd like to apologize for the state in which our investigators left your home. We tried to clean up most of the fingerprint dust, but you'll find some things disturbed."

Alma sat forward intently. "I just got home from the hospital a mere half hour ago. And my dear family hasn't let me look around yet." She scanned the room and aimed a laser beam of a glare at Rhett, Jacqueline, and her granddaughters. I shifted in my seat, uncomfortable with her censure.

"I'll get right to it." Truman sat down, uninvited,

on a severe-looking wingback chair near Alma. "After a thorough examination of your house, and in consultation with your son, his wife, and your insurance agent, it appears several items from your collection are missing. They include your first edition signed copy of *Gone with the Wind*, as well as your diamond and emerald replica Scarlett O'Hara engagement ring crafted by Fournier's Jewelry Store."

Alma closed her eyes and leaned back against her chair. Her hand fluttered to her chest, and we all leaned in.

"Grandma—" Becca leaped up to tend to Alma, and the older woman's eyes flickered open.

"I'm all right, child. Go on, Truman." Alma seemed to draw upon some well of inner strength, and appeared to blink back a cache of tears.

"We will be investigating this burglary and assault—" Truman began.

"Assault? Pfft. I was nearly murdered!" Alma sat forward so fast, the gun case ricocheted off her lap and fell to the floor with a clatter. Mercifully, the clasps held, and the gun remained safely inside. "Why, if Wilkes hadn't barked, I may not even be here with you today."

"I thought Wilkes was deaf?" Samantha cocked her head and studied the beautiful dog. Indeed, the Irish setter hadn't so much as stirred an inch when Truman had rung the rather loud doorbell.

"He is, but even he could tell I was in distress. Truman, let's not beat around the bush. I can think of one person who would wish to see me dead. She harangued me morning, noon, and night to purchase my famed collection. Not that she could afford it, I might add," Alma sneakily put in.

"And who might that be?" I could tell Truman's patience was wearing thin with Alma's theatrics.

"Felicity Fournier, of course!" Alma sat back in her chair triumphantly and slid the gun case under her coffee table.

Truman frowned and let a weighty silence permeate the room.

"Well, aren't you going to do something? Hup to it. Go arrest the scoundrel!" Alma glared at Truman, and Rachel stifled another giggle next to me.

"Ma'am," Truman began, "while there is no love lost between you and Felicity Fournier, I can't just arrest people based on hunches. We're thoroughly investigating your case."

"I can't think of anyone else desperate enough to try to pilfer my things," Alma seethed.

She had a point about desperation. Felicity's actions in Silver Bells had been downright bizarre. The woman had proved herself to be an inveterate *Gone with the Wind* nut, but did that make her a murderer? I shivered despite the warmth of the room, which seemed to be devoid of air conditioning. I wondered if Alma was a purist for historical accuracy, right down to matters of HVAC systems. My own inherited mansion hadn't had such amenities as air conditioning and radiators when it came into existence, but you can bet your fanny I'd upgraded the place to join the twenty-first century.

"I've drawn up the paperwork you'll need to

prove the absence of the items to start seeking re-imbursement from insurance. I can help you with any of the reports you'll need to file." Truman stood and donned his hat.

"What you can do is find my precious things. Then I won't need to file a report." Alma's crisp words came out as a command. "It sounds to me like you're already throwing in the towel, Truman Davies. Just like you did with my dear Glenn's murder investigation."

"I will stop at nothing until I solve both, Alma, and you know that." Truman was at once gruff but sincere. Alma dismissed him with a snort, and Truman took his leave, after bidding us all goodbye.

Rachel and I stood to go, looking longingly toward the ornate hall and wide door to freedom.

"Jacqueline, be a dear and make me a new pot of tea. Becca, please take Wilkes for his midmorning walk. Samantha, there's a bit of laundry that needs to be done, and some traces of fingerprint powder on the windowsills. And Rhett, you can start lunch." Alma gave her family stern marching orders, and the Cunninghams shuffled off to do her bidding.

"Mallory and Rachel, please wait."

Rats.

Rachel and I sank back onto our small couch and awaited Alma's orders.

"I need you to do some investigating for me." Alma grabbed my hand in her cold one and gave my knuckles a firm squeeze. I pulled my hand back as if I'd touched a live coal and tucked them in my lap.

"I'm a wedding planner, Alma, not a private investigator."

"Fiddle dee dee." Alma waved her hand dismissively in the air. "You're dating the chief's son, correct?"

"She sure is." Rachel was enjoying this too much.

"Yes, I am, but I'm not sure what that has to do with anything."

"Just keep an eye out for me, dear; that you can surely do? You seem fond of Truman, but the harsh truth is that he bungled the murder investigation of my dear Glenn. I don't want to be next."

I shivered at her concern and gathered my purse in my lap.

"I really should be going, Alma."

Her hand shot out and grabbed my wrist. Her eyes were filled with infinite sadness. "Please, just promise me you'll keep your ear to the ground. Especially concerning what happened to Glenn."

I gulped and extricated my wrist from her python's grasp.

"I guess I can do that," I whispered, regretting my acceptance of her plea as soon as it left my lips.

"Thank you, my dear. You won't regret it. Oh, and Mallory? You almost forgot this." Her slippered foot nudged the gigantic tome of a binder with The Duchess theater reopening plans.

"How could I have left this?" I picked up the binder and rested it in my arms.

Rachel and I made our way to the Butterscotch Monster.

"What a crazy bunch of characters." Rachel

shook her head in wonderment at the outside of Tara as she smoothed down her miniskirt. "And it only gets better." She gestured down the long drive, where Keith's navy BMW was pulling in.

"Mallory, wait." Becca's voice rang out over the yard, and she minced over, her heels sinking into the grass. Wilkes sniffed beside her on his leash, the doggy happy to be enjoying the late spring sunshine. His long snout opened in a cheerful canine smile. I knelt to pet his lovely auburn fur, and he rolled over for a belly rub.

"When can we schedule a final tasting for the *Gone with the Wind*–themed ceremony and reception?"

I carefully composed myself as I finished petting Wilkes. "There won't be a tasting, Becca. Don't worry. Rachel and I know what you like by now, and what will please Helene, and honor Alma. You'll love it, and it will be a fun surprise on your big day."

"But—" Becca's mouth twisted in a pout.

"You heard her, sister," Rachel snapped. "We've run out of time, and you just have to trust us, okay?"

"So you can't whip one up?" Keith joined his bride and gave Wilkes a feeble pat. "I thought you were gunning to be the premier wedding planning service in all of Western Pennsylvania. And you can't make a tasting happen?"

I narrowed my eyes, willing myself not to be bamboozled by his bullying.

"Of course we can! Be prepared to get your

socks knocked off." Rachel sneered at Keith and turned on her heel to the station wagon. I gave a final pat to Wilkes and joined my sister.

"I guess we've got a tasting to create."

Rachel offered a sheepish smile. "Oops."

CHAPTER SIX

"Third time's the charm," I muttered. I had ordered food for the Japanese cherry blossom–themed wedding and Helene's country club imitation meal and now was repurposing some of it for this latest iteration of the menu. But some food couldn't be used for the wedding. Helene was paying me an obscene amount to make this wedding come off, and it wasn't the change of plans that bothered me but the perceived waste of it all. Luckily, the food would be used by those in need, as I was going to donate much of it to the Helping Hands Foundation, run by my newly married friends, Owen and Dakota.

And today's tasting was going to be a more subdued affair. We would just be hosting Becca and Keith; the rest of the Cunningham clan had thankfully remained home, presumably to tend to Alma.

"Homestretch," Rachel muttered as she put the finishing touches on a miniature version of a cake for the couple. The confection was three tiers of

peach cake swathed in glossy light pink icing, with
pale green ribbon trim and magnolia accents scattered here and there. The beauty of the cake had
taken its toll on my sister. She'd spent extra time
with her under-eye concealer this morning in our
shared bathroom after baking the cake in the wee
hours of the morning.

"Whatever happens, it'll be over in less than two
weeks. We can do this." I slid trays of the representative meal into the oven to warm, and a trill of
déjà vu trickled down my spine. Of course it did.
I'd done this twice before. I didn't appreciate the
fire-drill atmosphere that catering to Becca created, but deep down, my heart still went out to her.
Her grandmother Alma had just been through the
ordeal of a lifetime, and Becca herself was about to
tether herself to Keith forever. And perhaps more
concerning, to Helene for the rest of her life. It
was enough to make a girl feel for her enemies.

"Let's do this." I held up my hand and Rachel
gave me a weary high five. We ferried an elaborate
place setting for two out to the gazebo near the
rear of our property. Rachel had insisted on wearing heels, in the form of sky-high wedges, the better to not sink down into the grass. We started out
on the herringbone-brick paths of the garden,
then off-roaded it to wend our way through the
smooth expanse of emerald lawn to get to the
gazebo.

The florist Lucy Sattler from the Bloomery had
arrived near dawn to work her prodigious magic.
I'd been shocked she'd agreed to decorate the
gazebo for this impromptu tasting. She'd had an
opening, and I was sure the obscene amount of

money Becca, Keith, and Helene had collectively pledged to spend on flowers hadn't hurt.

In three more trips, our work setting up the tasting was finished. The intricate white gazebo echoed the Italianate design of the mansion, with a gingerbread trim of curlicues, swirls, and flowers. A small thistle weather vane stood at attention at the top of the cupola, gently twirling in a slow circle from the wind. The columns of the gazebo were twined in swaths of magnolias and pink roses and ribbon, recalling the May Day festival the town had just held. A wicker table sat within, a sturdy and jaunty seersucker tablecloth laid over it. Dishes from the latest proposed menu for the wedding were served on a delicate china pattern featuring buttercups. I was proud of this latest tasting we'd whipped up for Becca and Keith, and couldn't help but hope they'd also love it.

"This weather is too cool. It had better warm up in two weeks." Becca bemoaned the temperature as she minced across the lawn in spike heels.

"Here we go," I whispered to Rachel, who grabbed my hand and gave it a squeeze.

"Mallory, can't you do something about this?" Keith frowned as he offered Becca his arm when she stumbled.

"About the weather?" I tried to wipe away the incredulous look I felt steal over my face. "I suppose we could rent some more heat lamps and set them around the property, although it might be too late. I think your guests will dress appropriately for an outdoor spring wedding." My eyes flickered to the couple themselves. Keith wore one of his ubiquitous sports jackets, but Becca was clad in a gauzy, insubstantial mint-green sundress. She pulled her thin cardigan closer to her to ward off some of the chill.

"It's pretty early in the morning now. Your mid-afternoon wedding will be warmer."

"No, no, no! Get the heaters." Becca's mouth twisted down in a frown.

"They're quite costly, especially this late—"

"Whatever she wants, get it," Keith said in a practiced monotone. Becca beamed at him, her frown turned upside down. But it quickly returned, as she found her four-inch spike heel mired deep in the grass.

"And we'll need a temporary path installed so guests can avoid this hideous grass on their way to the gazebo." Becca slid off her shoe, a pretty striped mint affair, but the footwear stayed stubbornly stuck to the ground. "What the—"

She pulled and pulled, and the shoe came free, unfortunately separate from the heel, which stayed in the earth as the shoe broke in two.

"Allow me." Keith gently removed Becca's other shoe from her foot and gallantly ripped off the other heel. It was a clever solution, and I smiled at his ingenuity. It was silly and reminded me of the old Keith I once knew and loved, the man I almost married. Buried inside his new quest for money and his blind allegiance to Helene was the person I'd once almost pledged my life to. Maybe I hadn't been crazy to have once been engaged to Keith after all.

Keith presented the newly augmented shoes to Becca, as if they were Cinderella's finest glass slippers.

"What have you done?" Becca's voice was a mere screech as she stared incredulously at her pair of ruined shoes. "Those are Balenciagas! Oh Keith, how could you?"

"Balenci-what?" Keith shook his head slowly at his bride. "Sorry, Bec, I was just trying to help."

Becca snatched the ruined shoes from his hands and slung them over her feet with vicious movements. "Let's get this over with."

I felt a shaking movement next to me, and jostled Rachel to stop her from silently laughing. If I caught the giggles from my sister, it would be all over.

"There seems to be some trouble in paradise," Rachel whispered as she stepped aside for Becca and Keith to enter the gazebo.

"I heard that," Becca snapped. "And everything is fine."

Rachel colored momentarily as she and I served the meal. The bride and groom sat down to collard green salad with roasted pecans and okra and honeyed biscuits to start. Next up was the main meal of tarragon fried chicken, fried green tomatoes, bacon and almond green beans, and savory cheddar shrimp and grits. Lemonades, shandies, and mint juleps stood waiting on the sideboard we'd set up.

Becca and Keith sat stone-faced as I named each dish, and I felt myself take a sharp breath as they finally tasted the meal. Keith did parcel out a mouthwatering gaze at the fried chicken. Becca let out an appreciative murmur of pleasure, despite herself, as she sampled each dish. Her fried chicken remained untouched, whereas Keith finished his chicken first, then reached to the center of the table for a second helping.

"No!" Becca reached out and moved the chicken away. "You need to fit into your suit."

"It's his favorite," I muttered, and it was like the music stopped. Becca, Keith, and Rachel all swiveled their heads in my direction as I clapped my hand over my mouth. Becca's look could cut glass, and I knew I'd done it. It was one thing to reflect privately on the fact that I was once betrothed to Keith. It was quite another to be dropping hints that I was privy to the knowledge of everything he liked.

"And now for dessert," Rachel smoothly recovered. "Peach cake, pecan cookies, and peach tartlets, along with tea, coffee, and brandy."

Becca oohed and aahed at the cake, as Keith made his move to snag an extra drumstick. Becca's hand shot out lightning quick, with the reflexes of a ninja, and batted the drumstick away. "I saw that, Keith."

Keith shot me a wounded look.

"And furthermore," Becca continued, "I wanted Southern couture for this *Gone with the Wind* wedding, not KFC!"

"You should try the chicken," I counseled calmly. "It's very nuanced." Not that there was anything wrong with some nongourmet fried chicken either. I'd been wrestling with this *Gone with the Wind* theme enough as it was. "I think this menu will be a nice compromise between the traditional Southern food Helene might approve of and a way to honor Alma."

"I don't know . . ." Becca neatly ignored the fact

that she'd finished every morsel on her plate except for the fried chicken, and continued to hem and haw.

"I know it's been a tough week," I soothed, sitting down next to Becca. "I'm not sure I would be handling things this well if my grandmother had gone through everything Alma has. But we're facing a time crunch. I'd like nothing more than to give you and Keith a lovely day. And to do that, I need to finalize the food orders." I sat on my hands to keep from grasping Becca's in a plea. She blinked twice and glanced at Keith, who gave her a nod.

"All right. This is the menu."

"No more changes," Rachel warned.

"No more changes."

I felt myself deflate with relief. It was going to be okay. Soon this wedding would be in the rearview mirror, and Becca and Keith would be out of my hair. Things were looking up.

"Are you coming with me?" Becca stared expectantly from her perch on the back porch where she was waiting with Keith. Rachel and I had begun our first trip back from the gazebo, our arms laden with plates and platters. Becca's question snapped me back to reality. I'd wondered why they were still here after the tasting.

"Um, coming to what?"

"To my dress fitting and repair session with Bev, silly. I thought you should attend in case I get more ideas for the *Gone with the Wind* wedding. You could take notes." Becca was entirely serious.

"You go," Rachel said with a smirk. "I'll break down the rest of the tasting."

So I soon found myself ensconced in Keith's backseat as we made our way to Windsor Meadows. We rode in a strange and not entirely companionable silence. I wondered what Keith and Becca would have said about the tasting had I not been in the car.

The hulking colossus of a maroon Rubik's Cube that was Becca and Keith's house came into view, never ceasing to momentarily jar me. But a stranger sight also greeted us.

"Whose car is that?" Keith frowned as he pulled behind a sleek silver Jaguar. "I'll have to call a towing company."

"We're not due for any visitors besides Bev, and she won't be here for another half hour," Becca said. "Is that her car, Mallory?"

"No, Bev drives a red Escape." The car in question didn't belong to the bubbly dress storeowner and seamstress.

"You ladies stay here," Keith commanded. "I'll check the place out." He stepped from his BMW with a swagger, and puffed out his chest as he made his way to the front door.

"This is silly," Becca said and got out of the car. I slowly followed suit, not liking the feeling I was getting.

I could see Keith poking around in the topiary by the side of the house as Becca and I made our way into the peach great room. An earsplitting shriek made me nearly jump out of my skin.

"My gown! It's gone!" Becca pointed to an

empty, crumpled silver garment bag lying in a ball on the floor in the kitchen.

"Someone stole the Scarlett O'Hara wedding dress?" I looked wildly around the room, but no gown could be found.

"First my grandmother, now me!" Becca pulled her hands through her hair and sat down, stunned. Then she stood up like a rocket and began ripping apart the room, searching in vain for the dress.

I helped her look until I heard a loud expletive uttered from the back of the house. Becca raced to the glass doors and slid them open with such force they jounced in their tracks. Keith stood rooted to the spot, his mouth open in a little round *o* as he took in the pool. Becca and I spilled out onto the sleek redwood porch, the obsidian rock garden calm and still.

As was the body in the pool. She floated face up in the gently bobbing waves, her gaze forever frozen on the brilliant sun above. She was clad in the famed wedding gown, the creamy silk and embroidered gauze now heavy and waterlogged. The voluminous dress fanned out around the body, appearing slightly blue-tinted from the pool's waters.

It was Felicity Fournier.

Becca's screams echoed around the backyard.

CHAPTER SEVEN

"Not you again."

Truman's words were as weary as the expression on his face. He'd just returned to Keith and Becca's living room after securing the pool and deck out back, and combing the scene for nearly an hour with his keen police chief's eyes. His partner Faith Hendricks stood snapping pictures of Felicity's semi-submerged body, while Keith, Becca and I sat huddled inside. If I sat up, I could just make out the white figure of Felicity in the Scarlett O'Hara dress, entombed in her watery grave. I closed my eyes and turned my body away from the glass doors, physically blocking the view, if not erasing the memory from my mind.

"I'm afraid so." I'd moved to Port Quincy a little less than a year ago, and was greeted with a dead body on my lawn the very first morning after I'd moved in. Since then I'd unfortunately found myself in close propinquity to some rather strange crimes in town. And it looked like my bad luck streak was continuing.

I shivered despite the temperate day. The 1980s splendor of a living room usually felt warm, with all of the peach and cream accoutrements. But a permanent chill seemed to have settled into my bones after seeing Felicity in the pool.

A ding emanated from my purse and I scrabbled to retrieve my cell phone.

"No communications for now," Truman warned.

"Uh-oh. It's Bev Mitchell." The text stated a quick apology for being late, and a promise to arrive at Becca's soon.

"What does that gossip queen want? Don't breathe a word of this to her." Truman leaned over my shoulder to scan the text. "Wait—she's coming here? You've got to stop her."

I texted back a laconic response canceling the dress fitting and dropped the phone back into my purse. A string of dings indicated that Bev's Spidey sense was up and running, and that there was more to my story based on my abrupt cancellation. She texted me three times before giving up. I felt guilty but obeyed Truman. I didn't want to be the one to inadvertently spread this sad tale by giving Bev a head's up. What had happened to Felicity was a bizarre tragedy, not grist for the Port Quincy gossip mill.

Keith stopped comforting a whimpering Becca and glared at Truman. "If Mallory is allowed to text, I'd like to as well."

Truman sighed and ran a hand through his salt-

and-pepper hair. "No can do, Keith. I don't need anyone else here mucking up my crime scene."

"And I'd like to call my mother and my sister Samantha." Becca's plea came out in between a jagged series of breaths.

Truman turned a kinder gaze on the bride-to-be. "Just let us do our work for a bit longer, then you can make your calls."

But Helene's own Spidey senses must have been alerted. A key turned in the door, and the dowager empress of Port Quincy let herself into the marble foyer, her kitten heels angrily striking the floor as she made her way into the great room.

"Police lights flashing, an ambulance, and crime scene tape! What will the neighbors think?" Helene glared at Becca for a moment before marching toward the glass doors to the deck. "I want this mess cleaned up immediately!"

Truman stepped neatly before the glass doors and held out his hand as if directing a traffic stop. "This mess, Helene, is what appears to be a murder. I'd appreciate it if you would leave the premises. We don't need all of these cooks in the kitchen."

Although the fire in Truman's hazel eyes was intense as he dismissed Helene, he wasn't even the most agitated person in the room.

"You *promised* me you'd get the key back from Helene! Honestly, Keith, who's more important to you, me or your mother?" Becca's tears evaporated as she sprang from the couch and took refuge behind the massive apricot-colored island in the kitchen.

Keith hung his head as Helene stared down Truman for a good thirty seconds, and then joined her son in the spot Becca had just vacated.

"I came as soon as you called, Son."

Truman's eyes turned positively murderous. "You called your mother?"

Keith merely tucked his head down another degree and refused to answer anyone. But I could see the red blush of embarrassment creep up his neck to stain his face.

Smart.

Keith practiced corporate law, primarily mergers and acquisitions. Criminal defense was not his forte, but be knew enough not to incriminate himself.

But what exactly does he have to hide?

And not talking at all didn't help to make himself appear less suspect in this situation. Still, Becca and Keith had excellent alibis. They'd been with me and my sister at the tasting for the hour before returning home. But that didn't mean that Keith, or Becca, or the couple together, hadn't killed Felicity before coming to Thistle Park. I gulped, and my eyes inadvertently strayed to the back of the house, where a crime scene technician had joined Faith.

"Come on, Keith." Helene stood and briskly brought him to his feet by executing a firm grip on his elbow. She was like a mama cat bringing its recalcitrant kitten back to the fold by the scruff of its neck. "I'd like for you to visit the family attorney."

"No one is going anywhere." Truman's command came out as a snarl. "Not until you've all been questioned." His lips twisted up in a rueful smile. "Including you, Helene, because you've chosen to wade into this crime scene."

Helene opened and closed her mouth, her coral-tinged lips finally settling into a firm line. She sat next to Keith with a harrumph.

"Well, you'll certainly be hearing from our attorney when all this is said and done." She stared imperiously down her nose at Truman, who met her gaze with an impassive look. Helene lost the game of chicken, looking away from his steely eyes first. But she wasn't done. "I know why this happened."

This earned her a second look from Truman, one of patient curiosity. We all leaned in to hear what Helene had to say.

"I warned you not to open your pool before the official benchmark of Memorial Day, Becca. Your impudence and classlessness brought this bad luck upon you." Helene gave a haughty wave toward the backyard, equivocating Felicity's death as a mere inconvenience for herself.

"What?" Becca stared at Helene with an incredulous gaze. "My opening the pool caused Felicity's death? You really have gone insane."

"I need some air." I stood and moved toward the glass doors, thankful Faith was bent over the pool, blocking my view of Felicity. Truman followed me out after a stern warning to Keith and Helene not to go anywhere. At the last second, Faith moved aside to ask Truman a question, and I caught a glimpse of the white dress. Truman must have noticed my discomfort and led me around to a copse of Japanese maples with a flurry of shiny plum leaves, which blocked our view of the pool.

"Thanks." My voice sounded shaky and woozy. "I'm not sure which is worse, being inside with Helene or out here with the body."

Truman sighed and took off his hat. "This doesn't look good. Whether it's a suicide *or* a murder."

He doesn't know the half of it.

Yesterday's melee in Silver Bells came flooding back, complete with the shoving match between my bride and the woman in the pool. And something told me Truman had no idea what had happened.

"Why do I get the feeling you need to tell me something?" Truman crossed his arms and waited for me to stop studying the ladybug crawling with infinite slowness on the trunk of the maple tree behind him.

"It might not be significant—"

Yeah right.

"I'll be the judge of that."

"Okay. Um, Becca and Felicity kind of got into a fight at the Silver Bells bridal shop yesterday."

Truman's bushy eyebrows shot up to his forehead, but he remained silent, the better to allow me to prattle on and spill the beans. I'd learned from Truman over the past year not to interrupt with questions when someone was telling their tale; they'd tell you more if you let them nervously fill the heavy silence. Which I did in spades.

"It was an actual fight. With shoving and name-calling and thrown champagne."

That was enough to get him talking. "Champagne?"

"Mm-hmm. In fancy wedding stores, the hosts like to serve champagne to the brides and family because—"

"I know, Mallory," Truman interrupted. "Summer likes to make me watch *I Do* with her." Truman smiled fondly as he mentioned his granddaughter Summer and the reality show her mother directed. "What was the fight about?" He turned back into inquisitor-cop mode with startling alacrity, the smile now wiped off his face.

"A Scarlett O'Hara–replica wedding dress." I gulped and limply gestured beyond the trees. "The one Felicity's wearing right now."

Truman's eyes nearly bugged out of his head. "They both wanted the dress, things got physical, and now one woman is dead. Thank you, Mallory." He abruptly left me to hover by myself behind the tree, twisting the topaz pendant I wore around my neck tighter and tighter. I felt like I'd just signed Becca's warrant papers. And floating up from the pool of guilt I found myself wading into was a niggling feeling that I hadn't told Truman all he needed to know.

"Wait!"

"This better be good."

"The altercation in Silver Bells yesterday? That's not all." I sheepishly stared through a lock of frizzy hair that had escaped my bun. It was getting humid by the pool now that the sun was high overhead in the sky. I felt an insect bite the back of my calf but decided it was more pleasant to remain outside with a corpse than to retreat to the house and deal with Helene. "I'm not sure if this is *really* relevant, but—"

"Spill it, Mallory." Truman's patience was wearing thin, and the hotter-than-usual May day was getting to him too. A bead of sweat gathered at his temple and rolled down the side of his face.

"Alma asked me to keep her apprised of what's going on in the investigation regarding her stolen memorabilia."

Phew. Now I feel better.

"What?" A look of utter disappointment stole over Truman's worn face. He quickly composed himself, but not before I caught a wounded expression. "Alma will never forgive me for not quickly solving the murder of her husband." Truman shook his head ruefully. "And although the best minds in the department have tried for a year to solve the crime, we haven't been able to. I don't blame her for her anger, although I do believe it's misplaced."

My heart went out to Truman. He always got his man, even if a case took decades to solve. If Glenn's killer had yet to be brought to justice, it wasn't through any fault of Truman's. Still, I could see why Alma would need to lay blame somewhere, what with the grief she felt for her husband.

There was one thing I was certain about. I wouldn't be telling Truman that Alma had tried to personally deputize me to help solve her husband's murder, as well.

"Is that all you have to tell me?" Truman's eyes seemed to bore into my soul. He could always tell when I was holding out on him.

"Um, I guess that's it. Becca and Felicity fought over the dress yesterday, Felicity offered to buy Alma's *Gone with the Wind* collection and Alma refused, and Alma asked me to keep my ear to the ground regarding her stolen things. Yup, that's about it."

Truman opened his mouth to rejoin when a figure stalked through the shiny maroon maples.

"That's enough, Mallory. I don't recall you being on retainer at the police department." Keith sent me a menacing glare that made me catch my breath. I felt woozy with the realization that just a year ago, I had been in the throes of planning my own elaborate wedding to Keith. He turned to Truman. "I want her out of here."

Truman opened his mouth to give Keith a piece of his mind when Becca's voice rang out over the backyard, clear and unwavering. "It looks like a suicide."

It was entirely possible. Felicity had seemed beyond distraught that she couldn't have the gown. Maybe she had decided to ruin it for Becca as well, as her last act on this earth.

"Excuse me, but you won't be making that determination." Truman left me in the maples as he emerged to face Becca. Keith and I followed suit. Truman kept his eyes on Becca, his gaze stoic. Yet his mouth twitched down in a frown.

Becca hugged her middle and turned her back to the pool. "Felicity tried to ruin *everything* in my life. She entered the Miss Port Quincy pageant the year after I won and copied my idea for the talent segment. She never had an original idea in her life. I went to college at Duquesne in Pittsburgh, and she transferred there after freshman year. I decided I wanted to go to law school, and she just *had* to go too. I bet Grandma Alma was right, that

Felicity tried to murder her. Maybe Felicity killed herself because of guilt over what she did to Alma." Keith materialized at Becca's side and gently tried to shush her, but to no avail. Becca batted his comforting arm away and continued. "Felicity killed herself in my pool in an attempt to ruin my wedding. I'm sure of it. And as God is my witness, she won't get away with it."

I wondered idly if Becca knew she had echoed one of Scarlett O'Hara's famous speeches from the movie and book versions of *Gone with the Wind*. Truman didn't look as impressed with Becca's performance. He studied Becca with a calm intensity. I tried to guess what wheels were turning in his head. My mind went to dark places where I didn't want it to. Did I dare to think that Becca's impassioned speech was just a way to throw us off her trail? Was my newest bride also a murderess? There had been real malice in the eyes of both Becca and Felicity as they fought over the gown the day before. Was Becca angry enough to kill Felicity over it?

"I have more questions." Truman looked at me, Becca, and Keith in turn. "For all of you. If you'd just return to the house, we can begin."

A screech of tires caused us all to look to the front of the house. A banging could be heard on the front door, and then a man came running around the side of the house to the deck behind. He was reed thin, with an Ichabod Crane frame and thick black glasses beneath a shock of floppy, sandy hair. He wore a dress shirt with the sleeves rolled up to the elbows, khakis, and moccasins. He appeared to be in his midthirties and moved with quick, precise movements. His eyes scanned the backyard, searching for something. Or someone.

"Where is she? Felicity?"

"And you are?" Truman blocked the view of the pool and placed both hands on his hips.

"Tanner Frost. I'm looking for my fiancée, Felicity Fournier. I just got done teaching my last class of the year. Felicity was supposed to meet me. She never showed, and she didn't answer her cell. She'd told me she was stopping by here earlier today. What's with all the police cars? What in the hell is going on?"

"Son—" Truman stopped when Tanner pushed past him to get a better view of the lower level of the deck and the pool.

"Oh my God. It's her. Felicity!" Tanner raced down the short flight of steps and stood before the water, tugging at his hair. "I've got to get her out of there." He reached for the body in the pool before Truman and Faith dragged him from the edge, where he fought like a tiger before succumbing to racking sobs. Truman led him back up the stairs and into the house, where Tanner limply fell into an ecru armchair covered in embroidered seashells. Keith and Becca claimed a peach couch across the room, staring at Tanner with suspicion-laden eyes. I hovered near the door, wondering when I could make an escape.

"What made you think you'd find Felicity here?" Truman was kind but ever watchful as he questioned Tanner.

"She got a text this morning inviting her to buy a wedding dress." Tanner was so distraught he appeared almost catatonic. It was no wonder; he'd barely had time to process his fiancée Felicity was gone for good. "She was beside herself with excitement."

Becca opened her mouth across the room. "That's not—"

"Stop." Truman held up his hand and his look brooked no wiggle room as he silenced Becca. "Go on, Tanner."

"She left my house to come here and buy the dress at the same time I left to teach class."

"So you're a teacher?" Truman slipped out a small notebook and scribbled something in the shorthand he'd perfected for interviewing.

Tanner seemed to bristle. "I'm a professor. At Quincy College, in the history department. This was my last class of the year."

"So you finished class. And then what?" Truman was patient, ignoring Tanner's affronted attitude.

"Felicity and I had a lunch date. She didn't show. She didn't answer my texts, and I got worried. Recently—" Tanner stopped talking, as if remembering something. His hollow cheeks glowed with a fast, creeping blush. "I was just worried about her, and because I knew she was supposed to stop by for the dress, I thought I'd see if she was still here. Her Jag was out front, and so were all the flashing police cars." He turned his head to look out the window at an unfortunate moment. Faith and the technician were removing Felicity's body from the pool, the heavy gown making the work ungainly and difficult. Tears began to silently stream down Tanner's face. I made myself useful and found him a box of tissues.

"I didn't sell her the dress." Becca could stand it

no longer and stood from her perch on the couch.
"I didn't even offer."

Tanner shook his head, as if clearing water from
his ears. "Yes, you did. I was there when Felicity got
the text. She even showed it to me. Felicity was surprised you'd changed your mind and decided she
was more deserving of the dress, but she figured
you'd just come to your senses."

Becca snorted, any sympathy she had for Tanner seemingly gone. "That's preposterous. I did no
such thing."

Tanner's tears stopped in midroll and he narrowed his eyes. "I bet her phone is still in her car.
I'm going to get it and show you."

"No one's touching a thing in Felicity's car,"
Truman intoned. "It's evidence now."

But Tanner was just getting started. "You probably lured her here, Becca Cunningham. You promised her the dress to get her on your turf, and then
you murdered her. You've been jealous of Felicity
your whole life, and you couldn't stand that she
was engaged and happy. How could you?" Tanner
stood and began pacing the kitchen.

Helene chose that moment to emerge from the
upstairs portion of the house, her senses keenly
picking up on the fact that someone had just accused Becca of murder. I could see the nefarious
wheels turning in Helene's head, and wondered
how she'd use this theory to her advantage.

"Now let's just settle down, everyone." Truman's
voice boomed, and no one said another word. It
was an uneasy standoff between Becca in the living
room and Tanner in the kitchen, walking nervous
circles around the behemoth island. It was like

being stuck in a cage with lions and tigers marauding around. Tensions were too high.

"And you hadn't had any disagreements with your fiancée lately?" Truman put away his notebook and turned to observe Tanner.

"Of course not!" Tanner's denial came out as a squeak. "We just got engaged two nights ago. This was supposed to be the happiest time of my life, and Felicity's. We were going to get married at the end of the summer. We were making plans." His eyes grew far away and his voice turned wistful. "We were going to get married right here in town. At Thistle Park. Then honeymoon in Venice. And now she's gone."

Say what?

"When were you marrying at Thistle Park?" I'd blurted out the question before I could stop myself, earning a withering glare from Truman.

"August. Felicity called and booked the date less than an hour after we got engaged." Tanner's laugh was tinged with aching sadness. "She was so excited, she started planning right away."

I had the grace to silently question Truman whether to go on with an imploring look. He nodded his permission, and I spoke again.

"I'm the owner of the B and B, and the wedding planner. I'll have to check when I return home, but I'm almost positive Felicity didn't book a wedding for August. In fact, I didn't speak to her at all about the matter."

Each weekend from now until October was spoken for. Several weekends this summer would hold weddings on Friday evenings, in addition to the usual Saturday. There was no way I would have been able to accommodate Felicity Fournier and Tanner Frost for a late summer wedding. He had to have been mistaken.

Tanner furiously shook his head. "That's impossible. I was there when she made the call and spoke with you. Just like I saw the text from Becca." He ran his hands through his floppy hair, and the speed of his pacing increased. "What's with you people? I know what I saw and heard. Is this all some kind of cruel joke? Are you trying to gaslight me?"

"I'll double check my messages," I promised lamely. I'd obviously upset Tanner, and that was not my intention, especially in his current state. "There's a possibility Felicity spoke to someone else besides me." I'd confer with Rachel when I finally got the heck out of this house of horrors, but I was willing to bet Felicity hadn't talked to my sister either. Even with the blur of new events we'd taken on, Rachel and I had insisted on keeping meticulous records.

"I don't have to take this from all of you." Tanner made a dash for the back deck and pushed open the glass doors.

My heart went out to the obviously and understandably agitated man. It hurt just watching him take in his fiancée, now retrieved from the pool, lying beside the water in the gorgeous but now-ruined gown.

We all wordlessly followed Tanner out and perched at the top of the deck, except for Helene, who stood quiet counsel from the kitchen window.

"Son, you can't touch her." Truman stood behind Tanner, who just stared at his fiancée. I didn't think Truman had to warn him.

Tanner's face registered acute shock as his gaze strayed to Felicity's left hand. He took in a sharp breath, and then reached for her hand.

"Tanner, you can't—"

He was trying with all his might to remove his fiancée's engagement ring. Becca, Keith, and I stood in horror as Truman and Faith pulled Tanner back.

CHAPTER EIGHT

"That sounds intense." My boyfriend Garrett pulled me closer on the porch swing. I sank my head into his shoulder, my hand resting on his chest. The soothing thrum of his heart beating against my hand worked to calm my racing mind. The day's events played on a frenetic loop in my memory. Truman had released me from Keith and Becca's house by midafternoon, and I'd rushed home.

The pressure and heat of the day had given way to cool, crisp night with the setting of the sun. Garrett and I sat on the porch swing in the gloaming, the sky an ever-deepening velvety blue behind the silhouette of Port Quincy. Garrett had popped over to lend an ear and share a cup of coffee. His was decaf, but mine was fully turbocharged, caffeinated java. It wasn't my first choice, as my nerves were a jangly mess. But I had to go over plans for a baby shower that was scheduled for the next day, and I needed to be alert after the adrenaline crash wore off.

"How's Summer doing in L.A.?" I changed the subject to something happier. I missed Garrett's fourteen-year-old daughter and couldn't wait to see her upon her return from her trip.

"She's having a fantastic time. She's been on set with Adrienne nearly every day, and they've taken some trips to the beach and to the mountains." Garrett smiled wistfully. Summer's mother, and Garrett's one-time, long-ago flame was the director of a newly revamped, popular wedding reality show that yours truly had once been featured on.

"Summer's flying back with her mother in three days." A grin lit up his handsome face. "This is the longest I've been away from her, and it'll be wonderful to have her back in Port Quincy. Just in time for your Mother's Day tea."

I winced as Garrett reminded me of yet another event we'd taken on. "All of Rachel's plans to expand the business seemed like a great idea." Before the murder of Felicity Fournier and the attempted murder of Alma Cunningham. "I'm excited to host more things here, but it would be nice for things to go back to normal too."

I shivered as the sun finally finished its journey beneath the horizon. I tried to train my thoughts on something more cheerful. "Tomorrow is Whitney's baby shower." I perked up at the thought. Whitney was one of my former brides, and Becca's cousin. "We'll be celebrating a new life."

Garrett hugged me closer, and we sat in companionable silence. But my racing mind wouldn't settle. I wondered about what Rachel had said when she'd teased about an impending engagement. I could detect no new undercurrents in my relationship with Garrett. He still thrilled me with his flashing hazel eyes and his sexy smile. He was my rock. But we'd settled into a comfortable rhythm. Things were fine just the way they were. Maybe Rachel was wrong about an engagement. Why should we change things just because we'd been dating for nearly a year? Especially in light of the fact it was just a year ago I'd been engaged to another man. I questioned myself frequently about what I'd ever seen in Keith. I'd finally come around to trust my judgment in the men department since I'd found Garrett. But that didn't mean I needed to move on to a new phase just to please friends and family who expected us to get engaged.

A police sedan pulled into the long driveway and broke my serious train of thought. I had enjoyed a cup of coffee with my boyfriend before I was to receive a private grilling from his father. Truman advanced up the brick path, his face pulled and tired. Despite his father's weariness, Garrett was nearly the spitting image of Truman. I had a preview of what my boyfriend would look like in twenty years' time.

"I'd better go." Garrett graced my lips with a tender kiss and bade me and his father goodbye. The hazy, warm feelings he instilled in me evaporated as I got a new cup of coffee for Truman and returned to sit in a wicker chair facing him. I set down a tray with shaking hands and winced as Truman flicked on the bright front-porch light. I'm sure he wanted to study my expressions as we talked. We started our genteel coffee service, but this was anything but a social call. My heart began to pound as I prepared to rehash the day's events.

Truman cut to the chase. "Did Felicity Fournier ever contact you about having her wedding here?"

"Nope. I checked my voicemail and the answering machine for the landline. Rachel checked her messages too. I'm certain she never called and talked to anyone here about her wedding."

"Tanner seemed pretty certain she had." Truman wasn't accusatory, just stating the facts.

"Could she have talked to someone who purported to be me?" The thought was disturbing. "Or maybe Tanner and Felicity got confused, and she spoke to another venue." There had to be some simple explanation.

"Or Felicity just wanted him to think she'd talked to you about booking their wedding." Truman's statement hung in the air between us.

"But why would she do that? What would be the point?" It was a shame we couldn't just ask her.

"Let's backtrack. What happened with that dress? Describe the altercation in the Silver Bells bridal shop. I want to hear it from you before I get Bev Mitchell's amped-up version."

I smiled at his rueful description of Bev. I'm sure she'd already spread her version of what had happened all over town, lighting up cell phones with the tale. I gave Truman what I hoped was a succinct and accurate recounting of the melee in Silver Bells. He took notes in his shorthand and stopped to observe my face as I talked.

"Oh, and there's one other thing. Two women were arguing in a dressing room."

"There was another argument, one separate from Felicity and Becca?" Truman leaned in.

"Well, I don't know if I'd call it an argument. There were raised voices, at least two women. And one of them left the dressing room. It was Felicity." I felt my face fall. "I don't know who the second woman was, and I wasn't watching the dressing room to see her leave." I wished I'd made note of the other woman. It seemed important now.

"That's okay, Mallory." Truman's face turned kind. "You observed and remembered a lot. This will help me greatly."

I relaxed and settled back into my wicker chair, drawing a sweater closer around me. Something was picking at the back of my brain.

"Tanner said Felicity received a text from Becca offering to sell her the dress after all. That just doesn't seem right after their fight over the dress. There's no way Becca would be willing to sell it, and she didn't mention anything to me about it either."

Truman sighed as he seemed to weigh how much to divulge. I had a habit of accidentally inserting myself into his investigations, and he would occasionally keep me privy to information if I gave him some in exchange.

"We'll need to subpoena the records from the phone company to get the official story. But Becca was very forthcoming about handing over her cell phone. And, at first glance, it appears like Becca is telling the truth. She didn't text Felicity to come over and buy the dress."

"Unless she erased the texts." I winced as the accusation flew unbidden from my mouth. I couldn't believe I'd just tried to implicate a bride I was working with, even if it was Becca.

Truman gave me an appraising look and raised one bushy brow. "That's why we'll need the official texting log. But it barely matters. We've had a chance to look through Felicity's phone, and sure enough, someone did text Felicity about purchasing the gown. Someone purporting to be Becca. We've run the number. It looks like it'll turn out to be a burner phone. We're putting a trace on it, of course, but that's what I expect to find."

"That doesn't mean it still wasn't Becca, trying to throw you off her trail."

"Becca and Keith were with you the entire time of the tasting. Did you notice them using their cell phones?"

I thought for a minute. "Keith did text, and he told us he was contacting his mother." I felt a rueful smile turn up the corners of my mouth. "He's still attached to Mama Helene's hip." My smile slipped from my face. "Becca did step out at one point to use the powder room. She could have texted Felicity from a burner phone then."

"I know there's no love lost between you and Ms. Cunningham," he said. "But I'm not willing just yet to make her my number one suspect."

"There's Tanner." I cocked my head and considered the lanky professor. "He seemed to be acting like a bereaved person would, under the awful circumstances. Until he tried to pry off Felicity's ring." I shook my head at the memory of Tanner's bizarre behavior poolside after Felicity had been taken from the water.

"Shock can make people do strange things," Truman agreed. "But we always look at the significant other, as a matter of course."

"And then there's the Alma connection." I brought up Becca's grandmother and carefully gauged Truman's reaction.

He was impassive and nodded. "I think Alma wants me to believe Felicity tried to murder her. According to Alma, Felicity tried to broker purchase of Alma's entire *Gone with the Wind* collection. Felicity would badger Alma at all hours, day and night. Alma never took her seriously because she didn't think Felicity had the funds to buy it all, and because she wasn't interested in selling." He shook his head and stared into the now-navy-blue night. "It's awfully convenient that Alma has insinuated that Felicity tried to strangle her to steal her collection and now Felicity is dead."

I couldn't stifle a guffaw. "Are you thinking that sweet little old lady had anything to do with Felicity's death?" It was laughable. Alma was a spitfire, but she wasn't capable of murder.

Truman gave me a withering look and settled back in his chair. "It's just something to keep in mind, Mallory. No one's accusing Alma of anything." He flipped his notebook closed. "I'm more interested in how this all fits together, or if these are just random occurrences. Felicity told Tanner she called you to set up a meeting for their wedding, yet she didn't. Why?"

"She seemed pretty excited about her engagement in Silver Bells," I mused. "Well, at least she was excited to shove her ring in Becca's face."

"Yes, according to Tanner, they got engaged two nights before she died."

I nodded my agreement. "That's what she said in Silver Bells too." I remembered what Becca had said on the deck. "Maybe Becca's right. Maybe it was a suicide."

"Let's not get ahead of ourselves. We'll need to do an autopsy. And Becca has reasons to cast doubt on Felicity being murdered at her home." Truman seemed to weigh whether to go on. "You're not from here, so you wouldn't know of their rivalry. Becca Cunningham and Felicity Fournier have been locking heads practically since toddlerhood. Of course, Becca wouldn't want her rival turning up dead on her property."

Unless she was behind it all.

I shivered again, and made a note to watch my step around Becca for the duration of the next two weeks.

"And how, or if this relates to the attempted murder of Alma and the robbery of her collection? Time will tell, and I hope to resolve this quickly." Truman stood to go.

A stray thought percolated in the back of my head. "And I wonder if this has any connection to the murder of Alma's husband Glenn last year?" I hadn't had a chance with the grisly whirlwind of events of the last few days to look into what the online newspaper archives said about Becca's grandfather's murder. I squirmed in my chair and tried to decide if it was a good idea agreeing to look into his murder at the behest of Alma.

Truman's affable face fell a degree and then took on a shuttered look. Clouds gathered in his hazel eyes, and I knew the conversation was over.

Oops.

I regretted at once bringing up the unsolved murder. A tidal wave of tiredness crashed over me. I thought of the loose ends I needed to tie up for tomorrow's baby shower before I could crawl up to bed. I hadn't even begun to leaf through the prodigious binder Alma had given me for her theater reopening. Rachel was right. I was overwhelmed, and we needed to hire more help to address our expanding business.

"Good night, Mallory." Truman's smile returned briefly. "Stay safe."

The next day dawned crisp and clear and sunny. I lay in my bed as rays of light spilled onto the honeyed wooden floors, and a series of birds trilled with delight outside my window. Soda, the little orange fluff ball, alighted on the bed to receive her usual morning cuddles and pets. Her mother, the calico Whiskey, remained dozing at the foot of the bed. She opened one eye as I threw back the covers, then got up and indulged in a resplendent kitty-cat stretch.

I showered and donned a yellow sundress and denim jacket to host my friend Whitney's baby shower. I was looking forward to a day of no drama, just good, clean fun. We'd be celebrating a new baby today. What could be more innocent than that?

Rachel and I ferried food out to the carriage house, where the event would be held. The space was decorated with murals in a nod to the vehicles that had once resided there. One long wall held paintings of turn-of-the-nineteenth-century cars. Model Ts and antique Rolls-Royces marched down the wall in a profusion of jewel tones. The opposite wall featured paintings of the elaborate horse-drawn carriages used at Thistle Park when it was first built. It was the perfect space to host a car-and-transportation-themed shower for a baby boy. The decorations Rachel and I strung up and placed at each table echoed the existing decorations in the space. Rachel placed the cake, a replica of a red toy windup car, at its place of honor on the sideboard. Caterers from the restaurant Fusion arrived with beautiful pyramids of sushi. The mom-to-be, Whitney, had been craving the dish but hadn't been able to partake of raw fish due to her pregnancy. The restaurant had crafted a careful menu of cooked and vegetarian sushi that Whitney could consume. I was excited the shower was coming together so nicely.

"I have to admit, Rach, maybe you were right. I'm having a blast putting together these extra events."

Rachel beamed and stood from scattering a smattering of mint leaves into the punch. "I told you it'd be worth it. And with the extra revenue—"

"What is this? Sushi?" Becca's reedy voice cut through our amiable chatter. "But I was going to have sushi at my Asian fusion wedding! Mallory, are you using this shower to upstage me?" Becca's pretty face was mottled with blotches of red. I glanced around, happy to find that the guest of honor, Whitney, had yet to arrive.

"Becca, take a deep breath." I tentatively laid a hand on her arm. "Your wedding is primarily *Gone-with-the-Wind*-themed, so there won't be any upstaging from this baby shower." I studiously avoided looking at my sister, who was giggling as she adjusted platters of food.

"I've had a change of heart." Becca's mouth took on a petulant pout. "After what happened with Felicity and my dress, I don't want to do a *Gone with the Wind* wedding. I'd wanted to honor Alma, but I just can't go through with it."

I don't blame you.

The ghastly scene at the pool yesterday was enough for me to agree with Becca. Though if I were being honest, I wasn't entirely sure Becca didn't have something to do with Felicity's murder.

"I see your point. I'll see what food we have arriving from our vendors, and we'll go back to one of the earlier plans for your wedding."

Becca's face relaxed a marginal degree, until a new voice ricocheted through the carriage house.

"I couldn't agree more." Helene strode purposefully over to us, her kitten heels striking the floor with such force, I expected to see brimstone. "There isn't time to come up with a new wedding plan with your big day so close upon us."

I found myself inexplicably agreeing with Helene and braced myself for whatever ulterior motive she had in mind. Becca took a step back and waited for that shoe to drop as well.

"I had to stop by to see you myself, Becca, since you won't deign to return my phone calls."

Becca cringed as Helene went on.

"So we will have no choice but to return to the ideas I proposed." Helene clasped her hands, dripping with jewels, before her. "I see white ostrich feathers, pink and cream peonies, and peach damask tablecloths. You can accent with cream pearls and lace and candles."

I felt my mouth open and close. I had to at least give Helene consistency points. This was the vision for the wedding she'd decreed for me and Keith a year ago. I'd grown so weary of fighting her every demand that I'd eventually just given in and planned the wedding to her specifications.

"And we already have the menu set. We'll go with the dishes you served at the tasting I attended. Prime rib, chicken piccata, potatoes, and white cake." Helene's face flushed and glowed with the thrill of victory.

Becca looked as if she'd cry. I felt a rush of empathy for her, and barely refrained from giving her arm a squeeze. It was mentally tiring going from pitying and understanding Becca to suspecting her for Felicity's murder.

"I guess so." Becca's voice was miserable, but she acquiesced.

"Good. I knew you'd come around. I must be off." Helene offered us a triumphant smile that didn't reach her eyes. She left as quickly as she'd arrived, more than earning her moniker of Hurricane Helene. She trailed a sharp cloud of Calèche in her wake.

I felt Becca deflate next to me. Her left eye

twitched. She unclenched her fists and gave a shaky laugh. "Helene always gets her way in the end."

I shivered as Becca stalked off.

"What if Helene orchestrated Felicity's murder to stymie plans for a *Gone with the Wind* wedding?" The thought popped out of my mouth as quickly as it had entered my head.

Rachel laughed and shook her head, her peacock-feather earrings skimming her shoulders. "Nah, that's too crazy, even for the likes of Helene. She's just up to her usual tricks. Ones you know very well."

Rachel was right, down to the act of Helene tracking you down in person if you dared to ignore her calls or didn't call back within half an hour.

"Speaking of crazy ideas . . ." A thought bubbled up in my head. I closed my eyes and thought of the basement, where a neat stack of boxes rested among extra tables, linens, and chairs for various wedding setups. The boxes of favors and decorations from my own defunct wedding to Keith lay calmly entombed in Thistle Park's cellar, waiting for their day in the sun.

"Rachel, what do you think of using the favors from my wedding for Keith and Becca's big day? Is that too tacky?"

Rachel shook her head, a slow smile lighting up her face. "I think it's perfect. Besides, desperate times call for desperate measures."

"No one would know, not even Keith." He hadn't taken much of an interest in our wedding decor back then. It was all Helene's whims and wishes come to life. And she'd decreed the same exact decorations, right down to the pearls and ostrich feathers. Which conveniently reposed in storage right on this property.

"Becca won't know either." Rachel's face grew solemn. Back when I'd been engaged to Keith, Becca had been the official other woman. She probably had never thought of what had become of my wedding decorations.

"Okay. It's a plan." I felt strangely better, knowing the old decorations would finally be put to good use. Not to mention there was one less task on my list.

"Mallory!" A gorgeous and hugely pregnant woman crossed the room to envelope me in as much of a hug as she could give.

"Whitney, you're glowing." It was true. Whitney had dressed in a simple, polka-dot blue dress for her shower, her lovely strawberry-blond hair curled over her shoulders. Her brown eyes shone as she turned a slow circle to take in the decorations.

"This space looks magnificent. This will be such a lovely shower." The mother-to-be gave Rachel a hug and nearly bounced on the balls of her feet with excitement.

"Whitney!" Becca embraced her cousin, and to her credit, seemed to have dropped the pouty act over dueling wedding plans and baby shower themes. Becca seemed genuinely happy for her cousin.

"And Samantha, I haven't seen you in so long." Whitney doled out an extra-long hug for her other cousin.

"I'm so glad I could be here for your shower

since I had to miss your wedding last fall." Samantha patted her cousin's back, and tears dotted the corners of her eyes.

The shower was soon underway. Guests dined on sushi and chicken tempura, and sipped two kinds of punch, one spiked with champagne, the other nonalcoholic. Soon Whitney was cutting into the car cake, which Rachel and I carefully served. Whitney ambled over after finishing her dessert.

"There's one guest missing." She sighed. "Felicity was supposed to be here." Whitney's pleasant voice was tinged with sadness.

I looked up sharply from the tower of diaper boxes I'd been straightening. "I hadn't realized she was on the guest list." It was true. I'd made sure I'd gotten an accurate head count for the event, and managed the RSVPs, but Felicity's name hadn't been on my radar until yesterday.

Whitney shook her head. "I'd been debating not extending an invitation. I was friends with Felicity, but she and Becca were famous rivals. It's horrific that Felicity ended up passing away in Becca's pool."

I nodded, speechless that word had traveled so fast and so far. There had been an article in the paper about Felicity being found on Keith and Becca's property, but the specifics weren't made public yet.

"Becca told me everything," Whitney rushed on, rubbing her ample belly. "I can't help but wonder what would have led Felicity to such despair. I hope it wasn't all because of a silly dress."

So Whitney thinks it was a suicide.

I was sure that's what others would think too. Especially because Felicity was found wearing the Scarlett O'Hara dress, and in Becca's pool no less. But what if someone just wanted everyone to think Felicity had committed suicide?

"So lovely to celebrate a new life." Alma materialized at my side, shuffling over while leaning heavily on her cane.

"Alma! I wasn't expecting you." I bent and gingerly gave the woman a hug, which she returned with full force. I recalled that Alma had been on the guest list for the shower but had assumed she'd still be home recuperating.

"I'm a little late," she apologized, waving to her granddaughters Becca and Samantha. "And Whitney isn't technically my relation. She's related to Jacqueline's side of the family." The sprightly woman gave a shrug. "But I'm always invited to her events. I'm the life of the party, you know." She gave a hearty chuckle, her scarf slipping a bit. Today's fabric was a vivid purple. Alma quickly retied the scarf so as not to treat guests to a view of her bruised neck.

"I'm so glad you could make it." Alma truly must have been on the mend if she could show up for the shower, late or not.

Her gaze grew wistful as she took in the pregnant Whitney. "My Glenn would have loved to have had some great-grandchildren. I'm so happy Becca is marrying Keith in less than a fortnight. Maybe I'll get to be a great-grandmother after all." She leaned toward me conspiratorially. "Have you asked Truman if he has any leads about my Glenn?"

I gulped a swig of punch down the wrong pipe

and sputtered into a napkin. Several heads turned toward me, and I quickly struggled to regain composure. "Um, I did mention your husband." I was squirming internally. I felt like I'd been thrust into the position of a spy, gathering secrets to report back to Alma. "Truman didn't really have anything to say."

"Not this time," Alma snorted. "Truman knows more than he's said to me, and I'm hoping you'll get to the bottom of it." She sighed, suddenly seeming all of her ninety years. "Although with the death of Felicity, he'll have his hands full." A small smile crept up over her lined face. "Bless her poor, dear heart." Her sympathy for Felicity was syrupy sweet, more akin to saccharine than maple sugar.

"I know Felicity was badgering you, but it's still a tragedy." I was inwardly appalled at Alma's apparent gloating regarding Felicity's death. But I was talking to thin air. Alma had spotted someone else she knew and had flitted away, leaning on her cane, before I had spoken my rebuke. It was just as well. I wondered if Felicity had annoyed others as much as she had Alma. Maybe her ending up dead at Becca and Keith's wasn't the result of her suicide.

I shivered, then shook off the macabre thoughts. After a rousing round of shower games, Samantha and Becca helped to divvy up prizes. Rachel and I served coffee, tea, and cookies. Whitney opened present after present and seemed delighted at amassing a tidy pile of baby onesies, booties, and hats. Behind her, her mother and mother-in-law worked to organize a flotilla of baby gear and gadgets. Women happily exclaimed over the loot, and all was merry and well. Ian, Whitney's husband, arrived, a slow smile lighting up his face, exposing his chipped-tooth grin. Women rushed to congratulate the parents-to-be.

Whitney and Ian stood hand in hand in front of their guests. "We want to thank you all for coming to celebrate our son. Thank you, Mallory and Rachel, for throwing this beautiful shower. We—" Whitney trailed off as her head swiveled toward the entrance to the carriage house. Whitney faltered, and didn't resume her speech. Her pretty face was pulled down in a frown.

I squinted against the sunlight to get a better look at the shower's newest arrivals. An unexpected man and woman walked in. The man was J.Crew handsome, with twinkling green eyes and close-cropped blond hair. The woman on his arm was lovely as well, her face reminiscent of that of a 1940s' Hollywood starlet, with large eyes, full lips, and the kind of cheekbones that could grace the cover of an old-time *Vogue*. She wore her jet-black hair in a daring pixie cut, the kind of hairstyle that few but those with her strong bone structure could pull off.

Becca gasped. Her flute of champagne slipped from her fingertips and shattered on the stone floor. The sound was impossibly loud because everyone had gone silent when Whitney had trailed off. A shard of crystal from the flute must have nicked the top of Becca's foot; a thin rivulet of blood trickled over her white sandal.

Ruh-roh.

Becca didn't even notice the state of her cut but laid her hand on her chest, where I saw her ribs rise and fall with her intake of breath. Why did I have a feeling the mystery party crashers were akin to the bad fairy arriving at Sleeping Beauty's christening? We'd already had one uninvited guest, Helene, but her visit had been mercifully brief. This duo didn't look like they were leaving anytime soon. Samantha stared in disbelief at the couple, as if she'd seen ghosts.

"Becca. Just the person I'm looking for." The man had a radio announcer voice, and the assembled baby shower guests sat up straighter to hear what he had to say. A gentle meow came from behind him, and it was then that I noticed he was holding on to a leash. A cat twined its way around the man's legs and stood next to him, as if in solidarity. It was a colossal Maine Coon, with sinuous muscles and tufts of hair decorating the tips of its ears like a bobcat. It proudly held its plume of a tail aloft like the mast and sail of a ship. It was a truly magnificent feline.

"What are you doing here?" Becca had finally found her voice. It came out barely above a whisper, full of anguish and despair.

What in the heck is going on?

Rachel leaned closer to my ear. "Okay, I've heard of wedding crashers, but baby shower crashers?"

Samantha had made her way over to me. "It's Eric Dempsey. He should handle this privately." Becca's twin was barely controlling the rage I saw bubbling deep within her blue eyes. Her mother, Jacqueline, had sat down in a cane chair, her face drained of color.

I recognized the name Eric Dempsey. I was hosting Eric and his fiancée, Piper Hamilton, for their wedding, scheduled for the day after Keith and Becca's Friday wedding. I felt a flood of relief well over me. I'd yet to meet Eric or Piper, as they lived in South America and had planned their wedding over a series of phone calls and emails. They must have arrived early and needed to see me about something. They should have recognized that they'd just walked into a party, but I'd help them as soon as the shower finished wrapping up.

Keith stalked into the carriage house and ran a handkerchief over the beads of sweat amassing on his forehead. He walked along the edge of the room toward Becca, and then seemed to notice the room's silence.

"Bec? What's going on?" Keith stared at a wordless Becca, then at Eric Dempsey. "Who are you? And why are you staring at Becca like that? What do you want with my fiancée?" Keith took a step toward Eric.

Eric snorted. "Becca may be your fiancée. But unfortunately, she's also still my wife."

CHAPTER NINE

Keith let out a rollicking laugh that bounced over the stone floors and echoed throughout the carriage house. When he realized no one was sharing in his mirth, the laughter strangled in his windpipe and spluttered out in an uncertain wheeze. Keith stared at Becca with dawning realization, then abject horror.

"Becca. Is what this man saying true?"

Becca wouldn't meet Keith's eyes. He seemed to have all the answers he needed. Keith's eyes went wide. He took a step back from his fiancée.

"You never told me you were previously married." Keith ran a hand through his thinning hair. He stared at Becca until she tore her eyes from the floor to meet Keith's.

Eric rolled his eyes and bent to pick up the giant Maine Coon. "My marriage to Becca was never annulled." He lifted his chin up high and set the cat down on the ground again. "I've come to ask you for a divorce, Becca. I'd like to remarry." Eric gave his fiancée, Piper, a warm smile. The woman more firmly grasped his arm and observed Becca and Keith with keen eyes.

"Becca." Keith's voice brooked no nonsense. "Is this true?"

Becca wiped at a stream of tears coursing down her cheeks and gave a barely perceptible nod. "I'm afraid so. I thought the annulment went through, but there were some complications."

Keith leaned against the wall, featuring a painting of an ancient Oldsmobile. His face was utterly crushed. A pin dropping could be heard in the carriage house. Then, all thirty ladies assembled began to talk at once.

"I'm glad you finally told her." Eric's fiancée, Piper, spoke, and I realized her voice sounded a bit familiar, though I couldn't place it. I must have just recognized it from the phone calls we'd had planning her wedding. She kept her arm possessively twined through Eric's, and I didn't blame her. Her fiancé was still apparently married to Becca after all. The woman leaned down to pet the impressive Maine Coon, who wound his way around her ankles. Piper sneezed three times in a row and delicately extracted a travel-size parcel of tissues from her tiny purse.

"It's time, Eric." She settled her large, liquid green eyes on Eric's face and arched an impeccably waxed black eyebrow.

Eric sighed and picked up the cat. "I'll miss you, big boy." He turned to Becca, who was in an intense discussion with Keith, and delicately tapped her on the shoulder. Becca yelped and turned around.

"Becca, Piper is allergic to cats. I know you originally wanted to keep custody of him. Piper has suffered enough, and it's time you two are reunited." Eric handed the leash off to Becca. The cat swiveled his regal, leonine head from Becca to Piper. Piper gave him a last fond pat, unleashing another trio of sneezes. "Catch you later, kitty."

Becca knelt close to the ground, and the big cat trotted over to her. She picked him up and buried her mascara-streaked face in his long coat.

"He remembers me." Becca stared up in wonder, a sheepish smile spreading across her face. The Maine Coon's purrs could be heard from several feet away as he shared the joy of being reunited with his former mistress.

"Absolutely not!" Keith stepped back from Becca in abject horror, seemingly more appalled that she was cuddling a cat than finding out she was still married to another man. "I forbid you to accept that cat, Becca. We have a lot to discuss. Come on." Keith held out his hand for Becca, a fierce glare turning his features menacing. Becca took in a sharp breath. She weighed her choice, stroking the cat's long fur as she peered into Keith's eyes.

"I'm so sorry, sweetie pie." Becca deposited the Maine Coon on the stone floor and reluctantly shuffled over to Keith.

"You have a lot of explaining to do, Becca Cunningham," I heard Keith sneer. He shuffled her out of the carriage house amid a buzz of chatter. Some of the baby shower attendees inched toward the exit, the better to hear Keith question Becca.

I searched for Whitney, and our eyes locked

from across the room. The mother-to-be looked stoic in the midst of her ruined shower. A soft flutter against my legs made me look down. The cat had come to rest at my feet. He blinked up at me with huge, citrine eyes that seemed to say, *I agree, they're all crazy.*

I picked up the cat and held him close to me, marveling that he certainly weighed more than both my cats combined. His enormous purr returned, and he looked quite pleased.

The shower was in shambles. Whitney finally made her way over.

"Hi, big guy. I never thought I'd lay eyes on you again." She stroked the big cat's fur and burst out laughing. "This will certainly be a shower to remember! Ian and I will have a good story to tell our son." Her laughter died. "Oh, but Becca sure is in a pickle, isn't she?"

The cat let out a soft mew and rubbed his head against Whitney's hand.

"He thinks you're saying his name," Samantha explained as she joined us. She rubbed the cat behind his tufted ears. "Hiya, Pickles. Fancy seeing you here."

"His name is Pickles?" I stared at the Maine Coon, who perked up when I said his name.

"Yup. They're his favorite. He adores them. He can distinguish the sound of a pickle jar being opened and run across the room to beg for some in three seconds flat." Samantha gazed fondly at the feline. "Dills are his favorite, followed by gherkins."

"A cat who eats pickles?" Rachel laughed and

took her turn petting the colossal cat. He continued to purr in my arms, soaking in all the attention.

"I guess it's not so weird. Whiskey's favorite food
is hot and sour soup." My older cat had spent
much of her life as a stray, and must have devel-
oped an interesting and varied palate in her forays
out in the wider world. She often begged for snippets of takeout, and I was continually surprised
that she ate it all with gusto. Perhaps a cat who ate
pickles wasn't so odd after all.

I helped Ian load the baby shower loot into his
Murano. I could see Keith still arguing with Becca
inside his BMW. He'd yet to pull out from the
drive. Not for the first time, I didn't envy Becca's
position.

Jacqueline remained at the shower, trying gamely
to engage in chitchat, but instead answering questions about her daughter's first, and apparently still-
current marriage. She finally tore out of the room,
a sour look on her face. She stopped to say goodbye as I loaded the last baby item, a heavy swing,
into Ian's SUV.

"Thank you for throwing my niece a lovely
shower." She squared her shoulders and seemed
to steel herself. "I'm sorry Becca's ex-husband had
to ruin it all. Just like he ruins everything." Jacqueline stared with malice in her eyes at Eric and
Piper, who were perched on the back porch of the
B and B. "Rhett said he'd handle the dissolution of
Becca's marriage." Jacqueline shook her head, her
pretty flaxen bob fanning out against her cheeks.
"This is just another thing he let fall through the

cracks." Jacqueline leaned in for a perfunctory air-kiss. I caught a distinctive whiff of Dior J'adore. Jacqueline stalked off to her car. I wondered about the state of her marriage to Rhett.

Samantha paused as she trailed after her mother. "I thought Eric would have had the decency not to make a show." She shook her head but returned Eric's wave to her from the back porch.

Interesting.

Becca may not have been on speaking terms with her ex, or, rather, current husband, but he seemed pretty friendly with her twin sister.

I was in no rush to check Eric and Piper in after the stunt Eric had pulled. But I wanted to be professional, and I was still scheduled to host their wedding. So Rachel and I made haste to break down the remnants of the baby shower. I soon joined the couple on the back porch, where they reposed with a mountain of luggage. They now looked appropriately sheepish in the aftermath of the show they'd put on. And a little bit spent too. Things had calmed down in the wake of Eric's dramatic announcement. All of the attendees had finally driven off, including Becca and Keith. I wondered idly what would become of their upcoming nuptials, now that it had been revealed that Becca was still married to someone else.

"I'm sorry we showed up a bit earlier than expected," Piper began.

Yeah, like a whole week early.

I was still salty that they'd almost ruined Whitney's shower. But then I remembered the ultimately amused look on Whitney's face and softened toward Eric and Piper.

"But we thought the annulment had been taken care of," Eric smoothly finished. "We needed some time to seek a quick divorce back in the States." I knew Eric and Piper were coming back to Port Quincy for their wedding from living abroad. Then it clicked. Eric and Piper currently lived in Colombia, where Becca's twin Samantha happened to be an attorney. I wondered if they traveled in the same circles in Bogota, and if that was why Eric had sent Samantha the friendly wave from the porch.

"It's all right. I can check you two in now and you can get started on your, um, divorce." I trailed off lamely and led them around the wide porch to the front of Thistle Park. Once inside, I unlocked the massive mahogany rolltop desk that served as a check-in kiosk in the front hall. Piper took in the two-story, open entryway, with its large glass bird chandelier. The peach, yellow, and blush sparrows seemed to chase one another around and around in concentric rings. She smiled appreciatively at the marble floors stretching back to the second hallway, and the passel of large rooms leading off to the right and left.

"This is going to be the perfect place for our wedding." But her wide smile slipped a degree. "Um, is that a cat?"

I followed her gaze to the top of the stairs, where Soda sat in a patch of sunshine. The stained-glass above rained down a kaleidoscope of colors on my little orange cat, who delicately washed one paw.

"That's my cat Soda. I have two, actually. I bet my calico is sleeping in the window seat in the library. It's her favorite spot." My prattle trailed off as I remembered a snippet of Eric's speech at the baby shower. "You're allergic to cats, aren't you?"

Piper nodded and stared warily at my kitty. "I've lived with Pickles for three years. I've been able to do it with an arsenal of Zyrtec and Benadryl always at the ready." Her Hollywood glam features softened. "And I'll miss the big guy. But Eric promised me I wouldn't have to deal with my allergies the week of my wedding." She sent me an imploring look, and I sighed.

"I can sequester my cats in my apartment on the third floor for the duration of your stay." I wondered if Piper had read the literature I'd sent with a packet of information that clearly stated there were cats on the premises, or the notifications of the same information on the B and B's website. She'd been given fair and ample warning that there would be furry little felines. No matter; in this business, the bride was always right.

"I guess we'll be putting this big fella upstairs too." Rachel had caught the tail end of our conversation, and sashayed over in her strappy heels with Pickles jauntily marching beside her on his leash. "Come on, Pickles." Rachel patted the leg of her short, electric blue dress, and the Maine Coon gamely ran up the stairs. He made a beeline for Soda, who took one look at the big guy and raced off down the hall.

Eric frowned at the cat interaction. "I'm sorry for the trouble. I hope your cats can get along with Pickles."

That makes two of us.

My mind idly took mental stock of the items in our kitchenette upstairs. I thought there might be a jar of pickles for the Maine Coon to enjoy a bite.

"You said Becca adores Pickles. I really thought she'd take him." Piper cocked her head in thought.

"Her fiancé would never consent to a cat," I rushed in. I felt a slow blush creep up my throat and surely stain my cheeks. I was always divulging personal information about Keith, though we hadn't been an item for almost a year.

I sat at the rolltop and clicked through my laptop, finally printing off a check-in sheet. "Here you are. I can officially offer you early check-in. You'll be in the lilac room, which is our honeymoon suite."

I doled out two keys and reached for a copy of the town newspaper.

"Please accept a copy of our local paper. If you'd like, I can leave a copy outside your door each morning. Just let me know your preference."

"How quaint!" Piper's eyes lit up. "I get all my news online. I haven't held a physical paper in years."

The paper slipped from her slender fingers onto the marble floor. It fell open to the society section, where a large color photo of Felicity Fournier and Tanner Frost stared up at us. I quickly bent to retrieve the paper and moved to close it, when something caught my eye. In the photograph, Felicity rested her left hand over Tanner's arm, the better to show off her impressive rock. Something skittered through my brain, but I couldn't quite catch it. I snapped the paper shut and handed it back to Piper.

Eric's phone buzzed, and he took a call, speaking in a flurry of Spanish. He moved several feet away from us and talked while walking in circles around the hall.

"He's a humanitarian and immigration lawyer in Colombia," Piper gushed, obviously proud of her fiancé.

"Like Samantha Cunningham?" I wanted to know for sure if Eric knew Samantha beyond being her once-brother-in-law.

Piper nodded, the chandelier lights glinting off her sleek pixie cut. "They work for the same NGO."

I filed away that piece of information. It was interesting to me that Samantha worked daily with the man who had once been married to her sister. Or rather, was still accidentally married to him.

I checked in Eric and Piper and left them to their day. The rest of the afternoon was blessedly uneventful, all things considered. I was initially worried about the custody limbo regarding Pickles the Maine Coon. But for now, he was happily ensconced in my third floor apartment. He'd properly met both Whiskey and Soda, doing a delicate cat do-si-do of sniffs and a few errant hisses. But my two cats seemed to be getting along well enough with the big guy. True, Whiskey pointedly ignored him, seeming to withhold her judgment for a later date. While Soda was more welcoming and engaged in a spirited game of chase with Pickles all around the apartment. He was quick for such a big cat, and gamboled around the place.

He was so heavy, he nearly thundered over the floorboards, sounding more akin to a small pony than a cat. Soda, in contrast, barely made a sound save for her clicking nails on the hardwood.

I sat at the desk I used to do work up on the third floor and rubbed my throbbing temples. Rachel had left for an early date, and I thought now would be a good time to turn to Alma's theater reopening.

Make that the only time.

I was running out of minutes and hours and needed to shore up this latest event. No matter; Alma had assured me again today at Whitney's shower that all I had to do was confirm with vendors and tie up some last-minute details with the contractor, Jesse Flowers, who I had worked with to renovate Thistle Park. I dialed the first vendor, PQ Catering.

"I'm sorry, but we heard that event was canceled. We've already rebooked the date. We won't be able to make it."

"What?" I toned down the incredulous and panicked tone from my voice and tried again. "The event is most definitely on. May I ask who called to cancel?" I willed myself to take some deep breaths and hoped the woman at the end of the line didn't think I was hyperventilating.

"Why, Alma Cunningham herself called three days ago to tell us it was off."

Call after call was met with the same response. Vendor after vendor claimed Alma had called them herself to cancel. I jabbed at my contacts list and called Alma in a panic.

"Of course I didn't cancel the vendor contracts!" Alma practically wailed from her end of the phone.

"Stay calm, Alma. I'll fix this."

I thought of her heart-rate monitor clanging in the hospital, and hoped I hadn't upset her too much. "I'll let you know when it's all straightened out."

"I knew I could count on you." The line went dead, and I stared at my cell phone.

Only one person in this town would have the gumption to try to ruin Alma's resplendent theater reopening. A certain person who had earlier this week been unceremoniously tipped into a swimming pool.

I called Helene's number again and again, but she wouldn't answer.

How convenient.

I got some quizzical looks as I led Pickles up the grand front stairs of the Port Quincy Courthouse. My two cats never would have consented to walk on a leash, but Pickles was a pro. He bounded up the steps on his white-tufted paws, graceful and sinuous despite his large size. Soda had been having a blast with the big cat. She'd just outgrown kittenhood, and she played vigorously with Pickles despite the cat visitor outweighing my tiny, five-pound orange ball of fluff by a good fifteen pounds. Whiskey was still wary, consenting to give Pickles the briefest of sniffs. I took Pickles with me to get some air, because he didn't seem used to being sequestered inside.

I unclipped Pickles's leash and advanced through

the metal detector once inside. I carefully shuffled my feet to help avoid setting the machine off. Pickles trailed behind me, staring warily at the metal doorway.

"C'mon, big buddy. It's just a metal detector. It won't hurt." I crouched down and held out my hand. The pretty Maine Coon gained his confidence and jauntily walked through the detector, but he balked when the beep went off. A security guard inspected Pickles's collar and gave the cat a cursory but gentle pat-down. Pickles seemed to enjoy the attention.

"He's probably not packing heat," the security guard joked as he waved us on.

"We'll have to try harder to remove that collar, Mr. Pickles." I resumed my walk with my new buddy, turning heads as we entered the central atrium of the building. I'd gamely tried to remove Pickles's collar, because he'd mainly be an inside cat during his stay at Thistle Park, however long that would be. Becca and Eric seemed to be in no rush to decide his fate, and I was happy to keep the cat. I didn't want his collar to get caught on any of the myriad antiques scattered around the mansion. Then again, because he was going to be sequestered to my and Rachel's airy and bright, mostly open third-floor apartment, maybe I'd leave his collar on.

Pickles got more oohs and aahs than the interior of the courthouse, which was no small feat. It was designed and built at the turn-of-the-twentieth-century, a jewel of a building clad head to toe in bright, Pepto-Bismol pink marble. The open-center atrium spanned three floors, topped with a massive dome consisting of an intricate stained-glass mosaic. But Pickles stole the show, his fluffy plume of a tail held high and proud as he trotted beside me.

I slipped into courtroom three and took a seat on one of the wooden benches in the back. Pickles settled on my lap, and I was happy I'd chosen to don a cat-hair-hiding gray skirt for this outing. I pet Pickles's soft coat and focused on Garrett, who was arguing a petition. He was skillful and calm, with a steady, confident courtroom manner. He finished his motion and moved to sit down. He scanned the back of the courthouse and caught my eye. The corners of his mouth flickered up in the beginnings of a smile, and he sat down.

I loved watching Garrett argue motions and petitions. It reminded me of my days as an attorney, but I didn't miss it. I was having more fun as a wedding planner, putting to good use the negotiation skills and persuasion I'd used as a lawyer. I still liked to see Garrett in action, and discuss his cases with him. I was proud of his successes and how he was continually building his practice.

Pickles stretched and yawned, then let out a satisfied little meow. The other attorney stopped talking and turned around to see where the kitty-cat noise had originated.

"You've done it now, Pickles," I whispered. He blinked up at me with impassive citrine eyes and curled up to sleep in my lap. The other attorney resumed his counter-petition, but the judge sent me a glowering look. I slid down further in the wooden bench and hoped I wouldn't be called out.

"Petition granted." The judge, Ursula Frank, was an imposing woman with a crown of gray braids wound around her head. She gave Garrett a smile, then, with a smart tap of her gavel, started to exit the room. Her tipstaff had to jog to keep up. I caught a flash of Judge Frank's Birkenstocks peeking out from her black robe as she nearly exited the courtroom.

"Judge, if I could have a word?" Garrett stood, and his voice rang out through the now-empty courtroom.

The judge wheeled around, nearly knocking into the clerks hurrying to keep up with her. "Yes, Garrett?" Her terse tone softened. I knew the judge taught a class one afternoon a week at Pitt, and that Garrett had once been her star pupil.

Garrett took a deep breath, suddenly seeming more nervous than when he'd argued his petition for his client. "Let me cut to the chase. I have a friend." Garrett stumbled over the last word, his face twisting into a momentary frown, belying the label. "A friend who needs a quick divorce. I have all the files and orders drawn up. Would you be willing to look this over and grant the divorce quickly?" Garrett stood with a sheaf of papers, an expectant and hopeful look now dressing up his handsome features.

Judge Frank let out a rollicking laugh. "I hear gossip too, Garrett. This is about Keith Pierce and his fiancée, isn't it? And I know he's no friend of yours. But, if you want to help him, you must have your reasons." She held out her hand for the small stack of papers, which Garrett deposited with a look of relief.

"I'm extremely busy, as you well know." Judge Frank now sent Garrett a stern look over her tortoiseshell reading glasses, which she'd donned to quickly scan the documents. "But since it's you asking the favor, I'll make time for this. When does this divorce need to be expedited by?"

Garrett cleared his throat. "Keith is scheduled to wed next Friday."

The judge raised her eyebrows and let out a slow whistle. "I'll see if I can get to this before then." She finally left the courtroom. I felt myself exhale a breath I hadn't known I'd been holding.

Garrett made his way back to me, a look of relief flooding his face.

"Keith owes me big." He shook his head.

"And I owe you big. Who would have thought some of my services as wedding planner would include facilitating the bride's quickie divorce so she could remarry in time?" I stood, and Garrett graced my lips with a quick, fleeting kiss. It deepened into quite a scorcher, until I felt Pickles brush by. Garrett pulled away and gave a laugh.

"So, this is the famous Pickles." The big cat pawed at Garrett's legs, and broke into a roaring purr when Garrett knelt to give him some pats. Garrett had once had a no-pets policy of his own, but he'd softened when his daughter had adopted my cat Whiskey's other kitten, Jeeves.

Garrett stood, suddenly all business. "If Judge Frank grants this divorce, which I expect she will, this'll be a quick end to an even quicker marriage." Garrett's eyes trailed up in the empty, vaulted space, deep in thought. "I wonder how long Keith and Becca will last."

"Tell me about it. I'm not so sure I believe in the

institution of marriage." I nearly clapped a hand over my mouth as I gave voice to some inner thought I hadn't realized I'd had.

Garrett let out a hearty laugh. "A wedding planner who doesn't believe in the institution of marriage?" His laugh died out when he realized I wasn't kidding. His deep hazel eyes took on an edge of alarm.

"I guess I haven't had the greatest experiences with marriage in the long run," I mumbled, digging my hole even deeper. "I think marriage is wonderful, and it works well for some. I love starting couples out on their journey together with a happy celebration. But my parents had such an acrimonious divorce, and you saw how it worked out with my engagement to Keith . . ." I trailed off into an uneasy silence, Pickles's purr working to fill the dead air.

"You're not with Keith now. And that's a good thing." Garrett stepped in closer, peering into my eyes with a burning intensity. I blinked and felt my heart go all aflutter in his heady proximity. We joined for another deep kiss, then finally exited the empty courtroom. I linked arms with my beau, feeling content. But my comments in the courtroom had cast a sneaking slip of doubt.

I wondered where Garrett and I were headed. I reflected on the real alarm that had gathered in his eyes like storm clouds when I'd blurted out my misgivings about marriage. Garrett and I had been together for almost a year. But my heart accelerated when I thought of the word *marriage* as it pertained to me personally, and not necessarily in a good way.

What are you waiting for?

I'd gotten engaged to Keith with no qualms, but look at how that had ended up. All of the goodness of our relationship had started to sour as soon as he'd slipped the too-big ring over my finger. But what I had with Garrett was different. I was happier than I'd ever been in a relationship. I didn't know if I wanted to change things; they seemed so perfect just the way they were.

We exited the courthouse into the bright May day. Pickles sniffed at the air and ignored passersby's comments about him walking on a leash.

"Look who it is." Garrett paused on the courthouse steps as Keith and Becca approached us.

"I trust the matter has been taken care of?" Keith nearly whispered his question when he met us on the steps. Becca knelt to pet and coo over Pickles, who seemed to be happy to reunite once more with his former mistress.

Garrett was barely able to suppress a smile and hide his mirth. "Yes. Judge Frank has the documents for Becca's divorce, and I'm sure she'll attend to them as soon as possible."

Keith winced at the mention of Becca's name, and crossed his arms. "That's not good enough. I need a guarantee that this will all be taken care of by next Friday."

"Um, Keith—" I began.

Garrett shook his head, and chose to address Becca instead of Keith. "The judge is extraordinarily busy. She said she'd get to your divorce, but I'm not about to ask her for a literal guarantee."

Keith rolled his eyes and let out a challenging

sigh. I couldn't believe how testy and ungracious he was being. Just kidding; I totally believed it.

Becca seemed to realize how delicate the situation was and made haste to repair Keith's damage. "I'm eternally grateful, Garrett, and Mallory. Thank you for your help in this trying . . . situation."

"Oh, great," I muttered under my breath as Eric Dempsey approached. He quickly reached our perch on the stairs and graced us with a megawatt smile of perfect, even white teeth. Piper joined his side, her arm possessively twined around his. They could have stepped off a movie set with their camera-ready good looks.

"Thank you, Garrett, for attending to this mess." Eric was far more grateful for Garrett's help than Keith had been. "I know the judge is busy, and that you went out on a limb to ask for my divorce to be granted so quickly." Eric wore his sincerity on his face, and Piper nodded vigorously in agreement.

The tense set of Garrett's jaw softened by a few degrees. "It's understandable in this situation. You genuinely thought your annulment had gone through, and came back early to Port Quincy to try to rectify things." He bestowed a gentle smile on me. "And I was happy to help when Mallory asked."

Keith narrowed his eyes and took a step closer to Eric. "How long have you known you were still married to Becca?"

Becca flinched beside Keith, and her left eye began to twitch.

"When I became aware that I was still married is none of your concern." Eric was cool and dismissive. Then a cunning look stole over his face. "But my fiancée, Piper, has always known I was married to Becca. What I don't understand is how you've just come to learn that Becca was married before."

I was no mind reader, but the look on Becca's face telegraphed that she wished the earth would open up at that moment and swallow her whole.

"You little—" Keith took a step toward Eric, his fists balled up next to his sides.

"Good afternoon, *gentlemen*." Truman advanced up the courthouse steps with an air of disapproval. Keith unclenched his fists and put some space between himself and Eric. Becca and Piper sported similarly appalled expressions. Truman's warning glare was brief as he continued up the steps to enter the courthouse.

"Let's go, Becca." Keith held out his hand to his fiancée, who had knelt to say goodbye to Pickles. The furry guy stared at Becca and sent up a plaintive meow. Two beads of moisture collected in the corners of Becca's eyes and threatened to spill.

"I just need a moment to say goodbye to Pickles again." Becca buried her face in the Maine Coon's fur and stifled a sniffle. My heart melted a degree toward her, seeing how much she missed the big cat.

"Oh, Keith, can't we take Pickles home?" Becca's voice was as pleading as Pickles's meow had been. Keith stared at the cat with disdain. I recalled my efforts to adopt a pet when we'd been together, and guessed the answer would still be a resounding no.

"Pickles is better off with Mallory," Eric smoothly interjected. A barely perceptible strain of worry graced his handsome brow.

Excuse me?

I wondered if I had just inadvertently become Pickles's new owner. I was growing attached to the big fellow, but if Eric's plans had been to rehome the kitty at Thistle Park, it was news to me.

Keith toggled a glare between Eric and Becca. "Fine. You can keep the cat." He appeared to change his mind based on what he thought would irk Eric more, rather than what would please his fiancée.

"Keith! You won't regret it!" Becca bounded up and showered Keith with a rain of kisses.

Eric frowned and knelt to pet Pickles. He scratched the kitty under his chin, simultaneously working to remove the cat's collar. The thick strip of leather wouldn't budge, and Eric finally gave up.

"Farewell, Pickles." Eric stared after the cat as Becca and Keith trailed away, Pickles firmly ensconced in Becca's arms. Becca wore an irrepressible grin on her face. It was a full one-eighty from the despair she'd been in when Eric reminded her that she'd never told Keith about her marriage. Keith didn't look nearly as happy. He stared at Pickles with open disdain. I hoped he'd warm to the cat, who would no doubt attempt to curl up on Keith's lap at the first opportunity.

"I'll miss that kitty," I mused to Eric and Piper. "Whiskey and Soda will wonder where their new friend went."

"He's a sweetheart," Piper agreed. "But I can't say I'll miss all the tissues and allergy meds I've dealt with for the past three years."

I bade them goodbye and set off to see Truman, who must have finished his business and was returning to the administrative police building across the street.

"Truman, wait up!" I gamely ran across the street in my low-heeled sandals, and caught up with the police chief right before he entered the building.

"This'd better be good." He glanced at his watch, all official business.

"Um, I have some information that may be of some interest to you."

Truman's face changed in an instant, the annoyed look replaced with frank curiosity. "Go on."

"All the vendors for Alma's theater reopening have pulled out. They claim she called them to cancel the event due to her attack. But Alma swears she made no such calls."

Truman cocked his head and considered the information. "It could be relevant to the attempted murder on Alma. Or it could be a relatively harmless prank."

Yeah right.

It wasn't truly harmless, as yours truly had to scramble to find new arrangements for Alma's theater unveiling.

"So you'll investigate who called to cancel each vendor contract? You could trace the number that called each vendor." I bit my lip, wondering if I'd gone too far. "I made you a list."

Truman shook his head, a mirthless chuckle escaping his lips. "I can always count on you to insert yourself into my investigations."

I bristled and straightened up. "I beg your pardon, but Alma has tasked me with taking over the planning of her theater reopening. I'm not just meddling," I lamely added.

This time Truman's laughter was real. But it soon died out. "I'll check out this list. But to be frank, I have enough on my plate investigating Felicity's murder."

"So it wasn't a suicide?"

Truman shot me a shrewd look. "The preliminary autopsy results came back. Felicity was hit in the head before she went in. She was most likely unconscious. It was no accident."

CHAPTER TEN

I left downtown with a heavy heart. The official news that Felicity had been murdered felt like a boulder resting on my chest. I drove on autopilot, wending my way through the yellow-brick streets of Port Quincy without really seeing my surroundings. I found my mind wandering back to Becca and Keith's pool and the day we found Felicity in the Scarlett O'Hara gown. I realized I'd tried to convince myself that she had indeed committed suicide, in some kind of bizarre payback on Becca for winning the right to buy the *Gone with the Wind* gown.

And now I had to consider the possibility that my newest bride was a stone-cold killer. There was no love lost between Becca and Felicity, and Felicity had been found in Becca and Keith's pool. Sometimes the most logical explanation was the winner. Keith and Becca had arrived at Thistle Park together for the tasting on the day we'd found Felicity, but that didn't mean Becca couldn't have murdered her rival. Keith could have been any-where in their cavernous house when Felicity went into the water.

I stole into the B and B, oblivious to the chirp-ing birds and warm May breeze. Rachel was in the kitchen. She wore a chef's coat over her short yel-low jumpsuit, and she knelt to continue applying icing in a complicated herringbone pattern to a delicate petit four.

She whirled around as I shut the back door, an irrepressible smile on her face. Her sunny smile faltered when she took in my expression. She set down her piping cone of icing and brushed her hands on her white coat.

"Felicity was murdered." I slung off my bag and placed it on the kitchen table. "It wasn't suicide."

Rachel took in a sharp breath. "I don't like this, Mallory. First Becca's grandmother is strangled, next Felicity is murdered in the pool. We could still cancel Keith and Becca's wedding."

"Not to mention Becca's grandfather was shot last year in his office at Quincy College." I'd finally searched the *Eagle Herald*'s online archives for news about Alma's husband, Glenn. The stories were brief. They reported Glenn had been found shot at his desk in the history department, with Wilkes the Irish setter by his side. A few small arti-cles followed up in the weeks afterward, mainly discussing the Port Quincy police having no leads.

"It's all fishy." Rachel rinsed a swath of icing from her hands and dried them on a dish towel. "Right down to Felicity telling her fiancé she'd called us to schedule their wedding when she hadn't."

"Well, there is one piece of good news." I sank

into a kitchen chair. "Garrett talked to the judge, and she seems amenable to granting Eric and Becca a lightning-fast divorce."

"That *is* good news. At least for Becca and Keith, and Eric and Piper." Rachel made a face. "Although to tell you the truth, I wouldn't have been unhappy if Becca had decided to cancel her wedding after all."

I nodded my agreement. "I kind of thought she might have done it after what happened to Alma." I winced. "And certainly after what happened to Felicity."

"What's the rush?" Rachel rested her chin on her hand and joined me at the table with a cup of coffee. "Keith and Becca asked to be placed on a waiting list for cancellation openings. Why not just keep their original wedding date of a year out?"

We sat in uneasy silence for a few moments as we pondered all the strange happenings going on in Port Quincy.

"And there's one more thing." I took a fortifying slug of coffee and dragged my eyes up from the kitchen table to meet my sister's inquisitive green ones. "I sort of told Garrett I'm having doubts about the institution of marriage."

"You what?" Rachel slammed down her coffee, and a slosh escaped the rim of her delicate rose cup. It spilled over the table in a brown rivulet and threatened to roll off the edge, before she caught it with a napkin. "Mallory, this is the worst possible time!"

"I regret saying it." I helped her mop up a bit of coffee and cocked my head. "I didn't even know I really felt like that until the words slipped out of my mouth." My eyes narrowed at my sister. "But what do you mean, this is the worst possible time?"

What is Rachel up to?

My sister colored, a pretty bloom of pink staining her cheeks. "I just think this isn't the time to be expressing doubts about marriage. I'm sure Garrett will be popping the question soon!" Rachel beamed, her thousand-kilowatt smile returned. She stood to get more coffee, and executed a series of actual hops on her high-heeled, bejeweled flip-flops.

"Whoa, whoa, calm down. No one is getting engaged around here. Certainly not me." I felt a coy look steal over my features. "Maybe you should look into getting engaged, if you're so smitten with the idea."

My sister had many suitors, all vying to catch her attention. But she seemed in no rush to settle down herself, preferring to go out on a fun series of dates with not-too-serious intentions.

"I'm not the one who's been dating Port Quincy's most eligible bachelor for the past year." Rachel raised one perfectly arched brow and returned with her new cup of coffee. "I'm not the one with a boyfriend spotted in Fournier's jewelry store."

My breath caught in my chest.

"*What?*"

Rachel nodded, the jaunty genie-style ponytail she'd placed atop the crown of her head spilling waves of honeyed hair. "I saw him at the jewelry store on my way out of yoga downtown."

"But that doesn't mean he was buying an engagement ring." My heart began to slow its staccato rhythm. I took a deep breath. "He could be getting something for Summer. Or his mom. Or having a watch battery replaced." I could think of several reasons why the man I'd been seriously dating had ducked into the jewelry store. And I secretly hoped each one led to a different outcome than an engagement ring.

"What if he was going to ask you right when you blurted out you aren't sure about marriage?" Rachel pouted and moved back to the sink to rewash her hands. She donned her white jacket again and picked up the piping cone. She squinted as she laced another lattice stripe on a petit four. "Nice going, Mallory."

My shaky breath returned as I recalled the lovely kiss I'd shared with Garrett. What if I had ruined the moment he was going to propose? A sickening feeling now settled at the bottom of my stomach. I was so confused. I was wary of marriage and entering another engagement after what had happened with Keith. Yet the thought of accidentally stymying Garrett proposing made me sad too. I wasn't sure what I wanted.

"Earth to Mallory." Rachel stopped in midpipe and wheeled around.

"Those are pretty," I remarked as I gestured to the little cakes. I had to try to change the subject before my head exploded. "What event are they for?"

"A church auxiliary party." Rachel stooped to glance at the petit four from another angle. "I'm taking on more cake orders." She straightened again and cocked a hand on her hip, leaving a smear of brown icing on her white coat. "I'm going to expand my side business, which means you'll need more help around here to run the weddings." A small, satisfied smile rested on my sister's face.

Check and mate.

If Rachel couldn't get me to agree to add on more events and book more Friday weddings, she was going to expand her baking repertoire. I'd be forced to hire a bigger fleet to make up for the time Rachel would be devoting to extra baking. My sister was one smart cookie, and she usually found a way to get what she wanted.

"I'm glad you're taking on more cake orders," I said evenly. "I suppose I'll have no recourse but to hire more people to help with the wedding side of the business."

Rachel let out a whoop of glee. "I'm so happy you've come around. It's time to take it to the next level. And not just with our business." She stopped and waggled her brows. "With Garrett too." Before I could respond, she rushed on. "And then we can host more events, and—"

I laughed, cutting her off. "Let's just get through this crazy month, all right? Speaking of which, I still need to find a solution for Alma's theater reopening or we really will have to cancel it."

And I couldn't do that. After all Alma had been through, I didn't dare break her heart by pushing off her grand reopening.

"I bet Helene was the one behind the vendors canceling." Rachel spoke with disdain lacing her words.

"She's done it before," I agreed. Just this February, she'd strong-armed a florist into not working with me as retribution for not following her decrees for a high school dance. Pretending to be Alma and telling all the vendors the event was called off had Helene written all over it.

"But be that as it may, the show must go on. I'm headed out to meet with Jacqueline, and we'll see what we can do to get the event up and running."

If I can make it happen in three days' time.

The thumping in my chest that pondering an impending engagement had evoked returned as I left Thistle Park and drove to the Cunningham residence. Alma's heavy tome of a three-ring binder rested on the worn leather passenger seat beside me. It held all her ideas, plans, and contracts for her theater-reopening event, but with each vendor erroneously canceled, it wouldn't do me much good. I had so little time to salvage the event, I didn't think I could afford to be picky. We would just have to go with what I could piece together, and try to make it a lovely party and debut for the small theater. I mustered these thoughts together as I pulled into the circular drive fronting Becca's parents' house.

Becca's family seemed well off but not ostentatious. Jacqueline and Rhett lived in a sprawling Tudor and brown-brick house with tall trees and a carefully cultivated front garden of hostas, geraniums, and impatiens. It wasn't as grand as Keith and Becca's Cubist monstrosity, but it was large and warm and inviting.

"Come in, dear." Jacqueline brushed my cheek with an air-kiss, a move Becca usually performed as well, and led me down a pretty tiled hallway to the spacious living room. Everywhere, there were pictures of Jacqueline, Rhett, and their twins. I could follow the progression of the girls' childhood, Becca salt and Samantha pepper. There were photographs of the girls with Alma, and an older man I assumed was Glenn. I recalled the annoyance Jacqueline had expressed at the baby shower regarding Rhett's failure to properly dissolve Becca's marriage. I wondered about the state of their marriage. In the pictures, they were a happy couple, doting on their daughters throughout the years. But pictures didn't always tell the whole tale.

"I hope chicken salad is okay." Jacqueline startled me as she entered the room. I sheepishly stood away from the bank of pictures I'd been examining and joined her on the couch. The consummate hostess, Jacqueline had served a pretty painted polka-dot tray laden with tiny sandwiches, iced tea, and scones.

"This looks delicious." I took a delicate bite of a sandwich and shoved the heavy binder with the theater reopening plans away for the moment. "I was just enjoying your family photos. You've taken some lovely pictures over the years."

Jacqueline smiled fondly and picked up a framed photograph from the side table. "They help me cultivate my happiest memories." She turned the picture outward and tapped the glass. "This is Glenn taking the twins for their first trip on a merry-go-round, at the county fair." In the picture, a delighted Becca and Samantha as toddlers sat on painted horses as the same older man from the other photographs smiled and kept watch.

"We miss him dearly," Jacqueline said as she set down the frame.

We ate the small chicken salad sandwiches on mini croissants and moved on to the matter at hand.

"These plans look wonderful. Unfortunately, as I said over the phone, they've all been canceled."

"That nasty woman." Jacqueline shook her head. "Helene Pierce has been absolutely horrible to my Becca. I've counseled my daughter to reconsider marrying Keith, if only so she isn't under the thumb of that woman."

I gulped a swig of iced tea and wondered if Jacqueline knew I'd once been engaged to Keith myself, before her daughter and Keith commenced their affair. It certainly wasn't an appropriate topic, so I chased the thought from my mind.

"Truman Davies said he'd look into who called all the vendors to cancel the theater event contracts. Let's just say I won't be surprised if Helene is behind it all."

Jacqueline and I bent our heads together over the binder, musing about what perfect plans Alma had amassed.

"No caterers in town are willing to step in just three days out." I bit my lip. "But we do have some food in our deep freezers we can repurpose into hors d'oeuvres. It may not follow a specific theme, but people won't go hungry."

Jacqueline nodded at the make-do plan. "And there were some last-minute construction details that were to be completed."

"I'm trying to get a hold of Jesse Flowers, the contractor. I've worked with him before, and I'm sure I can convince him to finish the job."

At least I hope I can.

"Alma planned on having some centerpieces in the lobby. The florist I usually work with, Lucy at the Bloomery, has agreed to put something together." I swallowed and broached a delicate subject. "Some of the vendors at the moment aren't willing to grant refunds to Alma because the cancellation happened so close to the event. They won't make an exception so far, even though Alma didn't cancel the contracts herself."

Jacqueline waved off my concern with a flick of her wrist. "Alma will take care of it. She has enough funds to reimburse whoever steps in at the last minute."

Phew.

Because for now, whoever was going to step in at the last minute would end up being me. I wasn't so sure if Rachel would be too keen on us taking on extra events if it meant we'd be footing the bills ourselves.

Jacqueline's eyes strayed to the photograph of Glenn with her girls. "Alma and Glenn couldn't wait to start remodeling the theater. They'd gotten the idea to redo the building on the eve of his retirement. This project was his baby." She smiled wistfully. "Samantha had a special bond with her grandfather. I know she misses him terribly. She said the other day that she regrets she was away in Colombia when he died."

"It's sad that he's gone." I gave Jacqueline's hand a squeeze. "The girls seem to have a close relationship with their grandmother as well."

Jacqueline winced, and I wondered what I'd said to upset her. She spilled the beans posthaste. "Alma seems to favor Becca, and you can't do that with children. Frankly, I'm appalled that Alma has offered her *Gone with the Wind* collection to Becca only. Alma seriously slighted Samantha, and she doesn't seem to care." Jacqueline's heart seemed to ache for her dark-haired daughter. I thought of all the ways Rachel and I had been treated differently growing up, even if it had been inadvertent. It must have been even harder for the twins because they were the same age, and were probably always being compared to each other.

"And I'm not even half as mad as Rhett. He's still furious that his mother bypassed him in favor of gifting her collection to Becca." She smiled ruefully. "Not that it matters now, with most of the collection stolen."

I tried to tread carefully but pressed on. "Was Rhett counting on the collection as an inheritance?"

Jacqueline gave a bitter laugh. "We don't need Alma's collection, impressive though it is. I brought quite a bit of my own money into my marriage. In fact, I paid for half The Duchess theater."

I dropped a scone in my lap, where it broke neatly in two.

"What?"

Why is Alma running the show if Jacqueline owns half the theater?

"I was a film major in college," Jacqueline mused. "Renovating and reopening The Duchess was supposed to be a joint venture between me, Alma, and Glenn. But Alma took over. As she usually does." A thin current of resentment seemed to boil through Jacqueline and threaten to spill over.

A shiver stole down my back as I inched away from the woman on the couch. What if her ire was enough to act upon? Could Jacqueline have strangled Alma in a spate of revenge for not letting her rightfully plan the theater reopening? Or did Rhett get some inkling that his mother was going to give her priceless trinkets to Becca instead of him, so he rushed to take her out?

"Alma seems to like to pull the strings," I said carefully. "Maybe she was giving away the collection to get some kind of response."

Jacqueline parceled out a shrewd look and wiped a crumb of scone from her lips. "Alma certainly does go after what she wants, whatever that may be."

Maybe I've hit a little too close to home.

I decided to switch the subject. "Alma tasked me with investigating Glenn's death last year. As well as the robbery of her collection and strangulation, for that matter." I blurted out Alma's request. I was met with a merry peal of laughter.

"Yes, I can imagine Alma asking you to do that."

"Tell me more about Glenn." I still didn't know much about him or his death, and I had promised Alma to look into it, no matter how misguided the request now seemed. I only knew the slim bits of information I'd gleaned from the spare newspaper articles.

"Well, for starters, Glenn couldn't stand *Gone with the Wind.*" Jacqueline took in my shocked look with another laugh. "He would be rolling over in his grave right now if he knew how much Alma has spent in the last year to grow her collection. Glenn was a professor of American history at Quincy College, and he thought the movie and book were inaccurate and biased representations of the Civil War and Reconstruction in the South."

I racked my brain for my remembrances of the film and the novel. I'd last seen the movie in college, and read the heavy tome in high school. I had planned on watching the film again this week at the theater reopening, because of course Alma had selected *Gone with the Wind* for the premiere.

"Alma plans on showing *Gone with the Wind* once a week." Jacqueline winced and raised her eyebrows.

"I think it will get some buzz the first time it runs, but there may not be enough continued interest to show it once a week." Not that I thought Alma would care. "What would you have chosen to run on opening night?"

A dreamy look stole over Jacqueline's delicate features, and she broke out into an impetuous smile. "*The Wizard of Oz.* It would be a nice nod to Port Quincy, with all the yellow brick roads downtown." She set down her scone and turned to me excitedly. "I would play *The Rocky Horror Picture Show* once a month. And run classics like *Citizen Kane* and *Casablanca* on Wednesdays. And all the newest indie feature films as well." The embers and sparkles died in Jacqueline's eyes as reality seemed to set back in. "But I'm not running the show. Alma is."

It was too bad Jacqueline didn't have more of a stake in what sounded like should have been a joint venture.

But was it enough to kill for?

The cherry grandfather clock in the corner chimed in a dolorous tone, making me jump.

"I've got to go." I bade Jacqueline goodbye. I was really no closer to whipping up a movie theater premiere worthy of The Duchess than I had been when I'd arrived. What I'd gotten instead was a whole host of reasons why Rhett and Jacqueline might want to murder Alma, and why Alma herself may have had an interest in killing her husband. I was happy to put the Cunningham house far in the distance as I made my way back to the B and B.

CHAPTER ELEVEN

Early the next morning, Jacqueline's revelations bounced around in my head like a game of pinball as I waded through a small village of box skyscrapers in Thistle Park's basement. I squinted in the dull light afforded by the few hanging bulbs in the cavernous space. I was looking for the containers of decorations I'd amassed for my own wedding to Keith that had, thankfully, never come to fruition. But I was distracted by thoughts of the complicated relationships in the Cunningham family, and by my mind's dogged pursuit to try to figure out why Alma had been attacked and Felicity and Glenn murdered.

"Focus. You're not Nancy Drew, you're a wedding planner." I delivered a stern admonition to myself and blew at a cobweb that had affixed itself to my nose. Truman would have a conniption if he found out I'd promised Alma to look into the death of her husband.

Pay dirt.

I found the boxes of decorations and favors in a particularly dusty corner of the basement. I thanked my lucky stars I'd chosen to stash them there last summer, rather than entomb them in a dumpster or set them aflame. I'd been pretty ticked off at Keith upon finding out about his affair with Becca, and trashing the decorations for my canceled wedding would have been cathartic.

But I believed things happened for a reason, and I couldn't erase the grin from my face as I ferried all twelve heavy boxes up the steep basement steps to repose in the kitchen.

"Yuck." Rachel sneezed and waved a hand in front of her face as I plopped down the last box. A layer of grime and dirt covered the cardboard.

"Help me wipe down the boxes before Samantha gets here." I tossed Rachel a dust rag, and we got to work tidying up the mountain of supplies. A tiny ribbon of guilt laced through my mind as we worked. I wasn't about to reveal to Samantha that the boxes were dirty because the decorations had been for my own wedding to Keith. If we'd had more time to come up with decorations for Keith and Becca's rushed big day, I would have started afresh with new trinkets and table settings.

"All better." Rachel surveyed our work with satisfaction and disappeared upstairs to clean up. I cut open several of the boxes to verify their contents, then showered to get ready for my meeting with Samantha.

Half an hour later, I paused at the head of the dining room table to survey the representative centerpiece I'd crafted to show Samantha. I'd gotten frissons of déjà vu as I placed the same white ostrich feathers, coral and pink glass orbs, and strings of pearls around the birdcages and wicker nests Helene had dictated I use last summer.

Rachel entered the room and slowly circled the table. "It's lovely. Too bad it's for those two ungrateful jokers."

I shrugged and adjusted a silk magnolia blossom. "Better Becca than me. And I thought I might be upset about going through my old wedding decorations." I reached for the tray of bagels I'd set up for my meeting with Samantha and used my knife to paint on a cream cheese mustache. I affected my best Clark Gable voice and smirked at my sister. "But frankly, my dear, now I don't give a damn."

Rachel whooped with laughter as I wiped off the cream cheese and reached for a bagel. "They'll soon be out of our hair."

I stiffened, hearing some movement in the hall. I'd left the front door open for Samantha, and not everyone rang the bell when they arrived. Rachel and I had learned to reflexively take care with our words, because we often had guests occupying the first two floors of the B and B. Thistle Park afforded so many nooks and crannies for guests to hang out and eavesdrop inadvertently, from narrow back hallways to window seats and the butler's pantry.

"Hi, ladies." Samantha materialized at the entrance to the dining room. I felt a slow heat climb my neck, and wondered how much she'd heard. "I let myself in, I hope that's okay."

Rachel sported two spots of color on her face but

recovered and offered Samantha a bright smile. "Of course. Help yourself to some coffee and bagels while you work."

Samantha sat down and let out a sigh. "I hate to say it, but being here making decorations will be less stressful than joining Becca and Mom at the dress shop."

I'd also decided to skip attending Becca's quest for a new gown, despite the bride's protestations. If we had any hope of finishing the preparations for this latest iteration of Becca and Keith's wedding, we needed to economize on time. And it appeared Samantha was happy to step out of the shadow of her domineering twin to steal some low-key downtime.

"Weddings can be stressful," I soothed. "They require as much preparation as the most complicated court case, and emotions can run just as high."

Samantha carefully slathered a swath of cream cheese on her bagel. "Becca told me you were an attorney before you became a wedding planner." A rueful smile slyly stole across her round face. "I'm beginning to see that maybe the law is the more tame profession."

"I don't know about that." I offered her my own grin.

"So, these were the decorations for your wedding to Keith." Samantha set down a melon-colored glass globe and sent me a level and even gaze. Rachel held a bagel in front of her open mouth, shocked into inaction right before she took a bite.

I felt my eyes widen and my heart begin to

pound. I feared Samantha could see the rise and fall of my rib cage. "How did you know?"

Samantha let out a rollicking laugh, the tension dissipated just as quickly as it had come on. "I may live in Colombia now, but I grew up in Port Quincy. And although Becca hid that Keith was involved with someone else when they got together, you can't hide anything from your twin sister." She frowned and set down the delicate glass ornament. "I'm sorry your engagement ended at the hands of my sister."

I shook my head, my brass-leaf-motif earrings fluttering around my shoulders. "I always remind myself that it was Keith's choice to step out of our engagement, not Becca's."

Samantha nodded and twined a cream ribbon through the top of the ornament. "Fair enough." She cocked her head in thought. "If it were me, though, I would have torched all this."

I smiled at Becca's twin, liking the way she thought.

"I don't want to spread bad juju by using this stuff, but time is of the essence." I threaded a strip of peach lace through the lattice of a sisal birdcage. "Maybe these baubles and pearls and lace and feathers will do some good in Becca's marriage to Keith."

"Maybe we should have them exorcised," Rachel murmured from the other end of the table.

"Pardon?" Samantha looked up sharply.

Rachel struggled to cover her tracks. "So, how did it come about that Becca is still married to Eric?"

Nice one, Rach.

I sent my sister a poorly concealed glare, and she shrugged.

"Oh, c'mon, Mallory. I'm just asking what everyone in Port Quincy is thinking."

Samantha laughed again, but this time her voice was tinged with weariness. She seemed to take no offense to Rachel's query. "I think Becca and Eric wanted to stay married at one point. Their trial separation just lasted and lasted, and they went on with their lives. My parents assumed Becca had taken care of it." An amused sparkle glinted in Samantha's deep blue eyes. "Becca is the ultimate procrastinator. Maybe she still had feelings for Eric. That is, up until she met Keith. Plus," she reasoned, "Eric was in Colombia. He wasn't here to handle the divorce in person until it became necessary to marry Piper. Eric is the king of efficiency. He probably just figured he'd get divorced while he was back in town. A quickie divorce, and then a new marriage right after."

"What's it like, working with your twin's ex?" I knew from Piper that Eric and Samantha had founded their NGO together.

Samantha tied a coral taffeta bow to the handle of a wicker basket. "It's surprisingly normal. Becca, Eric, and I all went to Duquesne for law school together." She set down the fussy decoration and seemed to stare into the distance. "Felicity too."

I recalled Becca's consternation and claim that Felicity had copied her decision to go to law school.

"Everything Felicity did, Becca had to do too. Or vice versa," Samantha said with a small, tight smile. "We all planned to go into humanitarian law once we graduated, except for Becca, who wanted to do corporate work at a firm. In the end, only Eric and I ended up doing humanitarian work."

I knew Becca had practiced law for a short time while she waited for her bar results, before she failed the test twice and left the law for good.

"Felicity decided she didn't want to practice, and moved back to Port Quincy to work in her parents' jewelry store. She used her law degree to expand the family business, but she stayed friends with Piper and Eric. I actually saw her more than I got to see Becca these last few years. She came to visit us in Bogota a few times a year."

The plot thickens.

It wasn't lost on me that Felicity had been murdered just as everyone from her past coalesced in town for Becca and Keith's, as well as Eric and Piper's weddings. It couldn't have been easy for Becca for her twin to be friends with her ultimate rival.

"What I don't get is how Becca's relationship with Eric ended in the first place. Becca may have her secrets, but she eventually tells me everything." Samantha took a fortifying slug of coffee. "They were so well matched, even though Becca was interested in a corporate career, and Eric wanted to work on human rights and asylum cases. I thought everything was going well with them. Then he suddenly left her. He asked me to get him a position with my nonprofit in Colombia. I wasn't happy he was leaving my sister, but I thought it would blow over. But on one of his trips back to

Port Quincy, Grandpa Glenn introduced Eric to Piper, and that was it. Eric was smitten. And I knew then it was truly over between my sister and Eric."

"Your grandpa introduced Eric to his new fiancée?" This time I had the pleasure of sticking my foot firmly in my mouth.

A flush graced Samantha's pretty, rounded face, belying her embarrassment. "Piper was Grandpa's star student at Quincy College. I don't think he realized anything would come of it, or that it would be the nail in the coffin of Becca's marriage. He certainly didn't want to hurt my sister. She was the apple of his eye."

Interesting.

I recalled my conversation yesterday with Jacqueline, when she'd made it sound as if Samantha had been closer to her grandfather than Becca.

"Your mom said yesterday that your grandfather didn't like *Gone with the Wind*." I decided to slip in a question about Glenn, in an effort to officially close my unofficial investigation of his death. I'd be seeing Alma later this afternoon, and I wanted to report that I would no longer be doing any off-the-clock sleuthing for her. This would be my last foray into the matter, and then it would be case closed. I had enough to do with planning weddings and events, without Alma deputizing me as an investigator.

Samantha set down her coffee cup and dabbed at her mouth with a napkin. "Alma and Glenn had a kind of James Carville and Mary Matalin relationship." A wistful smile stole across her face.

"About politics?" Rachel piped up from her end of the table.

"Oh, about everything," Samantha confirmed. "Sometimes oil and water do mix well, and that was my grandparents. Except for *Gone with the Wind*. He barely tolerated Alma's love of it, but her collection really flourished after his death." She winced and laid her napkin back across her lap. "Alma has sunk much of their joint savings into creating the premier, private *Gone with the Wind* collection."

"How do you feel about Alma's treasures?" I set down a willow branch and waited for Samantha's reply. Her dark eyes danced with laughter.

"I see both sides of *Gone with the Wind*, having grown up in its shadow my whole life. It certainly isn't a politically correct movie or novel when viewed through the lens of our current time." She cocked her head in momentary thought before seeming to carefully choose her words. "It's very problematic. But it also has its own history. I think it's a great teaching tool to examine history and consider it from all sides. As a history professor, Grandpa thought so too." She frowned, the thoughtful look from before slipping from her face. "Grandma never wanted to talk about *Gone with the Wind*'s negatives. I think the collection brought Alma much joy. But also a lot of trouble." Twin beads of moisture collected at the corners of Samantha's eyes. "To be honest, I'm a little miffed she gifted the entire collection to Becca." She straightened in her chair and resumed her work with the centerpieces. "But I can't say I was ever truly interested in it either."

I felt a rush of pathos for Samantha. Though she didn't seem to want Alma's collection, it still hurt that her grandmother had favored Becca in making the gift. Not that it would matter so much now that the prime pieces had been stolen.

"My dad is another matter." Samantha seemed to weigh her words before pressing on. "My father was absolutely furious that Alma gave the collection to Becca." A sheepish cast marred her features. "I think Dad was expecting a sizable inheritance from Alma, but she'd tied up all her funds in the collection. And she obviously didn't protect it very well." She let out a barely perceptible shiver. "I've never seen him so angry."

Rachel and I exchanged shared raised eyebrows across our opposite ends of the table. Samantha was studiously avoiding our gazes, seeming to realize she'd said too much. It was nearly time for our meeting to end anyway. The three of us had made some great headway. There now were the tidy beginnings of elaborate centerpieces, complete with glass peaches, lace ribbons, and willow and ash branches. The centerpieces would be placed back in their boxes. The night before the wedding, Rachel and I would reassemble them and twine them down the length of twenty long tables.

"We'd better wrap this up." I offered Samantha a kind smile. "I need to shore up some plans for Alma's theater reopening and then meet with her downtown."

Samantha nodded and rose to go. "I know Alma deputized you to look into Grandpa Glenn's death."

I felt my mouth open into a little round *o*.

Samantha laughed. "If one person can't keep a secret, it's Alma. Don't worry about her request. The situation is sad, but I believe Chief Truman is doing all he can. Grandpa was shot in his office. There was no sign of forced entry, but then again, Grandpa's office door was always open when he was at work, in case a student wanted to drop by. They found him with Wilkes, and that's all anyone knows."

It's too bad the doggy can't reveal his secrets.

"You can't think of any reason why someone would want Glenn gone?"

Samantha shook her head. "I've thought about it for a whole year. He did expect a lot from his students, but he wasn't so harsh with his expectations that someone would murder him."

There was one person who had a good, if not rational, reason to clear Glenn from the picture. I squirmed in my chair as dark thoughts about Alma needled their way in.

Samantha seemed to read my mind, and I wondered briefly if I'd accidentally spoken them aloud. "It doesn't help with the rumor mill," Samantha said softly, "that Alma broke ground on renovations to The Duchess a mere week after Glenn was killed."

She bade us goodbye and slipped out of Thistle Park.

Rachel let out a slow whistle. "And I thought our family was complicated."

* * *

I shook off my misgivings about Alma and sat behind my desk in the office I shared with my sister. The soothing green walls and poufy chintz furniture usually worked to put my mind in a great state for tackling the knottiest of wedding plans. I had practice negotiating, cajoling, and persuading brides and family members to come to agreements and put aside their differences during various phases of planning a wedding.

But this afternoon, I would be outright begging. I needed my former contractor, Jesse Flowers, to come back on board with Alma's project and finish the last few touches before premiere night.

"What can I do for you, Mallory?" Jesse's surprisingly high voice answered his cell on the third ring.

I decided to cut right to the chase, because time was of the essence. The Duchess would be opening in less than two days, and according to Alma, the elevators and bathrooms still needed to be painted. "I need a big favor."

"Anything for you, doll." Jesse and I had bonded over the particularly accident-laden restoration of Thistle Park last October. I knew I could count on him. It didn't hurt that I was on deck to host his wedding to Bev in a little over a year, right before the Fourth of July. I'd received a few panicked texts from the bridal storeowner herself right after Samantha had left. It appeared Becca hadn't been able to find a dress she loved as much as the ruined and forever cursed Scarlett-O-Hara replica gown. I didn't envy Bev's job right now, though it seemed like half the darn town of Port Quincy was either mobilized to make Keith and Becca's ever-changing wedding successful or to help Alma's theater reopening get off the ground.

"Um, I just wanted to ask if you'd be able to finish painting the last few rooms in The Duchess theater."

I heard a muffled swear and stifled a giggle. Jesse was six-foot-eight, a bear of a man, but his high-pitched voice coupled with his over-the-top utterance set me to laughing.

"I know Alma didn't really cancel the job. I could tell the person who called me was doing an impersonation of her."

"Then you know how dire the situation is. The theater opening is a go, and The Duchess isn't ready."

"I swore I was done working with Alma, whether she canceled the event and ended our contract herself or not." Jesse's voice grew more agitated. "Alma is an absolute nightmare to work with, and I'm glad to be through with her."

I winced at his proclamation and tried to come up with another angle.

"Now, if Alma had let Jacqueline in on some of the decisions, I might be ready to come back on board and get those rooms painted today."

Bingo.

"It just so happens Jacqueline is now in charge of the theater reopening." A tiny fib wouldn't hurt. While Alma hadn't technically ceded control of the event to her daughter-in-law, I had spent more time lately making decisions about The Duchess's debut with Jacqueline rather than Alma.

"Well, now, that's a cat of a different stripe."

Jesse's fondness for malaprops drew another smile across my face. "Okay. I'll get the last few rooms painted today. But let's be clear: This is to help out Jacqueline and you, not that *Gone-with-the-Wind*-crazed she-devil."

I hung up my cell with new theories swimming in my head. Alma had charmed me, but I was quickly learning that not everyone was simpatico with the feisty nonagenarian.

My stomach rumbled, reminding me of my upcoming planning lunch session with Eric. It would be my third stint of the day tending to a different event. I'd been neglecting finalizing the last-minute details for Piper and Eric's wedding, something I hoped to rectify posthaste. I needed a list to keep all the upcoming tasks straight. Due to some strange mishaps, all involving Becca and her family, I had grown our book of business this week. But we were now stretched to the limit. I added a task to my list to start hiring more employees as soon as I got a spare moment to create an ad. An extra assistant would be more than worth another salary. I chuckled to myself as I realized Rachel had gotten her wish.

CHAPTER TWELVE

I gave myself a mental pat on the back for deciding to meet Eric at one of my favorite local joints. The Greasy Spoon Diner was its usual cheery and bustling space, outfitted with gleaming chrome, shiny black and gold vinyl, and the rich and heady scents of comfort food. It was a Port Quincy institution, affording diners a chance to meet friends and acquaintances and share the latest gossip. Eric waved at me from his confines in a deep booth. He stood to greet me as I slid into my seat and took a sip of the iced tea he had already ordered for me.

"This is just what I needed. Thanks."

"I noticed you drinking it back at the B and B the first day we checked in." Eric leaned back in his seat, his dazzling, camera-ready smile on display, his blond hair close-cropped and gleaming. I wondered why Becca had dissolved her marriage to this kind and thoughtful young man. If what Samantha had said was true, Eric had just decided to end the marriage. I knew Becca was hard to please, but there must have been more to the story.

But it was none of my business. I inwardly chastised myself for dwelling on the past, and unearthed the binder of ideas and plans I'd created for Eric and Piper. I paused to put in my order with the waitress. I selected a Cobb salad with fries on top, and a cup of corn chowder. The businesses of Port Quincy had begun to blast the air-conditioning in earnest, and the coolness of the diner made me long for something warm to savor. Eric ordered the meatloaf with mashed potatoes and gravy. I privately tallied up my approval. I appreciated a man who could eat, something I enjoyed sharing with Garrett.

"Let's just confirm your choices and remind you of what you and Piper selected." I flipped open the binder and swiveled it across the table for Eric's approval. Piper was at a dress fitting and had handed off the wedding planning baton to her fiancé. She'd be joining us at the tail end of our meal, and Eric had already ordered her a dish to bring back to the B and B.

"I'm glad we're meeting here, rather than at Thistle Park," Eric said evenly.

"Oh?" I stopped buttering one of the diner's signature crusty rolls, my knife frozen aloft in the air.

"I hadn't known Becca's wedding was the day before mine. Samantha did tell me Becca was engaged, but I thought her wedding would be in a year. Besides Samantha, who I work with of course, I'm not too keen on running into members of Becca's family."

I blushed, thinking of an impromptu meeting I'd witnessed between Jacqueline and Eric. Becca's mother had stopped by to drop off some heirloom cookie cutters two days ago, to fashion some of the cookies for the wedding. She'd blanched when she saw Eric entering the front hall and had beat a hasty retreat out the door. She obviously still had acrimonious feelings toward her once-son-in-law.

"Becca and Keith wanted to marry as quickly as possible. I offered them the day before your wedding because we'd had a cancellation."

"I can't really complain about having to see Becca's family, because I'm technically still married to her." Eric's mouth turned up in a sheepish grin, and he turned to the binder.

"This all looks amazing. Though I have to admit, Piper made most of the choices."

"And she chose well. Your colors are navy and cream, with silver and green accents. Piper wanted the reception to be sleek and trim and bold."

Exactly like Becca's style.

I chased the thought from my head and went on. "Your guests will dine on a salad of radicchio, spinach, and pear. The soup will be gazpacho, with dilled salmon as the main course. And we'll follow up with devil's food cake for dessert." I flipped the page and showed a representative photograph of a cookie table, a Western Pennsylvania tradition. "And we'll present gift bags for your guests to sample and take home as many cookies as they wish." The cookie table would be more fun than the tame mints Helene had decreed as the favors for Becca's wedding.

A stray thought bubbled up in my head. "I just realized. Is the main reception dish a nod to Pickles?"

Eric let out a hearty laugh. "You figured it out. The big guy is wild about salmon with dill, his favorite pickle seasoning, and I wanted to incorporate something for him." A wistful look entered his eyes. "This is the longest I've been away from my cat." His mouth slipped into a frown. "Becca's cat, now. I wonder how he's doing."

And I wondered the same. Becca appeared to adore the colossal Maine Coon and relish their reunion, but I knew Keith would despise the cat's presence in their home.

Eric seemed to read my mind. "Is Keith a cat person?"

I barely stopped myself from squirming in the vinyl booth. "Um, I'm sure he'll grow to love Pickles."

Eric raised one brow.

"It's too bad you guys can't have joint custody," I continued. I knew I couldn't cope if I couldn't see Whiskey and Soda every day. The little kitties had become an integral part of my family.

"Piper and I will be returning to Colombia after our wedding and honeymoon." Eric folded his broad hands together on top of the yellow Formica table. "We live too far to share Pickles. I never thought Piper could convince me to give up my cat. He's traveled back and forth on my trips from South America to Port Quincy. He has his own cat passport," Eric proudly finished. "And I will get to see him later this summer, if Becca will arrange a meeting. Piper will be back in the States to defend her dissertation in August."

I'd known the bride was finishing up her history dissertation at Carnegie Mellon.

Eric stared out the front window of the diner and seemed to consider Main Street Port Quincy as he took a sip of his iced tea. "Piper really wants to come back home. She's been exploring getting a position teaching and researching as close to Port Quincy as possible."

I wondered what this would mean for the immigration and human rights organization Eric ran with Samantha back in Bogota. "So you're moving back?"

A dark cloud of annoyance marred Eric's good looks. "We're hashing it out," he mumbled.

Ruh-roh.

Maybe their future living plans were something this couple should discuss in depth before they walked down the aisle. Especially considering Eric was still technically entangled in his first marriage with Becca. But Eric had some things to get off his chest, protestations I wished I hadn't heard.

He took a deep breath and pushed away his glass of iced tea. "Seeing Becca when we arrived at the B and B surprised me." He tore a roll in two, then placed it back on his plate untouched. "I thought I'd gotten over her, but—"

Our waitress bustled over with a tray held high in the air. She carefully set down our plates of food, saving Eric from continuing his confession. We tucked into our food in weighty silence and ate without speaking for several minutes. When Eric opened his mouth to speak after we'd consumed most of our meals, I was certain, and hoping, he'd change the subject.

"I still have feelings for Becca."

My recently eaten lunch plummeted in my stomach like a stone in a pool.

This is a first.

I'd had several weddings canceled at the last minute, and had seen ample evidence of cold feet in some of the ceremonies I'd planned. The show didn't always have to go on, and it was always better to call off the big day than go through with a big party just because it was paid for and the guests were due to arrive. But I'd not yet heard a stark declaration such as Eric's on the eve of a wedding.

"This certainly complicates things," I offered lamely. It was good I'd devoured my delicious soup and salad before Eric's admission. I wasn't sure I'd have been able to eat anymore now.

"It was Glenn's meddling that ruined my marriage to Becca." Eric spat out the words and tossed his napkin on the table. "I have no love lost for Alma either. She was happiest when things got sticky with Becca."

I felt my eyes go wide before I could tamp down my alarm. What if Eric had something to do with Alma's strangling? He obviously despised the woman. I racked my brain for the details of his itinerary, then breathed an inward sigh of relief. If I was remembering correctly, Eric and Piper had been en route to the United States from Bogota after Becca's grandmother had been attacked.

I took a sip of my iced tea with shaky hands. Suspecting my clients of murder was wearing thin on my already jangly nerves.

"The Cunninghams aren't the perfect, happy

family they want everyone to believe they are," Eric continued. "They have their own nasty secrets."

I choked on a swig of iced tea and waited until my coughing subsided to stare at Eric. "What are you talking about?"

"Alma acts all sweet and innocent. But the murder of her husband, Glenn?" Eric leaned conspiratorially across the table. "My money's on Alma."

A shiver stole down my back that had nothing to do with the Greasy Spoon's overzealous air-conditioning.

"Jacqueline did say they had their differences," I wondered aloud. "But Samantha said it worked in their marriage."

Eric let out a mirthless chuckle. "Oil and water was more like it. They were one of those bickering old couples that should have just gotten a divorce, that is, if they'd believed in divorce." Eric's face suddenly shuttered, and he leaned back into the booth. He seemed to have realized he'd said too much about Becca, his marriage to her, and her family.

"But all that's in the past," he said smoothly, almost seeming to wish he believed it himself. "What I can't wrap my head around is Felicity."

I nodded, happy to leave the subject of the Cunninghams behind, even if it meant discussing a murder even more gruesome. "Samantha said she was one of your closest friends from law school, and that she still visited you and Piper in Colombia a great deal."

"Piper and I had looked forward to spending some time with Felicity while we were in town. She was going to be one of our bridesmaids." He seemed to hesitate, folding his napkin into an accordion shape, then letting it fall back onto the table. "I did wonder about her personal life."

I tried a tactic I'd learned from Truman, back when he'd had cause to investigate yours truly. I didn't say a word and let Eric fill the space with his own thoughts. He seemed eager to spill his concerns, and I did nothing to stop him.

"The last few times Felicity visited me and Piper, she was constantly texting. She used to text her boyfriend, Tanner, a bit while she was away, but this was new and incessant." A flushed look stole over Eric's features. He seemed to wrestle with going on. "This is hard to admit. The last time she visited, Felicity took a long nap right after she arrived. Her phone was absolutely blowing up with pings and sounds. Piper and I tried to turn it off and ended up reading the texts on her screen." He winced and leaned back from the yellow table. "I think there was a new guy in her life. One besides Tanner."

I blinked back my surprise and waded into the fray. "But she just got engaged last week. Why go through with it if she was seeing someone else?"

Eric nodded at my assessment. "Good question. Because she said on her very last trip to Bogota she wasn't sure she wanted to stay with Tanner. And this was before they even got engaged."

"Sorry I'm late." Piper appeared at the edge of the booth and plopped down next to her fiancé. Eric and I both jumped, startled at her sudden arrival. Piper didn't seem to notice and picked up a menu.

"I'm absolutely famished. All of this wedding stuff is exhausting!" She planted a quick kiss on Eric's cheek, and I couldn't help but wince. The blushing bride-to-be seemed to have no inkling that her fiancé was still smitten with his former, er, current wife.

I listened to Piper regale us with a silly and endearing tale of her latest dress fitting. Eric acted the part of the happy groom, attentive and sweet and sincere. Only I knew about his second thoughts.

This wedding is going to be a doozy. If it even happens.

I was relieved to bid Eric and Piper adieu and step into the cleansing, cheerful sunshine. Passersby strode down Main with errands to do and friends to greet. Fluffy white clouds stood out in stark white contrast with a vivid periwinkle sky. The rooftops of Port Quincy's eclectic architecture created a pleasing and varied silhouette, with Art Deco office buildings vying for attention next to Bavarian- and Edwardian-style buildings. I decided to put Eric and Piper and their relationship out of my head for the moment, and instead focus on Alma's theater relaunch. I was due to meet the spry woman at the theater in mere minutes. I hustled across Main to the corner of Spruce, and stood for a moment to take in the newly revamped Duchess theater.

The space was housed in an Italianate, white wedding-cake confection of a building. It was four stories high, an old-time office building that had been cleverly outfitted and given new life as a small movie theater. Until recently, the tall windows on the three upper floors had been blocked with wooden plywood. Now they featured posters of classic old films. One window showed Ingrid Bergman in *Casablanca*, another Charlie Chaplin. And the entire outside was gleaming, the white stone showing off tiny bits of mica embedded within, which seemed to sparkle as the sun lit up the building.

"Good afternoon, Mallory." Alma limped over, leaning heavily on her cane. She tsked as she stared up at the magnificent building and seemed to read my thoughts. "Glenn begged me to keep the soot on the facade." The town of Port Quincy had once been largely fueled by the glass factory owned by the family who built Thistle Park. Many of the buildings, including the police station, proudly wore the black grime of years past on their exterior walls as a nod to history. It was a preference I could imagine a former history professor such as Glenn Cunningham preferring.

"But I had the old gal powerwashed despite his misgivings. I'm sure if he were here, he would agree with me." Alma beamed and craned her fluffy white head back to admire the edifice.

I had to wonder how soon after Glenn's death Alma had restored the outside of the building, then inwardly chastised myself.

Alma is no killer.

The tiny woman could barely hurt a fly, despite her spirited opinions and gusto for life. She proudly held out her arm and gestured for me to take it.

"Come along, dear, and I'll show off the inside of the theater." I gamely reached out to link arms with Alma, when her heavy red macramé purse slipped from her shoulder. The rather large *Gone-with-the-Wind* replica pistol fell out of the purse and spun around in a circle on the pavement like an out-of-control toy top.

"Eek!" I instinctively jumped back, away from the weapon. Alma stepped on the gun to stop it from turning and nimbly deposited it into the confines of her purse. Other townsfolk hadn't noticed the gaffe, and continued to walk down the street, blissfully unaware. I wished I could say the same.

"Please tell me you have a permit for that thing." The words flew out of my mouth unbidden before I could stop them.

"Of course, silly!" Alma was totally unfazed by the appearance of the weapon. Her Southern tones were half-chastising, half-soothing. "What kind of heathen do you think I am?" She chuckled and snapped her purse shut. I felt marginally better. "Glenn hated guns." A faraway look stole over her wizened features. "We were the definition of *opposites attract.* I've been hunting since I was in pigtails. My father, Jeremiah, taught me how to shoot a gun when I was just seven, down in Georgia. Glenn couldn't stand the darn things. He was a pacifist to a T, thought all firearms should be confiscated." Alma sighed and smiled contentedly. "I miss that old fool so much."

She didn't seem like a woman who could have murdered her husband in that moment. Sure, it sounded like they definitely had their differences, but there was also a deep, abiding love present, that had seemed to transcend Glenn's death. I relaxed a few more degrees, especially now that the gun was confined to Alma's purse. Eric must have been wrong. There was no way Alma could have murdered her husband.

Alma gave her purse a sturdy pat. "And even Glenn would have found a Civil War–era replica gun at least marginally interesting, from an historical angle, of course."

I wished she'd stop patting her purse. "Is it loaded?" I held my breath, waiting for her reply. Guns made me nervous, no matter how skilled the user was. I knew Truman kept some in his house, but they were kept locked away in a safe.

"A lady never tells." Alma was enigmatic as she finally shuffled over to the glass door of The Duchess and held it open for me.

I gulped with a renewed frisson of nerves and allowed her to usher me in. The lobby space was truly magnificent. The remodel had Jesse's touch written all over it. The plasterwork had been painstakingly restored, with intricate curlicues and embossed patterns etching the high ceiling in a windowpane pattern. Gold leaf sconces held imitation gaslights recessed in the lobby's walls, between more posters featuring classic films. *Gone with the Wind* took pride of place, of course, lit by a small light above the elaborately framed poster. I could envision the party to be held tomorrow night in the lobby, with Port Quincy's finest gathering beneath the brilliant and traditional chandelier. In the afternoon light, the leaded crystal prisms caught the mid-May rays of sunshine and sent a spill of mini rainbows showering down on the lobby's walls. A busy evergreen carpet stretched out in the cavernous space, breaking up the distance between the old-fashioned ticket booth, partitioned off by red velvet ropes, and the large concession stand, also outfitted in retro style.

"Theatergoers will be able to enjoy modern snacks and popcorn," Alma mused. "And what will we be dining on during opening night?"

I offered Alma a tense smile and went with the truth. "In light of the caterer being canceled, Rachel and I are still coming up with a menu."

Alma blanched. "I trust we will be ready on time?"

"Yes." I was firm in my assent. The menu might not be cohesive in theme, but the guests at the premiere would not go hungry.

"I'm sure you'll make it right, dear." Alma patted my arm and motioned me toward the back of the lobby. "Let's continue our tour. The theater itself is designed to be a throwback." She led me through a wide, double set of brass doors to theater number one on the ground floor. The space was as opulent as the lobby, but quite obviously a movie theater. Plush velvet seats in dark persimmon red marched in procession across the room. They were packed closely together, in defiance of modern movie theaters' moves to adopt large, recliner-size seats.

"Jacqueline keeps warning me that we should have fewer seats in each theater room." Alma rolled her merry blue eyes heavenward. "But what does she know about running a movie theater?"

Well, she has studied film.

I found myself batting down a small edge of annoyance toward Alma. If Jacqueline truly owned half the building, she should be here with us now, helping to finalize the plans.

"Jacqueline seemed to have some good ideas when I last spoke to her about the theater." I broached the subject as tactfully as I knew how.

"Her?" Alma dismissed her daughter-in-law with a wave of her hand. "She can be helpful at times," she admitted. "She's more of a Melanie Wilkes, if you know what I mean. All quiet strength and Goody Two-shoes affect. But for this project, we need more of a Scarlett-type woman. Someone like you, dear, or me."

I winced. I wasn't sure if dividing up all the women in the world into a Melanie or a Scarlett dichotomy was very fair. And I wasn't sure if I wanted to be categorized as a Scarlett either.

Alma seemed to sense that she'd made me uncomfortable, and changed the subject. Unfortunately, her choice of topics only made me squirm inwardly even more.

"Have you made any headway on who killed my dear Glenn?" Alma deepened her Southern belle accent and blinked up at me in a plaintive manner.

I wished I'd never let her extract the promise to go poking around where I didn't belong. But her piercing blue eyes brooked no wiggle room, and I found myself spilling my thoughts.

"Why does Eric Dempsey blame Glenn for the breakup of his marriage to Becca?" I decided to counter an uncomfortable question with another one, and observe how Alma answered or deflected.

She gave a mirthless chuckle. "Glenn never

thought Eric was good enough for our Becca, that's all. Perhaps," her eyes focused on the stage where the red curtain was drawn, "if Eric had still lived in the United States when Glenn was murdered, I would have suspected him of exacting revenge for the dissolution of his marriage." She took in what must have been my shocked look and continued. "But he was far away from my Becca then, thank goodness. Canoodling with Piper by that time, as well." A wounded look stole over her features.

"Glenn introduced Piper to Eric."

"Yes, she ran off with Becca's husband, though their marriage was mainly over by then." Alma shook her head. "Piper was Glenn's star student. She was often over at Tara for dinner and discussion. She was like a third granddaughter to me. Until she hooked up with Eric, of course."

The irony wasn't lost on me. I'd loathed Becca when I first found out Keith had stepped out on our relationship to be with her. But then I'd come to realize it was Keith's betrayal that mattered, not Becca's choice to be with him. It stunned me to realize that Becca had gone through a similar situation with Eric and Piper.

But Alma continued to muse aloud, breaking me from my thoughts. "No, I've been thinking about it more, and I keep coming back to Tanner Frost."

"Felicity's fiancé?"

Alma nodded and leaned more heavily on her cane. "It didn't seem like such a big deal at the time, but it could have been significant. Glenn opposed Tanner making tenure in the history department at

Quincy College. He was going to recommend to his fellow colleagues that Tanner be denied tenure, and as chair, Glenn's suggestion would have had great weight."

I leaned against a plush red seat and nodded for Alma to continue.

"Glenn was murdered in cold blood, with only Wilkes as witness. With Glenn gone, Tanner made tenure. End of story." She neatly held up her hands in a kind of shrug, allowing me to draw my own conclusion.

"The timeline is significant," I agreed. "But don't you think Truman knows all this?"

Alma deflated and finally sat down in a theater seat. "One would assume he does. But why hasn't he acted on it?"

I shook my head and decided to defend my boyfriend's father. "I'm sure Truman has exhausted all the leads, Alma. That doesn't mean Tanner didn't do it, but if he did, there's some reason why Truman can't prove it beyond a reasonable doubt."

Alma bristled at my defense of Truman, and delicately folded her gnarled hands together. "Be that as it may, I won't ever rest until I find out what happened to my dear Glenn."

"Christmas on a biscuit." Jesse Flowers's voice rang out from the lobby. Alma and I hurried out of the theater, our tense discussion cut blessedly short. I waited with the door held open as Alma slowly made her way up the wide aisle and emerged into the lobby.

"What is it, Jesse?" Her tone was imperious and tinged with a dismissiveness I hadn't picked up on before. It was an affect perfected by Becca as well. No wonder Jesse was tired of working for Alma. Her sweet Southern lady routine was gone, replaced with a demanding tone.

"I stepped out to the hardware store while you and Mallory were touring the place." He ran a colossal hand over the brim of his Pittsburgh Penguins hat. "Someone trashed the bathroom I'd just finished." He motioned for us to follow, and we peered into the small space. The bathroom was as opulent and old-fashioned as the lobby, complete with a small sitting area with brocade fainting couches in an antechamber abutting the room with the sinks and toilets. The gorgeous gilt mirror facing the couches was dripping with magenta paint, a crudely drawn skull marring the smooth glass surface. A cryptic warning was spelled out in black paint on the opposite wall.

Mind your own beeswax.

Alma went white and sank into one of the couches. Her cane dropped to the floor.

CHAPTER THIRTEEN

I'd been happy to leave Alma and Jesse at The Duchess. Jesse had a full afternoon of work ahead of him if he was going to restore the bathroom in time for the grand reopening. But there had been one wrinkle: Jesse insisted on calling Truman to examine the scene, and Alma had been vehemently opposed. I'd left the two bickering in the theater bathroom to head home and figure out what food Rachel and I would serve at the premiere.

I found my sister pacing in the kitchen. She was gnawing on her shiny purple acrylics, a practice I knew belied some small crisis.

"What's up?" I slid into a chair and prayed whatever had come up would only be a minor catastrophe that we could easily handle.

"There's been a teensy, eensy, weensy mistake." Rachel grimaced and resumed her gnawing and pacing.

"Spill it, Sister." I wanted her to tell me now, and get it over with, akin to ripping a Band-Aid off a wound. Delaying the news wouldn't make it any easier.

"It's been hard to keep track of what's going on with Keith and Becca's wedding." Rachel held up one hand and ticked off themes on her fingers. "First it was Japanese cherry blossom–themed. Then Helene took over. Then it was *Gone with the Wind*. Then back to Helene's choices."

I nodded to encourage her to spit it out.

"I-forgot-to-cancel-the-food." Rachel hissed out her admission in a flurry of speech.

"You what?" I willed my brain to pause and tried to remember who was supposed to do what.

"I think you asked me to cancel the food for the *Gone with the Wind*–themed plans. I wrote it down, then immediately forgot." Rachel moaned and slid into a chair opposite mine. "I know I wanted to take on more events, but you were right. It's too much, and we've both been slipping."

I sat for a moment and considered what Rachel had told me. "Where's the food?"

"In the fridges and freezers downstairs." Rachel dared to look up. She stared at me quizzically as I felt a slow smile steal over my face.

"Rachel Marie Shepard, you're a genius."

"I am?" Rachel's eyes widened and she took a gulp of air.

"Alma's premiere is *Gone with the Wind*–themed. We'll just repurpose Keith and Becca's menu into the theater premiere hors d'oeuvres!"

Rachel's eyes sparkled as she considered the

idea. "Everything is ready for tomorrow's Mother's Day tea. We'll have to start right now on the prep for Alma's new menu if we want to get everything done on time for the theater reopening the next day."

I thanked my lucky stars that we'd had the forethought to prepare the food for tomorrow's event beforehand. We could use tonight to start on the now-finalized menu for Alma's event, and finish tomorrow night with hopefully some room to spare.

My sister and I tore into the basement and hauled food up the steep stairs to the kitchen. We fished out the recipes we'd crafted for the *Gone with the Wind* tasting and got to work. I beamed as I prepped, happy not to be wasting the food we'd accidentally procured for one of Becca and Keith's canceled wedding plans.

"Everything works out for a reason," I gushed. Alma would be ecstatic that we'd been able to whip up a themed menu for her theater relaunch.

"Except with Becca's family," Rachel countered. "All the hinky and crazy things that have happened are in some way related to the Cunninghams."

I cocked my head and considered what Rachel had said. It was basically true.

"First, someone broke into Alma's house, strangled her, and stole her collection." Rachel set down a gleaming butcher knife on the counter and raised her brows.

"And then Felicity was murdered in Becca and Keith's pool." I tidied my pile of sliced green tomatoes.

"Today, you saw the theater had been vandalized," Rachel added.

"And let's not forget Glenn was shot last year."

We stood in silence for a full ten seconds, contemplating the strange series of mishaps.

"So how does it all fit together?" I turned back to my pile of tomatoes, committing myself to keep working if Rachel and I were going to do some armchair sleuthing.

"Who would want to kill Alma? She's such a sweet little old lady." Rachel resumed her chicken carving. I gulped as the butcher knife flashed in her capable hands.

"That's the thing, Rach. Alma isn't all sweet, Southern hospitality." I recounted her imperious tone with Jesse. "And although Jacqueline technically owns half of The Duchess theater, Alma didn't include her in any of the plans for the reopening. Jacqueline studied film. She has some great ideas."

"Alma is a force of nature," Rachel considered "I could see her getting her way as a matter of course."

"She and Glenn may have gotten their way in regard to Becca's first marriage. It sounds like they were both integral in breaking up Eric and her."

"Then maybe Eric strangled Alma to get back at her." Rachel continued her butcher routine.

"I already thought of that. But Eric and Piper were still in Colombia when Alma's house was broken into. And," I admitted sheepishly, "I like Eric and Piper. I can't see them murdering anyone. One person who could have done it, and is conveniently out of the picture, was Felicity."

"Okay, now that you mention it, Alma does have some enemies." My sister separated chicken pieces into different piles.

"And according to some, she had a rocky marriage with Glenn." I pondered the different versions of her marriage I'd heard about. "Glenn apparently didn't like *Gone with the Wind*. Alma sunk their joint savings into expanding her collection after he died."

Rachel waved the butcher's knife in the air in a dismissive gesture, and I resisted the urge to duck. "Oh, c'mon. There's no way you could get me to believe Alma murdered her husband."

"I don't really believe it either." I recalled Alma speaking of Glenn with such love. But then again, as Eric and Becca had shown, who really knew what went on in a marriage?

"Well, then, maybe Tanner Frost did it, so Glenn wouldn't oppose his bid for tenure." I moved on from slicing tomatoes to creating a breading of crumbs and spices.

Rachel snorted from across the room. "Tenure isn't worth killing over."

"I'm not so sure. I bet Doug would disagree." I remembered our stepfather's nervousness about making tenure soon after he married our mother. He wanted the security of tenure to assure that he could provide for me and Rachel.

"And there's the connection to Felicity. She had just gotten engaged to Tanner when she was murdered." I gulped and stopped assembling ingredients. "And that's not all. According to Eric, Felicity was seeing someone besides Tanner."

Rachel sucked in her breath. "Do you think Truman knows all this?"

I felt a blush steal over my face as I pondered my sister's question. Truman would flip out if he knew I was asking people questions, and that Alma had deputized me to look into Glenn's killing.

"Let's hope so."

The inaugural Mother's Day tea event was off to a smooth start. I surveyed the setup of the backyard as I finished setting the small, round tables we'd placed around the back porch. We'd decided to schedule and serve brunch rather than a usual afternoon tea, so that our attendees could spend the rest of the holiday doing other things with their families. I was shaken by the dark whirlwind of events involving Becca's family but determined that this event would go off flawlessly. Though I couldn't help but also wait for the other shoe to drop. I'd lain awake in my bed the night before, Whiskey and Soda dreaming at my feet. I'd finally fallen into a fitful sleep. But now, watching the party come together, I chastised myself for worrying at all.

"This was a great idea." I beamed at my sister as she poured water into the glasses on the tables.

"It'll be a blast," Rachel agreed. "And I'm glad you hired more help for the occasion."

I'd put out a frantic call earlier this week for extra servers to help with the tea. Rachel was right; we needed to hire more to staff our gigs. I had plans to find some permanent additions to our team as soon as I had the Cunninghams out of my hair.

"If this goes well," Rachel beamed "we can regularly add holiday-themed events. And start advertising that we'll throw retirement parties, rather than accepting the occasional one that comes our way." Her pretty green eyes sparkled with plans of expansion and worldwide event-planning domination.

Give her an inch and she'll take a mile.

"Hold the phone, Sister. I like booking the random shower or retirement party at the B and B. It's good to expand our business organically, by word of mouth."

"And it's good for our pocketbooks and bottom line in general," Rachel interjected.

"True. But do you really want every week to be like this one, with an event scheduled nearly every day?" I placed my hand on my hip and put down the striped turquoise and lime-green tablecloth I'd been spreading out on a table. The jaunty colors heralded the upcoming change from spring to summer.

Rachel sighed in capitulation. "It has been a little nuts around here."

We scurried about for the next hour to finish setup for the tea. Although it was scheduled for mid-morning, we'd be serving traditional afternoon tea fare. There were scones with clotted cream, petit fours with cheerful flowers and vines scrolled across their precise rectangular tops, lemon cakes, and macaroons. We also were serving adorable crustless sandwiches in a range of options, including cu-

cumber, salmon, and chicken walnut salad. Guests could also munch on broccoli salad and coleslaw.

I bustled into the kitchen to help finish the food. Piper stood near the sink, grating lemons to create a tidy mountain of lemon peel to garnish the lemon cakes as a final touch. I was warming quickly to her. She'd offered to help with the tea while Eric was off at a coffee shop, catching up on some work regarding his asylum cases. He had plans to join her at the event later.

"Thanks for chipping in, Piper." I gathered the lemon peel and ferried it over to Rachel and the lemon cakes.

"It's no problem. It's a nice break from always slogging away at my dissertation, and from wedding planning details."

The three of us worked in companionable silence to finish the dishes. Our last tasks were to mix up a batch of mimosas and set out the six kinds of tea we were serving: Earl and Lady Grey, orange pekoe, jasmine, green mint, and lavender chamomile. Guests would drink their tea from ten elaborate sets we'd gathered from Thistle Park's well-stocked butler's pantry.

Thanks to the extra help we'd hired, we set down the last tray of food on the wide tables positioned in the garden as the first guests began to arrive.

"Mallory!" Summer Davies tore around the back porch and gave me a bone-crushing hug.

"Oh, sweetie, it's so good to have you back!" I embraced Summer in turn, then pulled back to examine the fourteen-year-old. She was sporting a slight tan, and her grin revealed her trademark magenta braces. She seemed taller than she'd been when she'd left, if that was possible. Garrett's daughter already had about five inches on me.

"I want to tell you all about my trip to L.A.," Summer gushed. She took in the backyard and porch as more attendees and families showed up for the tea. "Will you have time to stop by our table?"

"Of course, honey." I gave Summer another hug, and she was off to find her grandmother and mother's table. Garrett's daughter had become a fixture in my life, and I had to admit I was relieved she was home. I know Garrett had been counting the seconds until her return.

I moved easily among my guests for the next hour, unobtrusively observing how the event was running. If it went well, we could make this an annual Mother's Day event.

Most of our guests seemed to be enjoying themselves, save for a few glum tables. One held Tanner Frost and a woman I knew from the guest list to be his mother, Diane. Tanner was totally dejected, his tall, lanky Ichabod Crane–frame slouching over the table, his food and drink untouched. I didn't blame him, and suspected he was still understandably mourning his fiancée. Felicity's funeral hadn't even been held yet, according to the town newspaper.

"I'm so sorry for your loss," I murmured to Tanner as I paused at his table. The man looked up with dolorous, red-rimmed eyes and gave me a nod.

"Thank you. It's still quite a shock. My mother thought it would be good for me to get out."

I wasn't sure I agreed; Tanner seemed utterly devastated over Felicity's murder.

"Buck up, Son. Frankly, I think you dodged a bullet with that one." Diane Frost bit into a strawberry scone as if she hadn't just said something totally inappropriate.

"You don't have to gloat, Mother." Tanner slunk sourly into his chair and sent his mother a glare.

I left their table and tried to wipe the appalled look I was sure had appeared on my face. Perhaps Tanner and Felicity had had their problems. If Eric was right, she had been involved with another man on the eve of her engagement to Tanner. But that didn't make it all right for Tanner's mother to suggest he'd lucked out by not having to marry her through her unfortunate and untimely death.

I made my way over to Becca and Keith's table, where Helene held court. She did most of the talking, with her son hanging onto every word. But Becca's look telegraphed, *get me the heck out of here.* She appeared to be a hostage in the company of her future mother-in-law. She rested her chin on her hand and looked longingly to the table next to her, which held Alma, Samantha, Jacqueline, and Rhett. I'm sure Becca would rather be spending Mother's Day with her own family, but Helene often demanded allegiance.

"Mallory." Becca hissed at me from her table, and I paused to say hello.

"Meow." Pickles emerged from under the table and hopped up onto a wicker seat to greet me.

"I've missed you, big guy." I knelt down to give the gigantic Maine Coon some pets. He soon rewarded me with his rumbly, outsize purr. Becca looked on fondly, while Keith stared at the majestic cat as if he were an unusually large rat.

"Cats don't belong on furniture," Keith intoned. He reached out to give Pickles a shove from the chair, when Becca's fingers shot out and deftly smacked his hand away.

"Pickles is special. He's a member of the family now." Becca reached to gather the hefty kitty in her arms and buried her face in his long, soft fur.

"Pickles is no more a member of this family than you are, my dear." Helene raised one arch brow and picked at her salad. "Not officially anyway."

Tears beaded in Becca's eyes and she shuffled away, murmuring about getting some pickles for her eponymous cat. Keith stood so fast, his wicker chair toppled over in the grass.

"Now you've done it, Mother." He made haste to chase down his bride at the condiments table, and awkwardly gave Pickles a stilted pat on his fluffy head.

"That was uncalled for, even for you, Helene." I never inserted myself into family fights while wedding planning, but Helene and I had a history. And frankly, I was still mad at her for what she'd done to stymie Alma's event.

"I know you called around town impersonating Alma and canceling all her gigs for her theater opening." I inwardly seethed, but tried to keep my voice neutral lest any of my guests were listening in. "That was a low move."

Helene dropped her fork, a genuinely surprised look stealing over her sharp and surgically enhanced features. "Mallory Shepard, I did no such thing. And I resent your implication." She pushed herself up from her chair and gathered her tiny quilted Chanel purse. "I don't have to take this from the likes of you. I agreed to come to this event as a favor to you to bolster your reputation."

I stifled a laugh at the thought. "But you did get the florist to cancel her contract for Dakota Craig's wedding back in February. It's kind of your M.O."

Bull's-eye.

Helene froze in her tracks. Two spots of genuine color appeared over the carefully dusted-on peach rouge on her papery cheeks.

"I'm leaving!" She minced through the grass in her ubiquitous kitten heels and panty hose. Keith and Becca appeared moments later, with a dish of pickles for the cat.

"Where's my mother?" Keith narrowed his eyes as he pulled out Becca's chair.

"I think she stepped out." I sent Becca a wink in return for her grateful look and continued to mingle with the teagoers.

Eric and Piper waved to me from a far-off table that was occupied by a woman who was the spitting image of Eric. I finally arrived at Garrett's table. His mother, Lorraine, gave me a friendly wave, and Summer beamed.

"Hello, Mallory." Summer's mother, and Garrett's one-time fiancée, Adrienne Larson rose to give me a fleeting air-kiss. She was dressed impeccably in a St. John lace dress that probably cost as much as the food budget for this event. She pulled away, and I caught a whiff of Provencal meadows and flowery dew.

"So good to see you, Adrienne." There had been a time when I'd been intimidated by Adrienne's mere presence, and by the history she shared with Garrett, including their lovely daughter Summer. But that angst was gone now, and our past icy imbroglios had melted like the snow after the advent of a mellow spring.

"So good to see you again, kiddo." I accepted my second hug of the day from Summer.

"Grandpa Truman sends his regards," Summer said. "He's working overtime."

I imagined he would have to, with all the craziness that had gone down this week.

"Sit down and rest for a minute." Garrett gallantly pulled out a chair, and I gratefully sank into it. The event was going well, save for the tiff with Helene, and I was proud of my and Rachel's work. If this week hadn't been so jam-packed with other events, I would have enjoyed it even more.

"Let me get you a drink." Garrett rose and squeezed my shoulder. "A mimosa, maybe?"

"I'd love one, but I'd better not drink when I'm technically on the clock. How about a nice cup of Lady Grey tea?"

Garrett gave my shoulder one more squeeze and left to find the tea. I loved how thoughtful and attentive my boyfriend was.

Lorraine sent me a wry smile and set down her cup of tea. "Perhaps next year you can attend the Mother's Day tea as a member of the family, not as a hostess."

"Pardon me?" I crossed my hands in my lap to keep them from shaking.

Just what was she hinting at?

It seemed as if everyone had been bitten by the hoping-for-an-engagement bug. And things could be getting serious real fast, because Lorraine was the last person I'd expect to give me a verbal hint.

Summer cottoned on fast and sent me a megawatt grin, all flashing with her magenta and silver braces. Adrienne appeared less sanguine but covered her surprise well.

"Here's your tea." Garrett dropped a kiss on my forehead as he placed the steaming and fragrant forget-me-not-patterned teacup in front of me. I stared up at him with what was probably a flustered and reddened face.

"Everything okay?" Garrett's amiable face darkened for a minute as he searched my eyes.

"Yup. Thanks for the tea. I've got to get back to work!" I made haste to leave the table and sloshed a molten rivulet of tea on the skirt of my yellow sundress. But I didn't stop to mop up the mess and beat a hasty retreat from Garrett's family. I felt his keen hazel eyes boring holes in the back of my head, but I had to leave the stifling expectations of an impending engagement behind.

I'm just not ready.

I milled about the garden, communing with the angel statues, where the foliage ran from a lush mixture of wildflowers to the clipped, pruned precision of a classic English garden. My sandals made a pleasing sound on the herringbone-brick pathways. They mirrored those of the streets of Port Quincy, except these bricks were red instead of yellow.

Some families had finished their brunch and had moved on to playing bocce and croquet on the manicured lawn. I hugged my arms to my chest and considered them. Was I ready to officially join the Davies family? It would be an immense honor to be Summer's stepmother. I blinked back the start of tears, an overwhelming wave of sentimentality overtaking my senses.

"Mallory, you've got to help me." A veiny hand gripped my arm with a vicelike strength and whirled me around, breaking me from my weepy reverie.

"Hello, Alma." I made haste to dab my eyes and focused on the woman, who wore an intense and worried look on her lined but sprightly face. Her Irish setter, Wilkes, seemed to pick up on her strife and let out a low moan.

"I'm so embarrassed. I can't find my revolver!" She pulled open her cavernous red macramé purse to show me its contents. There lay her wallet, cell phone, and a package of travel tissues.

No gun.

"Let's just calm down." I said the words as much to myself as to her. I didn't want any of my guests stumbling upon what I guessed was a loaded firearm. "When was the last time and where was the last place you had the gun?"

"Maybe at the Greasy Spoon for lunch. No, I don't recall whether I'd lost it by then or not. It was still with me when I dropped it on the sidewalk yesterday. And you saw me put it back in my purse." By now, Alma was literally wringing her hands, and I placed mine on top of hers to still them.

"We need to call Truman and report the gun missing." I peered into Alma's eyes to let her know I brooked no wiggle room.

"Absolutely not!" Alma broke from my grasp and began pacing, albeit slowly and with the use of her cane, in front of an angel statue with one broken wing. "He'll never let me live it down. And I may lose my gun permit. Oh, I'm such an old fool." She clasped her hands at her throat, where she was still probably feeling some pain from the attempted strangulation. Her scarf, a white linen affair with a cheerful pattern of yellow chicks, slipped down and exposed her healing bruises. They were a mottled map of olive-green blotches on her papery skin. I winced and vowed anew to try to find out who had done this to the sweet woman.

"This is a terrible day already." Alma sniffed and stared heavenward. "Not that you haven't thrown a wonderful event, Mallory. I'm very much looking forward to what you and your sister have prepared for the theater opening. I'm just sad because today is the anniversary of Glenn's murder." She leaned against the angel statue and gave Wilkes a pat before she waved over to a distant table with her cane. "And to rub it in, there sits the man who probably did my poor dear husband in."

I followed the line of sight from her cane to take in Tanner Frost, still glumly suffering through the event with his horrible mother. A shiver ran down my spine despite the profuse May sunshine raining down on us in the garden.

"I must be getting back to my family." Alma gave

me one last pleading look. "I just thought you should know my revolver is missing."

I gave the woman a hug and good wishes. But I wasn't going to honor her request not to tell Truman. Alma shuffled off to return to her family, with Wilkes by her side. I whipped out my cell to text the chief of police. He texted back that he would be over as soon as possible, and not to announce the fact there was a loose weapon on the premises.

In the distance, a male voice rose and fell, the tone laced with anger and recrimination. Several guests at the tables farthest from the back of the house picked up on the tone and laid down their forks to strain their ears in the direction of the gazebo.

Just great.

Another male voice joined the fray. There was the unmistakable sound of a heated argument coming from the gazebo. Thankfully, the jewel of a building was hidden by a copse of trees. Or maybe that had been the wrong landscaping decision. It would have been helpful to know who was fighting at my event.

Summer bounded up to my place in the garden and gave me a fierce hug. "Dad said to say goodbye." I bid her farewell and watched her return to her table. I waved to her and her father, mother, and grandmother as they stood and left the tea. At the last second, Garrett turned around and sent me a slow, sexy smile. An electrical current ran from the top of my head to the tips of my toes. I sighed. I loved that guy. Garrett had thankfully been procuring my tea when the marriage talk had gone down, and I was glad he was none the wiser.

I was just about to play bouncer and break up the argument in the gazebo when the male voices went silent.

"I'm sorry my mother said that wretched thing about Felicity."

I jumped as the slender, now-stooped figure of Tanner Frost appeared at my side. "It can't be easy dealing with your fiancée's death. I'm deeply sorry, Tanner."

I considered the shell of a man before me and realized I didn't think he had anything to do with Felicity's death. My money was now on the mystery paramour Eric had made mention.

"I think I'd better get going. Between my mother expressing her happiness that Felicity's gone, and the death glares I've been getting from Alma Cunningham, it's time to leave." He seemed to have realized his poor choice of words and winced. "Alma's convinced I murdered Glenn." He snickered, the laughter hollow in his throat. "When I bet it's just an act. My money's really on Alma."

"But it's been a year since Glenn was shot," I protested, if not outwardly defending Alma. "If Chief Truman can't solve the crime, it may not be that obvious."

"It's obvious, all right. I had enough votes for tenure anyway, despite the fact Glenn was against it. I didn't have a reason to murder him. It's just a convenient excuse." He tossed a glare in Alma's direction. The woman was now peering into a deep thicket of daylilies, prodding the abundant leaves with her cane, no doubt looking for her lost revolver. I winced and turned back to Tanner. "Everyone knows Alma bumped off Glenn so she could spend their fortune on growing her ridiculously offensive *Gone with the Wind* collection." He spoke with such abject disdain, I didn't have to question whether he was a fan of the subject or not.

"It does seem to be a divisive book and film," I added lamely.

"It's an abomination of history!" Tanner's exclamation was so loud, he drew glares from some of the tea attendees. He modulated his voice and went on. "It's a racist text, romanticizing slavery and plantation life." He glared at Alma before returning to our conversation. "And Glenn thought so too. Their house didn't even look like Tara until he was murdered. She broke ground on the renovations and on The Duchess theater the very week after he died."

I blanched at the convincing case Tanner was building against Alma and longed to sag against the angel statue myself.

"I've heard they didn't have much in common." The thought slipped from my lips before I realized maybe I shouldn't be discussing these matters with a person hell-bent on accusing Alma of murdering her husband.

Tanner nodded vigorously, a shock of sandy hair landing in his dark-framed glasses before he pushed it away with long, skinny fingers. "They were one of those bickering couples who would have been better off apart. He wanted to keep the soot from the glass factory on the front of The Duchess for history's sake, and I thought she was going to kill him via heart attack when she made plans to have it powerwashed off."

Tanner's diatribe was cut short by the resumption of a male voice arguing in the gazebo.

"I'm sorry, but I have to break that fight up. Thank you for coming to the tea, Tanner. And again, I'm so sorry about Felicity."

Tanner sent me a shy but dolorous smile, and trudged off to the side of the garden.

I texted Rachel that I was going to head out to the gazebo. She texted back a second later.

Be safe.

I smiled at my sister's concern. It was rude as all get-out to be having such a loud argument at the Mother's Day tea, but I was sure I'd be able to keep the peace and the event could wind down in calm, sunny fashion. I headed off to the back of the property with a spring in my step.

Shots rang out from the gazebo, one, two, three. They were surprisingly close, and deafeningly loud. Silence reined for a nanosecond before most of the tea attendees screamed and instinctively ducked for cover.

Pickles and Wilkes shot out from the copse of trees. I couldn't stop the Irish setter, but I scooped up the cat as he tore by.

Tanner materialized at my side, his long face drained of every bit of color.

"Tanner, call 911." I handed him the Maine Coon and raced to the gazebo.

There lay Eric Dempsey, in all his movie-star-good-looks glory. But he wasn't playing a part. He wasn't moving. His hand lay over his left side, awash in blood.

CHAPTER FOURTEEN

"Eric, stay with me." I tore off the gauzy top layer of my polka-dot yellow sundress and applied it to the gunshot wound at Eric's side to try to staunch the flow of blood. The delicate fabric was soon consumed with the red stuff, and I looked around in dismay for something better to press on the wound.

Glinting on the gazebo floor, just beyond Eric's hand, was a massive diamond ring. It was done in Edwardian style, a colossal old European cut diamond in the center, surrounded by a dainty encrusted pattern of milgrain platinum and hundreds of tiny diamonds.

I snapped my attention away from the pricey bauble and focused back on Eric. He shifted a millimeter and let out a groan. I nearly whooped with joy that he was still alive. I raced to the entrance to call for help. A small audience of tea attendees had let their morbid curiosity overcome their sense and had gathered in a crowd in front of the gazebo.

"Get back."

Thank God.

I was relieved to see Truman parting the sea of guests as he made his way to the gazebo with long, purposeful strides. Behind him rushed the paramedics, their stretcher at the ready to ferry Eric to the hospital.

"That's my fiancé! Let me through!" A hysterical Piper pushed and shoved her way to the front of the line, beating Truman and the first responders to the scene. She flung herself atop Eric and spoke to him in a low, insistent tone. It was a scene I would never forget. We'd taken down the decorations we'd used to stage Becca and Keith's Southern couture tasting, but the gazebo was as opulent and fussy and white as it usually was. But now it was marred with a slick of blood, a dying man groaning on the floor, and his fiancée begging him to stay with us on this side of the earth.

She peered up at me with her face awash in tears. "It's too bad Wilkes and Pickles can't talk."

The two pets had indeed seemed to have witnessed the shot.

"Although poor Wilkes is so hard of hearing, he can't even perceive a gun going off." Piper clasped Eric's hand and kept prattling on, trying to keep him awake.

I stepped aside for Truman and the paramedics. Minutes later, Eric was carted away from the gazebo, thankfully still moaning and groaning. The woman I'd guessed to be Eric's mother joined Piper in the back of the ambulance, and the vehicle drove away in haste, crushing several flowerbeds, the sirens flashing.

Truman had exercised some impromptu crowd control, and the Mother's Day tea guests had been moved from their rubbernecking station in the garden to the back porch, where many scanned the horizon of the grounds with their hands shielding their eyes from the sun.

Rachel finally found me and flung her arms around me with such force, she nearly knocked me over. "Thank God you're all right." She brushed tears from her eyes. Her skills at makeup rivaled her baking skills, and there was nary a streak of mascara on her face.

"You too." I held my sister at arm's length, thankful she was unharmed. "Eric seems to be the only person hurt."

"The only person targeted," Rachel quickly amended. A wash of icy nerves trickled down my back at her observation. Someone had tried to murder Eric Dempsey in cold blood at our inaugural Mother's Day tea. Rachel and I left the police to do their work and rushed back to the house to attend to our guests. Truman had the place on lockdown, and no one was happy they were now sequestered at Thistle Park for the remainder of the afternoon.

"I'm not sure why we need to be held for questioning," a woman complained as she glanced at her watch. "I was nowhere near the garden when the shots rang out."

Rachel and I freshened up the food and drinks as best we could and bustled about to make our guests feel as comfortable as was possible in the macabre situation. I sent up a silent prayer that Garrett, Lorraine, and Summer had already left the tea when the incident occurred.

There was one person, or should I say feline, who was enjoying the situation. I spirited Pickles up to my third-floor apartment to decompress, and the big cat was thrilled to see Whiskey and Soda again. The kitties did their delicate sniffing-as-greeting routine, and Soda and Pickles were soon playing in the living room.

"It's too bad we can't just ask you what happened back in that gazebo, Pickles." I wondered what the cat had witnessed before the shots went off, and what Eric had been doing with the Maine Coon. I'd last seen the cat with Becca.

"And it would be good if Wilkes could spill the beans too." Wilkes had stood counsel over Alma before we'd arrived to find her strangled, and I was sure he knew who the perpetrator was.

I rushed back downstairs and ran smack into Truman.

"Come with me."

He led me out the back door, down the porch steps, and to the garden.

"I want to know exactly what you saw, heard, and even smelled right before the shots went off. Of course, everyone has a different story, but several people have said you and Tanner were closest to the gazebo when the shots went off."

I gulped and nodded. I recalled learning in my evidence class in law school that most people make pretty lousy witnesses. With that in mind, I told Truman the facts as I knew them, trying to be faithful to what had happened, and letting him know when I also wasn't sure. He listened, his hazel eyes intense and attentive.

"Thank you, Mallory. I hope I can release your guests soon."

He turned to go, but I couldn't resist.

"Do you think this has something to do with Felicity's death?" She had been good friends with Eric, good enough to visit him in Bogota several times a year. And it couldn't have been a coincidence that she'd been murdered mere days before someone had made an attempt on Eric's life.

Storm clouds gathered in Truman's expression, and I regretted my prying.

"It's very likely." He dropped the laconic act and took off his hat. His salt-and-pepper hair was beaded with sweat. He sighed and glanced back at the guests held captive for the time being on the back porch. "It could be that Eric's would-be murder has something to do with Felicity or Alma." He stopped and winced. "Or Glenn, for that matter."

I swallowed hard and decided to keep butting in, with Truman in a sharing mood. "I know you said Felicity's death wasn't a suicide. Do you think it was Tanner? He seemed genuinely upset, devastated even, today at the tea."

I realized I didn't want Felicity's killer to be her fiancé.

Truman's brows knitted together in a grim fashion. "We've finished the financial forensics on the case. Felicity had amassed a questionably large fortune, with no apparent clues to explain how she obtained the money. Her father, Roger Fournier, was shocked. He said she received a small salary from the family jewelry business, but not enough to make up what she had. Plus, a large part of that small salary went to paying off her law school loans. Her parents said they helped her to save money by letting her live in the loft apartment above the jewelry store. But there were large cash deposits nearly every month to her account."

I bit my lip, a trickle of sweat running down my spine. "Um, I heard something about Felicity."

Truman perked up and leaned in intently.

"Eric told me the last time she visited him in Colombia she was texting a man. Romantically. A man who wasn't Tanner."

"Dammit, Mallory!" Truman shook his head and clapped his hat back atop his head. "Just when were you planning on telling me this tidbit of information?"

I felt like sinking straight into the garden ground and blinked up in contrition. "I thought you'd interviewed Eric about Felicity."

Truman muttered some choice words. "I did, and specifically asked if there was anyone else in her life. Mr. Dempsey must have conveniently forgotten the information at that point."

"Well, I did confirm with you that Felicity never did call to set up her wedding." I tried to score some brownie points by reminding Truman of what I had told him.

Truman nodded. "And just as we suspected, the call logs don't match up. Felicity never made that call to you or to Rachel. Not from her cell, Tanner's cell, or the landline at the jewelry store." He narrowed his eyes and spoke his next words in a skeptical tone. "You're not hiding anything else from me, are you, Nancy Drew?"

I placed my hand near my heart and felt my eyes go wide. "No, sir. I'm just very busy, that's all. Rachel's been scheming to expand our business to include more nonwedding events, and that's how this Mother's Day tea came about." I glanced around at the once-pleasant day, now irrevocably mired in scandal and doom. "Not that we'll be hosting another one of these, I'd imagine. And then Alma was strangled, and she asked me to take over her planning of The Duchess reopening. Which reminds me." I shielded my eyes from the sun and looked over Truman's shoulder at the remaining sequestered guests. Helene was among them. "I kind of accused Helene of canceling Alma's vendor contracts on the eve of the theater reopening. Rachel and I have had to scramble to get the event off the ground."

"And how did she respond to your claim?" Truman swiveled his head in the direction of Helene sitting sourly on the back porch.

"It's funny, but I actually believe her that she didn't do it." Helene was no Oscar-caliber actress, and I thought I'd know if she'd lied to me in her denial.

"Oh. There is one more thing." I felt a trail of heat rise up my neck and undoubtedly stain my face pink. "Someone broke into the theater right before Alma gave me a tour. They painted a skull on the wall and a threatening note."

I thought Truman was going to blow his stack. "Why doesn't Alma tell me these things? Why did you have to let me know that silly ninny lost her gun, a weapon that could have been used to try to murder Eric Dempsey?" He shook his head. "She doesn't think I tried hard enough to solve Glenn's murder. She couldn't be more wrong."

I bit my lip and carefully studied the ground.

Truman would really flip his lid if he found out Alma has asked me to investigate Glenn's death on her behalf.

But a new thought eddied up from the recesses of my brain, chasing the guilt of my secret away.

"That ring in the gazebo."

"It's a pretty pricey specimen, if it's the real deal," Truman mused. "And it's also very distinctive. What about it?"

"I think I've seen it before. Yes, hold on a minute. I'll be right back." I nearly ran through the grass and through the mazelike brick of the garden to the back porch. Bored and testy guests stared as I tore into the kitchen and dug through the recycling bin. I raced back to Truman with a several-days' old Port Quincy *Eagle Herald* under my arm.

"Recognize this?" I was truly panting now, and a further line of sweat running down my spine glued my sundress to my back. I'd hastily folded the newspaper back to the engagement announcement section, and thrust the photograph of Felicity with Tanner under Truman's nose.

"I'll be." The fancy ring residing on the gazebo floor was the very one ensconced on Felicity's finger in her engagement photograph.

"That wasn't the same ring—" I began.

"That Tanner was trying to remove from Felicity's finger at the pool," Truman finished. He glanced around, and our eyes both rested on the figure of Tanner. He was glumly picking at a hangnail from his perch on the porch, his mother several feet away gossiping with another woman.

"That must be why he was trying to take it off." The bizarre action poolside finally made sense. "He realized his fiancée was wearing someone else's ring."

"Truman, you've got to see this." Faith Hendricks, Truman's young partner, motioned him over. "Hi, Mallory."

It was all the invitation I needed. I wordlessly followed Truman to where Faith stood. The young officer took several pictures with her digital camera, her blond ponytail swishing behind her. She then looked to Truman in silent counsel. He nodded, and Faith slipped a pencil from her uniform's front pocket and poked it into the thicket of fragrant honeysuckle that grew around the base of the gazebo. She retracted her hand, the *Gone with the Wind*–replica revolver hanging from the writing utensil, literally smoking.

"Oh, crap." Alma's lost gun had been used to shoot Eric.

"How convenient," Truman muttered. "This day is just getting started." He made a beeline for Tanner.

Faith and another officer finished up getting statements from everyone who had attended the tea. They gratefully gathered their belongings and beat a trail from Thistle Park, having been detained for several hours after the tea was due to dissolve. It would be a Mother's Day they'd never forget.

"That's one less event we'll be hosting next year." Rachel grumpily flounced into our living room and flung herself onto a puffy pink chair with a tiny and surprisingly subtle flamingo print. She wore a silky robe and shorts ensemble, and carried a nail kit in her hands.

I wasn't sure whether to laugh or cry at her pronouncement. Maybe both responses were appropriate.

"At least Eric is still alive." If not well. Piper had texted me that he had pulled through surgery, his major organs intact. But his spleen had been nicked, and he'd lost quite a lot of blood, requiring several transfusions. The once-white gazebo bore testament to that fact. I dimly wondered when we'd be able to hose off the evidence, then felt a wave of guilt crest and crash over me.

"And who in their right mind would want him dead? He seems like a good-enough guy to me." Rachel retrieved a sparkly bottle of nail polish from her robe pocket and began to paint her toenails a vivid, blingy purple. My sister had had some unfortunate relationships as of late and didn't always trust her own judgment in the men department. But I did agree with her on this one. Eric seemed like an honorable person. I thought of his immigration and asylum cases in Colombia, and sent up a prayer that he would make a speedy and complete recovery.

"Although." Rachel waved at her big toe and capped the polish tight, "he was once married to Becca. That's some questionable taste right there."

I raised my brows and shook my head. "Not even 'once married.' He's still technically wed to Becca. I don't think Judge Frank has granted the divorce yet. Garrett would've told me."

We sat in silence for a few minutes as Rachel carefully painted her nails with the same steady hand she used to decorate her gorgeous confection creations. Soda approached her to sniff at the formaldehyde-laden polish, while Whiskey appeared and curled up on her favorite spot in my lap. I thought I'd imagined it, but the kitties seemed a little glum since their new pal Pickles had left the Mother's Day tea with Becca when the guests had finally been released.

A sick thought raced through my mind, and I struggled to comprehend it. "If Becca is still married to Eric, but she wants to marry Keith—"

"Maybe she wanted to bump off Eric to speed up her road to being a free woman." Rachel read my mind and moved on to painting her fingernails, this time a startling shade of electric blue.

The laws of succession and inheritance swirled around in my mind from a long-ago trusts and estates class. "And what if she tried to kill Eric to inherit from him right before he divorced her? That would be an added bonus for wanting to kill him."

I racked my brain, trying to recall where Becca had been when the shots had gone off. The last I'd seen her, she was hurrying away from Helene, with Pickles in her arms and Keith close behind. It was possible she'd made her way back to the gazebo in the half an hour between my last seeing her and Eric getting shot.

"Or," Rachel capped the second bottle of polish, "maybe Keith shot Eric."

"Hmm. It's totally possible." I'd thought I'd heard two masculine voices in the gazebo, at least for part of the argument I'd overheard. "Maybe Keith was afraid the divorce wouldn't go through in time for his Friday wedding, so he tried to take Eric out." I shivered despite the still-warm May evening air breezing through our open windows. A year ago, I'd been engaged to Keith myself, and now I suspected him of being a stone-cold killer.

"Would he kill for Becca?" Rachel cocked her head in thought. "Maybe Keith did it at the behest of his fiancée."

My phone trilled out its announcement of an incoming call. I shifted to retrieve the phone from my pocket, gently depositing Whiskey next to me. "Speak of the devil."

It was Becca.

"Mallory. I need your advice. Right now."

I sent my sister a quizzical look and took a deep breath. Some brides ended up using my wedding planning services more like sessions with their shrinks. They ended up seeking counsel and asking me to weigh in on bad momzilla behavior, meddling mothers-in-law, and general feelings of cold feet. But in light of what had been going down in Port Quincy this week, I wasn't sure I wanted to be privy to Becca's deepest, darkest thoughts.

"Um, Becca—"

"Meet me at my house. It's an emergency." The line went dead.

I smirked at my sister. "Becca's been taking lessons from Helene. She just summoned me and hung up before I could wiggle out of it."

Rachel giggled as I stood to get ready for my apparent meeting with Becca.

Fifteen minutes later, I found myself turning into

Windsor Meadows. My interest had been piqued. I was also genuinely worried about Becca. Her grandmother Alma had been strangled, her childhood rival was murdered in her very own swimming pool, and a serious attempt had just been made on her still-not-divorced husband. If Becca said something was an emergency, it probably was.

I pulled into the circular drive in front of the Rubik's Cube of a house and cut the Butterscotch Monster's engine. I hesitated as I swung my legs out of the car. Perhaps I should call Truman. If Becca truly had some newsworthy revelation, he should probably hear it first. I decided at the last minute to hear her out.

"You came." Becca flung open the red-lacquered double doors before I had a chance to ring the bell. She pulled me into the hall and the peach great room beyond and offered me a seat. I sunk into a deep white couch covered in a pattern of seashells and starfish, and accepted the glass of white wine she pressed into my hands. Becca carried her own glass of the stuff, more like a bowl-like goblet. She paced around the great room as she gathered steam.

I took a sip of the wine, a delicious chilled dessert Riesling, then set it aside. I hadn't eaten much today, what with the running around at the event, then later nerves killing my appetite. I had to drive home, and I hoped to do so soon. Becca shared no such concerns and took a healthy swig from her glass.

I noticed that the view to the redwood deck, obsidian rock garden, and pool was now occluded by a bank of new peach curtains. They shut out the darkness, both the literal kind, which had appeared as the sun set on my drive over, and the figurative darkness of the memories of what had happened to Felicity in the pool.

"Where's Keith?" I glanced around the mostly quiet house. Pickles snored softly on a grand cat condo installed by a window overlooking a bird feeder. He seemed quite content in Becca's company, and I relaxed, thinking he was a truly happy kitty, reunited with her.

"He's still at work in Pittsburgh." Becca waved her hand dismissively, a slosh of wine running down the edge of her goblet. I didn't envy the long hours Keith still had to put in as an attorney, now partner at his big Pittsburgh firm. I still pulled long hours as a wedding planner, but I enjoyed my work much more.

"I'll get right to it." Becca set down the goblet and turned to me with a look of utter anguish marring her pretty features. "I wonder if I should remain married to Eric."

I felt my mouth open and quickly shut it. This wasn't what I'd expected when I'd been summarily summoned over.

"Well, you *are* technically still married to Eric," I added lamely.

"I'm considering canceling my wedding to Keith." Becca resumed her pacing and avoided my gaze.

I took another swig of wine after all.

"Lots of brides have second thoughts. And I'm no marriage counselor, but depending on how strongly you feel, maybe going through with it isn't the best idea." I didn't want to be responsible for jettisoning Becca and Keith's nuptials, but if the bride was still interested in her former husband, that was a pretty big seismic shift to attend to.

"Why did you end up calling off your wedding to Keith?" Becca stopped in her tracks and searched my face for an answer.

Are you joking?

Keith's infidelities no longer stung. In a strange way, canceling my wedding to him, and the effects of his affair with Becca, had led to some pretty wonderful things. I'd inherited Thistle Park from his grandmother Sylvia, started my wedding planning business, and fallen in love with Garrett. But the inciting incident had been Keith's affair with Becca.

My face must have telegraphed the answer, because a furious blush stole over Becca's face. She pulled her blond hair into a hasty ponytail to give her fidgety hands something to do, her trademark stripe of roots still visible.

"I've been thinking about why I dragged my feet on divorcing Eric. I used him being out of the country as an excuse. But maybe there was a reason we stayed married." She perked up. "I think the stars are aligning for us right now."

I thought those must be some crazy celestial patterns if they were aligning to give us this messed-up week of murder and mayhem, but I didn't share my thoughts with Becca. She dreamily stared off into the distance, and I wondered if she'd had an earlier glass of wine from that big goblet before I'd arrived.

"I'd like you to take me to the hospital to see Eric." It wasn't a request really, but a command.

Becca scooped up her Louis Vuitton bag and slung it forcefully over her shoulder. "Let's go."

"Is this a good idea?" I glanced at my watch. It was already evening. "I bet visiting hours are over."

"But I'm his wife." A slow smile stole over Becca's face as she reclaimed the title.

Oh dear.

"Plus, I got a text from Keith that he'll be spending the night in Pittsburgh. He's about to wrap up discovery on a big case. One he wants to finish before our wedding." Becca realized what she'd just said and colored anew.

I felt sick as I took my spot behind the wheel. I recalled the long nights Keith had been away from our shared apartment in Pittsburgh. Some of them had been legitimate work sessions, while others had been dates with Becca. And now I was trapped in my station wagon with the woman in question, helping her to elude Keith to see her former paramour.

"You're close to Truman, right?" Becca squinted in the glare of another driver's high beams and caught my glance in the rearview mirror. "Who does he think tried to kill Eric?"

"I haven't a clue." And even if I did, I wouldn't share it with Becca. But I could do some sleuthing of my own. "Do you think Felicity's death has anything to do with the attempt on Eric's life?"

Becca's hopeful look soured, and she sent me an impressive glare. "That woman has nothing to do with Eric."

"According to your sister and to Eric, she visited him and Piper quite a bit in Colombia."

And collected quite a bit of extra cash, according to Truman.

Becca appeared to have been sucker punched at the mention of Piper's name. "I haven't the slightest idea. But I'm sure the murder of riffraff like Felicity has nothing to do with the attack on my Eric."

We drove in testy silence the rest of the way to the hospital complex just south of town. One thing was obvious: Becca was firmly in Eric's camp, and hadn't gotten over him at all. I wondered if she'd been having these feelings since he crashed Whitney's baby shower, or if Eric's brush with death had reawakened her ardor.

"I'll just wait here." I parked in a lot near the front entrance and waved my phone. "Just text me when you're done." I'd aided and abetted Becca enough.

"Don't be silly. I need you." Becca leaned across my seat and opened my door. I numbly followed her through the lobby to the waiting room of the ICU.

"You came!" The woman who bore a striking resemblance to Eric rose from her couch and gave Becca what looked to be a bone-crushing hug. She glanced down the hallway with a nervous movement, and it was then I realized Piper was nowhere to be seen. She hadn't been at the B and B when I'd left to see Becca, and I'd assumed she'd be at the hospital with her fiancé.

"Judith, it's so good to see you." Real affection shone in Becca's eyes. "Is Eric awake?"

The older woman shook her head, but a well of

hope shone on her face. "He isn't at the moment, but we got to talk to him briefly after surgery. He was groggy, but still with us, if you know what I mean." She brightened. "Would you like to see him?"

Becca followed Eric's mother to the nurses station, and the three women engaged in what I'm sure was an odd conversation. The nurse stared at Becca incredulously, then led her to a nearby room. I bet she'd seldom had the opportunity to meet a patient's fiancé and current wife in the same evening.

"Eric never should have left Becca." His mother sighed as she returned to the couch. "Becca is so much better suited to him than Piper. If only Eric will see that when he recovers."

I winced as I recalled Eric's confession of renewed feelings for Becca at the Greasy Spoon. Little did Eric's mother know, he was on the same page as Becca.

Becca retreated from Eric's room with tears coursing down her cheeks.

"Thank you, Judith," she whispered.

"What are you doing here?" Piper emerged from the elevator and stopped as the doors closed behind her. She held a candy bar in her hand, and her classic-cinema-era good looks were tinged with sadness and fatigue. Her sleek, shining pixie cut clung to her skull, and her shoulders were hunched. Yet she seemed to draw on some inner reserve as her eyes narrowed on Becca.

"I'm here to see my husband." Becca held her chin up high and proud, and reached for Eric's mother's hand.

Oh no she didn't.

"Get out." Piper's voice was low, clear, and threatening.

"I have every right to be here." Becca stood, and I realized three nurses were now listening in from their station. "In fact, as Eric's wife, I have more of a reason to be here than you do."

"You little—" Piper lunged for Becca, but I managed to pull her off. Judith similarly contained Becca, but it was too late. Hospital security materialized ten seconds later, and summarily ordered everyone out but Judith. I'd never been happier to be kicked out of a joint in my life.

CHAPTER FIFTEEN

Becca's declaration of renewed affection for Eric occupied way too much real estate in my mind as I worked with my sister to put together the finishing touches for Alma's theater gala. I'd eventually pushed thoughts of Becca and her confusing love life from my head in order to give The Duchess theater my full attention. Rachel and I spent the day finishing the prep we'd started a few days before. We'd succeeded in repurposing the full courses for the *Gone with the Wind*–themed wedding into bite-size hors d'oeuvres for Alma's premiere.

I'd managed to hire back the canceled servers Alma had originally booked, although at a steeper, last-minute price. I was still grateful Rachel and I wouldn't be handling the event by ourselves. We unloaded food from the van we'd rented and quickly set up hot plates, china, stemware, and napkins on the tables we'd been able to rent last minute, also at a healthy surcharge.

"Now that our portfolio has expanded, we should buy our own van." Rachel's eyes took on a dreamy cast as she unwrapped a foil-topped tray of canapés.

"That's a nope." I lined up bottles of red and white wine inside the bar and stepped aside for the bartender. "Purchasing a van like the one we rented tonight would bust our budget for a whole season."

Rachel pouted at my attempt to ground her back on planet Earth, but quickly brightened as we neared the finish line of our setup. We stopped as we ferried in the last bit of linens and craned our heads back to take in the beautifully refurbished theater. A few guests were already lining up to take their places near the door.

The Duchess gleamed, every bit as fancy and stately as the inaugural moviegoers in their black tie. I marveled at the transformation the building had undertaken. When I'd first arrived in Port Quincy last summer, the building had been shrouded in drop cloths and scaffolding. It must have been soon after Glenn's death, when Alma kicked her renovations into high gear.

And maybe she was able to do so because Glenn had been standing in her way and was conveniently murdered.

I shuddered at the macabre turn my mind had taken, and determined that the evening would be a success. Rachel and I waited in the wings as more and more denizens of Port Quincy assembled on the red carpet we'd rolled out on the sidewalk in front of the theater entrance. Attendees pulled up and got out of cars whisked away by valets.

Alma positioned herself near the front door, greeting each person as they arrived. She wore a deep plum ensemble with a chiffon skirt and matching sequin jacket. Her cane had a shiny new silver topper. Alma deposited a rather perfunctory kiss on Jacqueline's cheek as her daughter-in-law and son arrived. I knew how painful this evening must be for Jacqueline, because Alma hadn't let her participate in the planning and resurrection of a theater that she technically co-owned. Jacqueline hissed something at Rhett, and the jolly look slid right off his face. I wondered what they were arguing about, and what had upset Samantha as well. Becca's twin was dressed in a pretty black cocktail dress with a smattering of dark sequins, with a matching dark look on her face. She narrowed her eyes at the back of her father's head, then ducked into the theater before the movie began, without getting any refreshments.

I held my breath as I glimpsed Becca's trademark dark stripe of hair flash before me on the red carpet. She wore a daring dark-blue velvet dress, the neckline a deep V. She sported a choker of sapphires around her neck, and her princesscut engagement ring from Keith was firmly anchored on her ring finger. She entered the building on the arm of Keith, clad in a tuxedo. Their appearance together didn't ease my racing thoughts. I wondered if Keith would ever find out about her visit to Eric in the hospital. And if Becca had made any permanent decisions about which man she would choose to be with.

One of the last couples to arrive, Keith and Becca stopped to converse with Alma. Their friendly chitchat was broken up by a rousing chant brewing outside.

"What are all those people doing?" Rachel squinted out the front glass windows of the theater for a better look.

"I think they're protestors." I spotted Tanner Frost, and gave an inward sigh of relief. If he was free to be out and about protesting, then Truman hadn't arrested him for either Felicity's murder or the attempt on Eric's life. Tanner was surrounded by about thirty other like-minded protestors. They held hand painted and professionally printed signs with slogans like, "Educate, Not Hate!" and "*Gone with the Wind*, Be Gone."

"What gives? It's just a movie." Rachel straightened a pile of napkins and gave a shrug.

"There are some theaters that won't show *Gone with the Wind*." I thought back to Tanner's impassioned diatribe against the book and movie. "Some think it hasn't held up well to the test of time, and that even when it was written and filmed, there were depictions that were racist or romanticized slavery in the South."

Rachel's eyes widened. "Then why is Alma showing the film?"

I cocked my head and pondered my answer. "There's a lot to learn about the history of the movie itself, and the writers, producers, and directors' decisions. But I think Alma just adores the film and the novel for the story itself. It's timeless, much beloved, and part of the American canon. I honestly can't wait to see it again, and decide for myself."

"I'm going to chase them out." Alma peered outside the front glass at the pavement and the chanting protestors. "I won't let them ruin my theater reopening!" Alma flung open the door and stepped outside to confront the crowd. Just then, a TV station from one of the Pittsburgh news outlets pulled up to film the protest and interview the attendees. Alma appeared beside herself. She seemed to be weighing the boon of getting her theater reopening on television with the reality that they were filming a protest against her film choice.

Just as Alma opened her mouth to give the protestors a piece of her mind, the eggs began to fly. Raw yolks and shells splattered on the pavement and the front of the glass as the protestors lobbed them with precision.

"Arggh!" Alma beat a hasty retreat into the theater, just in the nick of time. A large brown egg splattered the glass door and cracked into gooey smithereens as she slammed the door behind her. The lobby of the theater erupted in chatter as Truman appeared outside to break up the protest.

"They've nearly ruined everything!" Tears sprung at the corners of Alma's usually twinkling blue eyes. "How could they?"

"Free speech is important, Grandma," Samantha gently stated at Alma's side.

"Be that as it may," Alma sniffed. "They didn't need to throw the eggs."

The protestors' appearance colored the rest of the party portion of the evening even after they'd disassembled. Eggs littered the sidewalk and red carpet outside the Duchess, and guests exclaimed over them just as much as they did over our menu. I couldn't wait to actually start viewing the film, to see if my viewpoint lined up more with Alma's love for the film or the protestors' critique.

"Despite the interruption, I think we can call this evening a success." I hung back to observe the attendees noshing on our menu and sipping sparkling wine. Even Alma seemed to have settled down, and stopped to thank us for whipping together the event from the ashes it had been last week. She did cause Rachel to raise her eyebrows when she declared my sister's daringly cut ruby satin minidress worthy of Belle Watling. Thankfully, I didn't think Rachel was aware of the character's role in the film.

Guests sipped on lemonade, shandies, and mint juleps in addition to sparkling wine. There were fried green tomatoes and bite-size portions of the tarragon fried chicken Keith had been so smitten with. We'd repurposed the savory cheddar shrimp and grits into tiny puff pastry cups, and served the same pecan tartlets we'd dished up to Becca and Keith at their tasting. A photographer from the *Eagle Herald* wandered around snapping digital photos of all that could be considered the glitterati of Port Quincy, except for Helene, whose absence was notable. I'm sure after her dip in the pool at the hands of Alma's cane, she would never set foot in The Duchess theater.

And Garrett was missing too. I let out a sigh of relief as I finally got a return text from him, explaining that he was tied up with work and would join me soon. I caught a whiff of my sister's perfume, all sweet strawberry and musk, as she leaned over my shoulder to read my screen.

"That's too bad he'll be late. This would be the perfect occasion to propose."

I dropped my phone back into my purse with a

little yelp and stared at my sister. "Do you know
something I don't?" My heart began to beat a fren-
zied rhythm in my rib cage. If there was one thing I
couldn't handle, it would be a showy engagement.
Or any engagement, for that matter. I was happy to
lose those thoughts and attend to the small fires
that needed to be put out before the actual movie
showing began. We ran out of shrimp cups and
needed to bring out more, and had to attend to a
flooding toilet in the bathroom Jesse had re-
painted, as well as find an attendee's missing cell
phone. Rachel and I handled each mini crisis with
smooth aplomb.

I edged closer to a corner, where Jacqueline was
having a heated discussion with Rhett. I tried not
to openly snoop as I retrieved an empty bottle of
wine someone had dropped on the floor.

"And you can stop moping about her." Jacqueline's tone was pure acid as she strode away from
her husband. I wondered who the *her* in question
was and carried on with my tasks. It was finally
time to take our seats in the theater. I settled in a
plush red-velvet chair with my sister, who blended
into her seat with her similarly hued dress. I saved
a spot for Garrett and felt myself relax as the lights
dimmed. Alma had employed old-fashioned ushers, who moved down the aisles with flashlights to
guide latecomers to their seats. The ushers reminded patrons to turn off their cell phones, and
before the lights dimmed, Alma walked before the
red curtain at the front of the theater.

"I wanted to thank everyone who helped make
my dream come true to remodel and reopen The
Duchess theater." Alma beamed a nearly incandes-

cent smile over all seated in the audience. "I'll be showing one of the greatest films ever made, based, of course, on the incomparable novel by Margaret Mitchell. I hope it brings you as much joy as it has to me over these long decades." Alma shuffled off the stage as she received a rousing round of applause, and the theater finally went black.

"Thanks for saving me a seat." Garrett slipped in beside me moments before the opening credits rolled, and I squeezed his hand in the darkness.

I soon got lost in Margaret Mitchell's world. The sweeping score set the tone, reinforced by the panoramic vistas of a South long gone, if it ever really was the way it was depicted in the film. I found myself alternatively carried away by the emotions of Scarlett, as played by Vivien Leigh, to questioning the historical accuracy with disquiet for certain scenes viewed through the lens of the present. There was no doubt it was a grand film, with a history all its own. It was gorgeously and sweepingly shot, but there was enough to be uneasy about too. I watched the film with fresh eyes, at once extremely entertained, but also questioning. I saw the points of both Alma and the protestors.

I squeezed Garrett's hand harder as Rhett and Scarlett, larger than life, began their treacherous drive with a purloined carriage out of Atlanta as it fell, Melanie and her newborn in the back. Garrett slung his arm around my shoulder and pulled me in close. I involuntarily bit my nails as the poor horse on screen balked at walking among the burning embers of the city engulfed in flames. I watched with bated breath as Rhett gave the horse makeshift blinders, and they barely crossed. It was so believable, I could almost feel the heat and smell the flames. It was a truly magnificent movie, and I felt transported, my heart racing.

"What's that smell?" Rachel's bell-like voice rang out over the theater, and several people turned around to shush her.

Gasoline.

A slow flame licked up the edge of the curtain surrounding the screen, mirroring the flames depicted on film. The accelerant used quickly caught on, and the screen itself was soon engulfed in flames, both real and cinematic.

"Fire!" Someone voiced what we'd all just seen, and pandemonium officially broke out. Someone pulled the fire alarm to add to the melee, and the stampeding began in earnest. Rachel grabbed my arm, but we were soon separated. I felt stilettos jab into the top of my foot, and stumbled before Garrett hoisted me to my feet. The smoke was thick in the air, and I coughed as my eyes filled with tears.

"Wait." Garrett's voice was eerily calm as he pulled me lower to the ground and guided me down a row of seats. I could barely make out his actions as he poured some of his lemonade onto a napkin and pressed it to my face. The tangle of limbs of theatergoers pushing and shoving to leave finally abated in what must have been a mere minute but seemed like a lifetime.

"All right. Keep your head low. Are you ready?" Garrett spoke to me through a series of racking coughs, and we made a run, or rather a crawl, for it. We'd finally reached the exit to the lobby when I heard a weak cry to my left. I dimly wondered why it had started to rain on the inside of the theater, when I realized the sprinkler system had kicked in. Garrett pulled my hand as he desperately crawled the last few feet to the door. But I couldn't leave the person behind.

My lungs screaming for clean oxygen, I felt around me until I connected with something.

Alma's cane.

The distinctive silver top, fashioned as an acorn, was immediately recognizable. I dragged her small body toward the door with some inner reserve of strength and made it to the threshold.

After that everything went black.

CHAPTER SIXTEEN

I awoke on the sidewalk, cradled in Garrett's arms.
Right where I'm supposed to be.

The protestors were gone. The sky was a black-velvet canvas with a smattering of sequin stars. A brisk wind rustled in from the west. But what should have been a lovely evening was unquestionably, irrevocably ruined.

I was exhausted from dragging Alma from the smoke-filled theater. My muscles ached and my feet were sore from taking the brunt of so many stampeding, panicked theatergoers. My lungs were searing, and my eyes felt like a watery, rheumy mess. I was thankful for the oxygen mask first pressed to my face by the paramedics, and now by Garrett. All around me, women were shivering in their evening gowns and light wraps, boleros, and pashmina scarves. The night had grown cooler than expected. I shook violently, and realized I was freezing, having gone from the heat of the engulfed room, to getting doused by the sprinklers, to finally making it out into the now-cool night.

"Take this." Garrett shouldered off his jacket and tenderly wrapped my shoulders in the smooth wool.

"You're all right!" Rachel appeared at my side, and the oxygen mask fell to the concrete, forgotten, as I hugged and hugged my sister. I swiped away more tears and stared in disbelief at the black smudges left on my hands.

"Alma!" I suddenly remembered who I'd gone back to save and tried to stand on woozy legs.

"Sit down." Garrett gently pushed me back to the front stairs of the theater, then gently turned me around and pointed to the top of the steps. There sat Alma, with her own oxygen mask firmly tied to her face. She gave a weak wave, and an even feebler thumb's-up.

Thank goodness.

She was going to be okay. I'd thought she'd been unconscious when I dragged her out of the theater, but now I wasn't sure.

"Are you all right?" Truman's face appeared close to mine, and he peered intently into my eyes.

I nodded and tried to stand, helped by Garrett. We stood with arms wrapped around each other, taking stock of what had happened.

"This was most definitely arson." Truman could barely contain his anger, his usual investigator's attitude stretched too thin over the past week with its murder and attempts at murder.

"It was the protestors." Alma had slowly made her way down the steps to where we were, moving down each stair as she sat and held on to the railing. She stared up at us with reddened eyes and dirty, sooty water marring her once-fluffy corona of white hair.

"Unless one of the protestors disguised themselves as a theatergoer, I don't think that's the case." Truman was gentle in offering his opinion, but it still made Alma wince.

"All I've worked for is gone in a cloud of ash and rain." Alma appeared her true age of ninety for the first time since I'd met her. The strain from seeing her dream to fruition, then watching it all go up in literal smoke was too much for her. She began to weep.

"I have some good news." The fire chief knelt in front of Alma and gently lifted her chin from her hands. "Believe it or not, it could have been much, much worse. The fire was mostly contained to the curtains and the screen. Luckily, your sprinkler system kicked in. There'll be some water damage, and cleanup, and you'll need to repaint. But you should have The Duchess up and running in no time."

Alma's tears slowed to a dribble, and she thanked the fire chief profusely. "You're a true hero." She took in her granddaughter Becca, who had made her way over to see her grandmother. "Not like Eric."

"Grandma!" Becca took a step back from Alma and placed her hand over her heart. "I won't have you besmirching Eric's name."

Uh-oh.

Keith let out a guffaw, which turned into a string

of coughs. "Why not? It's me you're marrying, not Eric. If you can even remember that."

I took note of Keith's protestations, but my embattled mind was really interested in what Alma had said. What had she meant when she'd stated Eric wasn't a true hero?

"It's time to go." Garrett gently steered me to his car. Rachel slipped into the back, and we traveled to Thistle Park in his Accord, leaving the rented van we'd used to ferry over the food behind the theater. It seemed like ages ago, not mere hours.

Rachel ducked into the bathroom for a shower, and I waited my turn as Garrett wiped off my face and hands with a washcloth. His touch and his gaze were tender and full of affection and care. I nearly laughed at my previous worry about getting engaged.

Of course I want to be with Garrett.

"I'll be glad when this week is over, and you're done with Keith and Becca and her whole family as clients." Garrett let out a low chuckle and seemed to read my earlier thoughts. "If Keith and Becca are any indication of the sanctity of marriage, I can understand why you're hesitant."

He bestowed a tender kiss on my lips an hour later, after I'd showered, choked down some tea, and crawled into bed. As I fell asleep, I made quick plans for tomorrow. I'd skimp on breakfast fare, as our only current guest was Piper. I hoped she wouldn't mind I'd now be serving muffins, bagels, and bacon instead of the elaborate breakfast I'd posted on the B and B menu board. As I drifted off, a kitty cat ensconced on either side of me, I thought again of Garrett. I was so happy he was a part of my life, and that I was a part of his. There was no one else I'd rather want by my side.

Despite the events at the theater, I drifted off to sleep with a smile lilting at the edges of my lips.

"What in the world happened?" Piper gasped as she alighted on the bottom stair of the back steps leading into the kitchen.

Rachel and I shared a glance, taking in each other's red eyes, which was what Piper was no doubt commenting on.

"There was a fire at The Duchess theater's reopening." I moved to bring a plate of muffins and bagels into the dining room, when Piper stopped me.

"Sit down and relax." She clucked over Rachel and me like a mother hen and remained in the kitchen rather than taking the food to the dining room, where the B and B guests ate. She poured us the coffee we'd made to serve to her. "You poor girls."

She sank into a chair opposite us and her exquisitely shaped brows knitted together in concern. "Is everyone okay?" Her green eyes widened as she awaited the answer.

"Thankfully, yes. I had to go back to get to Alma, but everyone made it out."

A flood of relief washed over Piper's face. "I don't think this town can take any more tragedy." She selected a poppy seed muffin and stood. "I hate to grab and go, but I want to be there when Eric wakes up for the day."

"I'm so relieved Eric is doing better." I heard the grateful note in my voice as I met Piper's eyes. I would carry the image of her fiancé in the gazebo with me forever, and was thankful that he seemed to be on the mend.

Piper offered me a warm smile and smoothed down an errant lock of her pixie cut. "He'll make a full recovery." Her perfect 1940s movie-star smile dimmed a few watts. "I just wish he'd stop criticizing himself for not being able to remember what happened in the gazebo."

I felt my eyebrows involuntarily shoot up. "He doesn't recall who shot him?"

Piper shook her head, her frown now deeper. "He remembers following Pickles into the gazebo, and then waking up in the hospital." She blew out a puff of air that made her bangs rise from her forehead, then settle back. "Truman questioned him for hours, but it was all for naught. He can't produce a single detail."

We sat in silence for a whole minute, digesting this info, if not our food. Piper glanced at her delicate antique rose-gold watch and winced. "I really should head out."

Rachel and I bid Piper goodbye and tucked into the food she'd left mainly untouched. I was surprised at how famished I was but didn't relish the scratchy feeling still present in my throat.

A rat-a-tat-tat on the back kitchen door made my sister and me jump.

"It's just Truman." Rachel stood to let him in and poured him a cup of coffee as he sat down across from us.

"My son assured me you two were doing just fine,

but I wanted to see for myself." Truman doled out a gentle smile for me and my sister before helping himself to a bagel and a tub of cream cheese.

"We'd be better if we knew the person creating all this mayhem was behind bars. No offense." You could always count on my sister not to mince words.

"And I agree." Truman didn't seem offended and took a vicious bite of his bagel. "The attempts on people's lives are ratcheting up. Alma, Felicity, and Eric's attacks were on them alone. Whoever did this last night didn't care how many people they took out in their quest to wreak havoc."

A clammy feeling of dread welled up in my chest as I realized what Truman had just said. "You think the person who set fire to the theater meant to kill one person, and they were willing to kill everyone present to make it happen?" I was stunned at the escalation of terror being wrought upon us.

"It's not a stretch." Truman took a slug of coffee and set the cup down with some force. "But right now, I have to admit there are too many possible suspects for this latest incident."

"I bet it was the protestors." Rachel echoed Alma's sentiment and reached for her own bagel.

"We're looking into it," Truman admitted. "But my guess is, it's more personal." He scratched at his chin and seemed to ponder whether to share his theories with us.

I tried not to look too eager and carefully studied my coffee before raising the cup to take a sip. I'd just give Truman a little nudge.

"There's Tanner." I sat back and waited, turning Truman's interrogation technique around on him.

"Alma's husband tried to block his achievement of

tenure." Truman took the bait. "Maybe he wanted to destroy the theater because it was originally Glenn's dream to open it too. It seems like a stretch, but it's somewhat plausible."

"Or he wanted to get back at Alma herself, not just destroy the theater." I considered the possible motive. "Maybe he was mad that Alma wouldn't sell her collection to his fiancée." My reasoning sounded lame even to me.

"Or," Rachel mused, "he thought Alma murdered Felicity and was getting back at her."

We all chuckled at the thought of tiny Alma overpowering Felicity. I was glad the motives attributed to Tanner weren't airtight. His despair over the death of Felicity seemed genuine, and I didn't want to consider him a killer.

"But Tanner's not out of the woods concerning Eric's attempted murder," Truman said. "I just can't prove it yet."

I hoped he was wrong.

"But Tanner wasn't in the gazebo when Eric was shot," I reminded Truman.

The chief raised his brows. "That's not what some of my sources have said."

Interesting.

"What about Samantha?" Rachel retrieved her bagel from the retro chrome toaster and slathered it with a healthy dose of cream cheese. She turned her inquisitor gaze on me. It was double effective with her eyes still red and irritated from the fire. "Wasn't she ticked that Alma gifted her *Gone with the Wind* collection to Becca?"

I shook my head vigorously. "No, it can't be Samantha."

Or you just don't want to believe it could be Samantha.

I couldn't imagine the sweet woman wanting her own grandmother dead, even if Alma had rankly favored Becca by gifting her her prized collection. But a series of concerning details marched with precision through my head.

"What aren't you telling us?" Truman's tone was gentle. "C'mon, Mallory."

I took a deep breath, already regretting my words. "Last night, I noticed Samantha went into the actual theater way before anyone else. Like when people were still milling around in the lobby drinking and eating." I frowned and wiped up a trail of poppy seeds from a bagel. "But that doesn't mean she was up to no good. Maybe she just wanted to take a peek into the theater."

Truman and Rachel exchanged glances that told me I'd just said something more significant than I'd meant to.

"And there's more." My voice got even quieter. "When Alma didn't show up for Keith and Becca's initial tasting, we all rushed back to Tara to check on Alma." I reflected for a moment to confirm what I was about to say was true. "Everyone rushed up the path to get to the front door and make sure Alma was okay." I swallowed and met Truman's eyes. "Everyone except Samantha."

"So it was like she already knew Alma was in trouble."

Maybe.

Truman filed away the info in silence and nodded for me to go on. I realized the tables had turned. I'd wanted him to spill his insight and information, and he'd somehow gotten me to do the very same.

"Well, if we think Samantha could be targeting her grandmother over the collection, maybe Rhett is too." I recounted how peeved Rhett had been at the hospital when Alma gifted her collection to Becca, and how Jacqueline had confirmed it.

"And then there's Jacqueline herself," Rachel interjected and shook her head. "I'd be mad too if I owned half The Duchess and Alma hadn't let me plan a darn thing."

"Especially because she's the family film buff. She studied it in college, when Alma's true love of film seems limited to *Gone with the Wind* itself." I finished my coffee and tried to recall something else. "And I also heard her arguing with Rhett about something last night." My tired mind finally failed me. "But I can't recall any of the specifics." Another idea did surface. "I do know Jacqueline isn't happy with how differently Alma treats her daughters."

"But is that enough motive to kill?" Truman drained his coffee. "Is there anyone else you can think of that would want to hurt Alma Cunningham?"

"Well, there's Helene." She would never live down being pushed into the pool. "And Eric, if he blamed his marriage to Becca dissolving because of Alma." I slammed down my coffee cup in excitement. "And Alma said something last night about Eric not being a hero."

Truman smiled at this tidbit and stood to go. "Thank you, ladies."

We'd definitely been had.

* * *

After Truman left, Rachel and I spent the morning rehashing his theories as to the various motives, means, and opportunities of each suspect. It made our work freshening up the B and B more enjoyable and helped to pass the time. We'd gone from scrambling earlier in the week to make several events happen, to wondering if the next two weddings would even go on.

"If Becca is truly having second thoughts, she should just cancel her wedding to Keith right now." Rachel fluffed Piper's pillows while I headed for her bathroom to change out her towels.

"And if Eric can't leave the hospital in time for his wedding, that'll be a no-go too." I doubted Eric and Piper could go through with their large wedding even if Eric could leave the hospital on time. I couldn't imagine the recently shot man struggling through a big day of meeting-and-greeting guests and being up to the task.

Then again, he'd once seemed awfully keen to wed Piper. It was the only thing that had spurred him to finally get a divorce from Becca. That is, before his confession in the Greasy Spoon that he still had feelings for Becca. But maybe Eric and Piper would still want to go through with getting married in a few days' time, if not have a big wedding.

A kernel of an idea formed in my mind. "How far along are you on that online class to become a wedding officiant?"

Rachel stopped her fluffing. "I just have to take the final test, then I'm done."

"I have an idea."

An hour later, I was pulling my station wagon into the parking lot at the McGavitt-Pierce Memorial Hospital. I made my way to the ICU and peeked my head in Eric's room.

"Mallory!" Piper jumped up from her fiancé's bedside and gave me a quick hug. "Look who's here, sweetie."

Eric gave me a kind smile as I sat next to his bed. He appeared to be truly on the mend, despite the tangle of wires and IV lines hooked up to him.

"I can't wait to get out of here and marry this girl." He turned his gaze to Piper.

I had one answer. Eric probably didn't want to postpone getting married. His earlier ardor for Becca seemed to have dissipated.

"That's why I wanted to talk to you two. What do you think of getting married on the appointed day, even if you don't have your actual wedding?"

Piper nodded, seeming to warm to the idea. "We could marry right here in the hospital."

"Rachel can do it, if you'd like. And I'm willing to reschedule your reception for any date in the future when I have an opening." I liked this couple and wanted to accommodate them. "Or, in the alternative, you could just postpone getting married until you're all better, Eric."

"No!" He shook his head and turned to Piper. "I'll ask the doctors today when I can get out of here. If I'm able to leave, we'll go through with our wedding."

Piper tsked over her fiancé. "Is that really the best idea? The wedding will take a lot out of you, maybe more than you can give right now."

I had to privately agree. Eric seemed to grasp

the reality of the situation and sighed. "Fine. We'll see what the doctors say. They were hopeful I could be discharged as soon as tomorrow. If I feel well enough to go through with our wedding, I'd at least like to try."

Piper leaned down and squeezed her fiancé's hand.

"And if I'm still here on Saturday, Rachel can marry us."

"I can't wait." Piper dropped a kiss on Eric's forehead and headed for the tiny bathroom in the corner of the suite.

"How is Pickles?" Eric endeared himself further to me by asking about his cat.

"I think he's in good hands with Becca." It was true. He'd seemed content the last time I'd observed him at her home.

"And how is Alma?" Eric's voice was suddenly sly. "I read what happened at the opening of her theater."

I took a step away from the bed, not liking the gloating tone I picked up on in Eric's voice.

"She's fine, thankfully. No one was hurt too badly in the incident, although many suffered from smoke inhalation." Including yours truly. "And the theater didn't burn down, but there's some damage."

Eric shook his head in mock regret. "Alma would have an easier time of it if she treated people better. She's not the sweet little old lady people think she is."

"And why is that?" My heart pounded while I awaited his answer.

"She and Glenn never thought I was good enough

for Becca," Eric nearly spat. "They broke up our marriage. Isn't that enough?"

An icy rain of nerves danced down my spine. I tried to recall where Alma had been when Eric was shot. She'd claimed she'd lost the replica revolver, and I'd peered into her purse myself. But what if she'd just stashed the gun near the gazebo and attempted to murder Eric to keep him from sweeping Becca off her feet a second time?

Don't be ridiculous.

I barely kept myself from shaking my head at the preposterous turn my thoughts had taken. Alma may not have been a sweet old lady to everyone, but there was no way she was an attempted murderess.

"Piper mentioned you don't recall much about the incident in the gazebo." I tried to tread carefully and kept my voice neutral.

Eric let out a sigh laden with regret and rubbed at his eyes in a weary motion. "I can remember nearly every detail of each asylum case I'm currently working on back in Colombia. I can recall the exact moment I laid eyes on Piper." The weariness dissipated and a gentle smile lit up Eric's handsome face. But then a cloud of annoyance stole over his features. "But besides following Pickles out to the gazebo, I can't remember a single thing about being shot. Nothing."

I took in the anguished look on Eric's face and silently castigated myself for opening this line of questioning. I should just have let the man recuperate in peace.

I quickly bade Eric goodbye and slipped from

the room. But I couldn't get the thought of his anger toward Alma out of my head. I was glad Eric had been accounted for during the arson, safely tucked away in his hospital bed. I was starting to think if he hadn't, he'd be suspect numero uno.

I left the hospital and drove through the outskirts of town to Becca and Keith's house. Boxes containing the decorations for their wedding slid around in the wide trunk with each turn I took. Becca and I had made several trips hauling the loot into her living room, where we'd be finishing the centerpieces for her wedding.

If she and Keith even go through with it.

We put the finishing touches on the busy collections of ostrich feathers, pearls, lace, candles, glass fruit, and willow branches. Pickles had a grand time playing with the feathers, and Becca made no move to stop the big cat. I loved watching her interacting with the Maine Coon. It softened and humanized her, despite her usual prickly persona. And I had to chuckle at Becca's passive-aggressive ruining of the decor Helene had decreed by letting Pickles systematically shred each ostrich feather.

"Hello, Mallory." Keith descended the wide set of cutout stairs from the second floor of his mansion and gave me a cool stare. "Has Garrett made any headway on finalizing Becca's divorce?"

I was glad Becca's back was turned to her fiancé, so he didn't witness her rolling her eyes.

"Not yet." I was beginning to doubt Judge Frank would get around to reviewing and signing the papers anytime soon. And maybe that would play perfectly into Becca's new plans to possibly get back together with Eric.

"See to it that he does." Keith's tone was high-handed and haughty, and it was my turn to roll my eyes. Pickles dropped an ostrich feather and made his way over to Keith. He sent up a meow and twined around Keith's legs, looking for pats from the one person in the room who didn't want to dole them out.

"Shoo. Get away, Pickles." Keith took a step back from the cat, who ignored Keith and luxuriantly stretched against his khaki-covered legs. "Ouch! He scratched me!" Keith glared at the cat and angrily retrieved his golf bag from the corner.

"I'm out of here." He slammed the lacquered front door behind him.

"It's okay, pal." Becca buried her face in Pickles's luxuriant fur and glared at the front door. She absentmindedly worked the clasp of the cat's collar, failing to remove it as I had.

"That thing will need the jaws of life before it can be removed," I said.

Becca opened her mouth to respond when her cell phone trilled out from the table. The name *Judith* popped up on the screen.

Eric's mother.

Becca swiped at her phone and must have accidentally put it on speaker. Judith Dempsey's kind voice filled the room.

"I asked Eric the information you wanted, dear. He doesn't have a will."

Becca quickly colored and jabbed at her phone, silencing Judith. She held the cell to her ear and continued her conversation for a few more minutes, only now I wasn't privy to what was being said on Judith's end.

Why does she care about whether Eric has a will?

A sickening realization washed over me. Of course. Becca was still married to Eric, so she was the presumptive beneficiary of all his property as his wife.

And perhaps his presumptive killer.

Becca ended her call and turned to face me. "I guess wills are on my mind." She shrugged and picked up a glass peach to glue to a centerpiece. "I happen to be the executor of Grandma Alma's will." A rueful smile appeared on her face. "I didn't know I'd fail the bar twice, by only a few points each time. We all assumed I'd get to be an attorney, and I was still living in the States, unlike Samantha, so Alma made me executor." She waved another ostrich feather in Pickles's direction, and the Maine Coon executed an impressive balletic move to leap for the feather. "A month ago, before all these crimes started happening, Alma asked me to change the sole beneficiary of her will from my dad to my mom."

I cocked my head, not sure if I'd heard her correctly. What reason would Alma have had to change who inherited from Rhett to Jacqueline?

I must have worn my puzzlement on my face.

Becca nodded at me. "I was confused too."

Before I had time to ponder that tidbit of information, the doorbell clanged out notice of a new caller.

Becca left and returned with my boyfriend in tow. I sighed with relief when I saw Garrett.

"I thought I'd let you know in person the good news." Garrett bestowed a kind smile on Becca. "You're a free woman now. Judge Frank just signed the divorce decree."

I turned to Becca, not sure what her reaction would be.

Garrett mistook Becca's stunned silence for happiness. "Congratulations, Becca. You're officially divorced."

Becca sat on the couch, the wind seemingly knocked out of her at hearing the news. "I made a horrible mistake," she whispered.

"No. I'm the one who made a mistake." Keith strode into the room. "Rebecca Scarlett Cunningham, we're through."

CHAPTER SEVENTEEN

I was now thoroughly convinced the wedding decorations from my own defunct ceremony were bad juju. They hadn't been used in celebration of my canceled marriage to Keith, and now they wouldn't be used by Becca and Keith either.

"Now get out." Keith slid his golf bag from his shoulder and stood before Becca, his arms crossed.

"How dare you!" Becca screeched at Keith and tore at the diamond on her left hand. "You can't break up with me, because I'm breaking up with you!" She threw the ring down the long hallway, where it landed with a metallic *plink* and jounced across the smooth, glossy floor like a stone skipped across a pond. Pickles leaped after the bauble and batted it around on the marble.

"That's not how it works, Becca. As I recall, I just dumped you."

The two former fiancés argued for a good five minutes over who had done the initial breaking up. Garrett send me an incredulous look that turned into one of mirth as Keith and Becca went on and on. My ribs ached as I tried to stifle my laughter. I shouldn't have been happy about the dissolution of Keith and Becca's engagement, but it also meant this wedding was done, once and for all.

"Whatever, Keith. We're leaving." Before I knew what was happening, Becca had linked arms with me and started pulling me up the stairs.

"Um, what?"

Becca yanked me into the bedroom she shared with Keith and pulled suitcase after suitcase from under the high bed.

"I'm moving into the B and B." Becca dumped hanger after hanger bearing designer clothes into her cavernous suitcases, not pausing to gauge my reaction.

Like hell you are.

"Piper is staying at Thistle Park." I broached the subject obliquely. "Perhaps it would be better for you to stay somewhere else—"

"Let's go."

Garrett was a gentleman and made several trips to ferry Becca's last flotilla of luggage into the blue room back at the B and B. I sent up a silent prayer that Piper wasn't around. I wasn't in the mood to referee the same kind of tiff they'd had at the hospital when we'd all gotten kicked out. But I needn't have worried; the evening passed uneventfully. Becca enjoyed takeout in her room with Pickles, and Piper didn't return from the hospital until after Becca had presumably turned in for the night. I prayed Piper's allergies wouldn't start acting up now that Pickles was back in the guest portion of the B and B.

But I couldn't hide the fact that Becca had moved in for long. As the sunlight streamed across my comforter the next morning, I prepared myself for the World War Three that might ensue when Piper realized Becca had come to live with us at Thistle Park. Rachel left me to fend for myself as she attended her yoga class. I nervously fed Becca a breakfast of egg white omelet and turkey bacon, per her request. She sat at the kitchen table rather than the guests' usual seats in the dining room. Her dark hair part stood out more than usual against the dyed blond, and big bags lurked beneath her eyes.

"I can't believe I'm divorced from Eric and I've broken up with Keith." She picked at her food with listless hands and eventually shoved the breakfast away. "What am I going to do?"

I carefully sat down before her and pushed a cup of tea toward her. She took a fortifying sip and stared at me expectantly.

"What do you want to do?" It was a simple question I'm not sure would earn me a simple answer.

Becca sighed and ran a hand through her hair. "The truth is, I think I just went to law school because my sister and my rival were going. And then I realized I had to actually practice law." She made a face. "I wanted to pass the bar, but I couldn't do it in two tries. I just assumed I'd marry Keith and we'd make our life here." Her eyes grew wistful. "But then Eric walked back into my life. And now everything's changed."

Uh-oh.

What Becca failed to realize was that Eric may not have wanted her in his life, despite his mother's seeming preference for Becca over Piper. His close brush with death had seemed to renew his commitment to Piper.

A car door slammed outside the kitchen window, and Becca ran to see who had arrived.

"Eric!" She set down her tea and raced to the front hall to greet the man who had graduated from his hospital stay.

Double uh-oh.

Becca flung open the door and stopped herself from running down the porch steps in the nick of time. Piper pushed Eric in a wheelchair up the herringbone-brick walkway with an ear-to-ear grin on her face. Becca took refuge in the library, her face sullen and defeated. Piper took the long way up to the front porch, using the series of ramps at the side of the house to avoid the steps. She finally pushed Eric into the front hall.

"Welcome back." I gave Eric my hand and congratulated him on his recovery. I resisted the urge to turn to see where Becca was.

"I owe my health to this lovely lady." Eric impetuously pulled Piper onto his lap, and she let out a lovely laugh. "I can't wait to carry you over this very threshold after our wedding." Piper leaned in for a deep kiss, and I heard a soft yelp behind me. Becca stole into the hall and made for the back of the house. I distantly heard the kitchen door slam and wondered if now was the time to tell the two love-birds that Becca was also staying at the B and B.

"I have some interesting news." I heard the false cheery note in my voice and attempted to tamp it out. "First off, you're officially divorced from Becca Cunningham."

"Whoo-hoo!" Eric deftly spun around in his chair, Piper still giggling and ensconced on his lap.

"That's the good news." I waited for the spinning to stop.

"What's the bad news?"

"Keith and Becca broke up. She's moved into Thistle Park." I said it in a rush, hoping swift delivery of the bad news would somehow lessen the blow.

"She *what?*" Piper hopped off Eric's lap and began pacing the hall. "Absolutely not. I won't stand for it."

"Now, now," Eric soothed. "It's a great big house. We can just ignore her."

But Piper was already gone. She stalked away from Eric into the recesses of the house, leaving the two of us alone together.

"I can show you the new elevator," I added lamely. We'd just had one installed in a thin shaft of hallway at the rear of the kitchen, where the back staircase resided.

Eric gave me a kind smile. "Don't worry about Piper. She'll be all right. She knows I only have eyes for her."

But Becca didn't know that, and that was what I was worried about.

My ears picked up the sound of a vehicle out front, and I flung open the front door to witness Keith extracting more of Becca's belongings from the trunk and backseat of his BMW. A whiplash of déjà vu hit me hard. He'd performed the same ritual last summer with my things. Eric peered around me and couldn't resist coming onto the front porch to gloat.

"I'm sorry to hear about you and Becca."

Keith emerged from his car with a small bowl in his hand. "You don't know what you're talking about."

I held my breath as Keith advanced up the walk and the stairs to the front door.

"I think I do." Eric wheeled back into the B and B and tossed a final parting shot as he made his way toward the elevator. "Good news travels fast in Port Quincy."

I was left alone with Keith. I could sniff out some ulterior motive a mile away, stronger than his cologne.

"I didn't pack this. It's Pickles's favorite cat dish." He held up the small ceramic bowl embossed with purple and silver paws and began to walk it to the kitchen.

I eyed the bowl warily, thinking it was a Trojan horse kind of a cat dish, designed to get Keith through the door and into the house that had once belonged to his grandmother.

"Well, thanks so much. I'm sure Becca and Pickles will appreciate it."

But Keith made no moves to go. Instead, he dropped into a kitchen chair with a heavy sigh.

"I just wanted to talk."

Bingo.

I was willing to therapize the brides I worked with, and help them figure out knotty problems associated with their weddings. But I'd be damned if I was going to include Keith in my ministrations.

"I'm sorry you and Becca broke up. But this is a very busy time. You came here to drop off Becca's belongings, and you've done that. So it would be best if you'd go now."

Keith stood and placed his hands on my shoulders. "I made a grave mistake last summer."

Alarm bells clanged on DEFCON one and I attempted to slither out of Keith's grasp.

"You're the one I should be with, Mallory."

And with that Keith planted a kiss on my lips.

And all hell broke loose.

"Get off me!" I broke away from his octopus grasp and put five feet between us.

"You hussy!" Becca stormed into the kitchen with a look of vengeance etched on her pretty features. And behind her stood Garrett, a stunned and miserable look on his handsome face.

"Whoa, whoa, whoa." I turned in a slow circle, not sure whom to address first. "That was *not* a sanctioned kiss, Keith."

"I know what I saw." Becca crossed her arms in front of her, seeming to forget that she was no longer engaged to Keith.

"You heard the lady." Garrett took a step toward Keith, with murder in his lovely hazel eyes. "You can't just go around planting kisses on people who don't want to reciprocate."

Keith stared at me, then Garrett, and finally seemed to realize the gravity of his mistake.

"I'll be going now." His voice was small and dejected. He made his way out the back door, Becca trailing after him.

I crossed the room in three steps and buried my head in Garrett's chest. He wrapped his arms around me, and I knew then he believed me.

Garrett left almost as swiftly as he'd arrived. I'd assured him that Keith had forced the kiss, and being the wonderful, calm, and collected man I'd come to love, of course he knew it was true. The one person who didn't trust me was Becca. She stared glumly out from the parlor, but interestingly made no moves to leave.

"I never would've moved in here if I'd known you'd try to poach Keith the minute my back was turned." She glared at me from behind the cover of the Italian *Vogue* she was reading. I ignored Becca and retreated to the library. There was no use stating my position again that Keith had kissed me and not the other way around. I booted up my laptop and made a stop at the online version of the Port Quincy *Eagle Herald*. The screaming digital headline made my heart stop.

Area Man Arrested In the Attempted Murder of Eric Dempsey

The article was accompanied by a grainy mug shot of Tanner Frost, Felicity's fiancé. I skimmed the article in disbelief. While I'd had a hunch Tanner had argued with Eric in the gazebo that fateful Sunday of the Mother's Day tea, I didn't think it had been possible for him to shoot Eric. We'd ended our conversation before the shots rang out, but Tanner had been in my line of sight the entire time. I snapped the laptop shut and headed for the front door.

"Where are you going?" Becca's voice was plaintive and needy. I poked my head into the parlor.

"To the police station."

"You're sure you're not off to canoodle with Keith?" Her voice was laden with hurt. I stopped myself from rolling my eyes at the last minute and controlled my voice as well. "Don't be silly, Becca."

I willed myself to obey all the stop signs and traffic lights on my way to the Port Quincy jail. I got stuck behind a poky truck, and the trip downtown over hill and dale seemed interminable. I finally arrived at the jail and handed over my purse for inspection. I shuffled through the metal detector and soon nervously sat in the visitor's waiting room, not sure if Tanner would consent to see me. But after a ten-minute wait, Felicity's former fiancé was led into the room in an orange jumpsuit. The fabric was ridiculously loose for his skinny frame and hung off his body at weird angles.

"Mallory." Tanner took a seat across from me and folded his hands in front of him.

"I know you didn't do it." Our time was brief, and I wanted to cut to the chase.

"Which crime?" A rueful smile temporarily turned up one corner of Tanner's mouth. He was oddly professorial, even in his prison garb.

"Eric's attempted murder. I remembered I could see you in the garden when Eric was shot."

"Tell that to the police." Tanner seemed to scoff at my words.

"I intend to remind them."

"Well, I'm their man now, and I doubt they'll just let me go." He glumly picked at a hangnail and slouched down further in his metal chair. I wondered where his proud professor persona had gone.

"I shouldn't have been carrying around that stupid ring."

"The one they found in the gazebo."

Tanner nodded. "Felicity flung it at me the day she died. She told me she no longer wanted to get married." He took a deep breath and went on. "I knew she was having an affair. I just couldn't figure out who the guy was."

"Do you think he murdered her?" I was willing to bet if the police thought Tanner was their perpetrator for Eric's shooting, the assumption would be that he'd killed his cheating fiancée Felicity as well.

Tanner considered my query. He was silent for an excruciatingly long time, seeming to weigh his options. "Felicity was a mysterious woman. At first it excited me, but later in our relationship, it just became tiresome. She had so many secrets she wouldn't share, and now I can't piece them together to figure out who killed her."

"Like what?"

Tanner glanced around the room, but we were the only ones in the visitors' area.

"Well, for one, she started bringing peanut butter on her trips to Colombia."

"Peanut butter?" I frowned. "What could she want with that?"

"She told me she just wanted some snacks, and that it was hard to find what she wanted in Bogota. But I realized later she was probably smuggling something."

It fit. I recalled Truman's admission that Felicity had amassed a questionable fortune that didn't line up with her small salary at the family jewelry store.

"Did you tell Truman that?" I couldn't imagine the chief would hold Tanner if he knew the whole story.

Tanner let out a gruff laugh. "He has his man, and I'm it."

I tore out of the jail and headed on foot toward the municipal building that housed the police headquarters. I passed the pink palace of a courthouse on my way to the low-slung, 1960s' limestone building covered in the same soot Alma had powerwashed off The Duchess. I took the steps two at a time in my haste, and burst into the front office.

"Truman Davies, please."

I tapped my foot against a metal chair leg as I waited what seemed an endless amount of time but was really only twenty minutes. I couldn't expect someone as busy as Truman to be able to see me at a moment's notice. But an innocent man was currently reposing in the Port Quincy jail for a crime I knew he couldn't have committed.

"This had better be good, Mallory." Truman materialized in front of me. His bark was worse than his bite. He sounded annoyed, but the twinkle in his hazel eyes belied his good nature.

"Tanner Frost is innocent."

The kind look in Truman's eyes evaporated in a haze of annoyance. "Back to my office. Now."

I nearly trotted to keep up with his lanky frame as he made it back to his desk in record time.

He shut the door behind him and crossed his fingers in front of him. "And why do you think Tanner Frost is innocent?"

"Okay, so he probably was arguing with Eric in the gazebo. That'd be when I heard two male voices."

Truman nodded. "And?"

"And I'd just finished talking to Tanner about Glenn when the shots rang out. I could see Tanner walking away from me. It would have been impossible for him to shoot Eric then. He couldn't have been in two places at once."

Truman ignored my revelation and instead focused on the other part of my declaration.

"And just why were you talking to Tanner about Glenn Cunningham's death?"

I squirmed in my chair under Truman's microscopic gaze.

Time to come clean.

"Um. Because Alma sort of asked me to look around regarding the murder of Glenn."

"Dammit, Mallory." Truman hit his desk with his fist. A framed photograph of Truman, Lorraine, Summer, and Garrett jumped off the desk, then resettled. "Don't ever deputize yourself in one of these cases. What if the killer thought you knew something important, something you didn't even realize you knew?" His eyes welled up with concern. "I consider you to be family." His hazel eyes pierced mine, as caring and concerned as his son's. "I just don't want you to get hurt."

CHAPTER EIGHTEEN

Truman's declaration that he considered me to be family was like a knife twisted in my heart. I hadn't meant to deceive him or cause him any strife. I'd just wanted to help Alma. But now I saw I couldn't do both without the prospect of someone getting hurt. And his concern about the effects of my sleuthing made ice run in my veins. What if someone did target me, or someone I loved, as the result of poking around in places where I had no business?

I'd left Truman, but not without delivering a heartfelt apology. He'd grudgingly accepted it, but made me promise not to stick my nose where it didn't belong with renegade, unauthorized sleuthing. I'd vowed to stick to wedding planning rather than detective work and had shuffled out of his office with a dejected cloud hanging over my head.

I emerged from police headquarters to a light rain that had just begun to fall. The weather mir-

rored my chagrin, the sky a leaden gray. I turned
my face up toward the rain and let the light mist
cool my still-heated cheeks. I'd been so embarrassed to admit I'd been looking into the string of
violent crimes at the behest of Alma that my face
had still felt warm when I'd left Truman's office.

My phone snapped me back to reality. I answered a call from Rachel as I hustled back to the
Butterscotch Monster before I became completely
drenched.

"He's getting a ring."

"What?" My heart accelerated, and the sound of
a distant ocean came coursing into my ears with a
rush of blood to my head.

"I saw Garrett in Fournier's Jewelry Store picking out a ring! He's going to pop the question,
Mallory." Rachel's jubilation was easy to hear over
the phone, and I could picture her dancing a jig as
she informed me of the good news.

But was it good news?

I'm just not ready.

It was the truth. I loved Garrett, his daughter
Summer, and his family. But I didn't want to rush
into another engagement. Not to please my sister
or my mother. Not to adhere to an invisible timeline decreed by the denizens of Port Quincy. Not
to avenge my broken engagement with Keith.

A thought skittered through my mind. Truman
had said he was upset about the prospect of me
getting hurt because I was like family. My mouth
went dry. Maybe Garrett really was planning to
pop the question. And I was the last one to know.

Rachel's voice became more insistent. "Say something! Mallory, this is fantastic. I just knew your engagement would be right around the corner. We'll have a blast planning your wedding. I know you were going to wed Keith in June, but how do you feel about winter? It would be all cozy and fresh. You could have the small wedding you always wanted. Mallory? Are you there?" Rachel trailed off in a confused tone and waited for my response.

"How can you be sure Garrett is going to propose? Maybe he was in Fournier's for another reason. Like getting a new set of cuff links."

"Garrett doesn't wear cuff links, Mallory." Rachel's sigh was practically loud enough to be heard without the aid of the cell phone. "Tell you what. You seem skittish about this, even though it'll be the happiest time in your life, I promise. Let's just find out right now."

"You mean ask Garrett if he's going to propose?" My question came out in a high-pitched squeak.

"No, silly. We'll just pop on over to the jewelry store and find out what he bought for you. Easy-peasy."

"Rach, I'm not so sure that's a good idea." I'd just promised Truman I'd lay off the sleuthing.

My sister seemed to read my mind. "This isn't like prying into a murder investigation. We'll just drop some hints that you're the soon-to-be lucky lady, and we want to confirm that Garrett was indeed buying an engagement ring."

"Won't that ruin the surprise?" My breath was coming fast now, and I was trying to stall in any way possible.

"That's just it, Mall. You don't want this to be a surprise. I'll meet you at Fournier's in ten minutes."

My sister hung up on me. I jammed my phone into my purse and took the long way to the jewelry store, willing my pulse to slow down. Finding concrete evidence that Garrett was about to propose would make the possibility too real, and too near. I felt like I was on a collision course to a place in my destiny I wasn't sure I was ready to comprehend.

The light drizzle tapered off, and the sun showed its face from behind a break in the slate-gray cloud cover. A passerby gasped, and I followed her line of sight. A gorgeous rainbow stretched from the Monongahela River in an impressive arc over the town of Port Quincy. The lines of color were defiantly bold against the dark sky in the west, backlit by the rays of the newly emergent sun.

No matter what happens, it will all be okay.

I thought back to Garrett pulling me from the smoky depths of The Duchess theater, and soon after cradling me in his arms. About the first kiss we'd shared, and the joy of spending time with his daughter Summer.

A feeling of peace and clarity stole over me as I gazed at the rainbow. I would be ready for the next step, whatever that may be.

"You showed." Rachel grabbed my hand and gestured toward the window display at Fournier's. It was more subdued than Bev's riotous paean to spring but no less dazzling. A bed of rich brown velvet served as garden soil, where gems and sparkling wares reposed like newly planted seeds. A silver shovel and spade lay next to the display, and a watering can suspended from the ceiling poured out a rain of crystals suspended by invisible fishing lines, mimicking water droplets in the sun. The tiny prisms cast mini rainbows over the display, echoing the natural rainbow currently presiding over Port Quincy.

But Rachel didn't have time to marvel at the wonders of Mother Nature. "I can't wait to see what he's considering for you." Rachel nearly pulled me into the shop, where the tinkling of bells announced our arrival.

"Can I help you two ladies?" Roger Fournier greeted us with a failed attempt at a smile that didn't reach his dark brown eyes. I couldn't blame him for not feigning enthusiasm. His daughter was to be buried today.

"We were wondering where your engagement rings are kept." Rachel hungrily took in the glass cases laden with decadent jewels and rich platinum and gold.

"*Where* in the store?" Mr. Fournier raised one brow and gestured to the middle of the displays. I'll admit it was an odd-sounding request. "These four cases house our more traditional offerings. Most feature diamonds, although some contain gems like sapphires and rubies as complementary stones." He paused and seemed to try to get a read on Rachel. "Was there anything in particular you had in mind?"

Rachel's eyes twinkled conspiratorially. "It's for my sister," she said in a rush. "I saw her boyfriend in here, but he wasn't looking in these cases. I always thought he'd be a diamond man, but he must be getting her something more unique."

You'd have thought Rachel had pulled out a can of paint and begun spraying graffiti in the resplendent space. Mr. Fournier drew himself up to his full height and glared at my sister. "I will not be giving out information about what my customers have purchased."

Rachel blinked back in surprise and swiftly adopted a flippant tone. "It's not like we're asking for medical records. I just wanted to see for myself what he was considering."

"Young lady, an engagement is quite a serious affair. It symbolizes betrothal, and commitment, and a public declaration of fidelity and intent." Mr. Fournier took a deep breath and gathered further steam. "And it is initially an agreement meant for two people to agree upon. A sacred contract, if you will. One Fournier's has been a part of for over one hundred years, as my father and his father before him supplied most of the engagement rings in Port Quincy. So no, I will not be ruining the surprise of a beautiful symbol and start of a new journey for some couple. So stop snooping."

Rachel's mouth dropped open, then closed again. "I just thought it would be neat to see what he was considering for Mallory." Her voice was small and chastised. She appeared even more horrified when Mr. Fournier burst into tears.

"This is a bad time. I'm burying my only child today. Forgive me. I think you're asking about Garrett Davies. He was looking at this case." Mr. Fournier gestured to a glass shelf holding a row of pretty gemstone rings, all with an antique cast about them. But I didn't care about the rings, and neither did Rachel. She reached into her purse and handed Mr. Fournier a tissue, trailing the scent of her strawberry and musk perfume. He blew his nose and sniffed back another spate of tears.

"We're so sorry about Felicity." A wave of pathos welled up inside me for the jeweler. "I can't even imagine."

Mr. Fournier nodded. "You were there when she was found, were you not?"

I swallowed and gave a brief nod.

"I knew she and Becca were feuding over some silly *Gone with the Wind* wedding gown. But I never imagined it would lead to my daughter's death." He seemed to try to compose himself and closed his eyes. "But I didn't realize all the secrets Felicity was keeping either."

My mind immediately went to the affair Eric claimed Felicity had been having, the evidence she'd been smuggling something that Tanner had witnessed, and the mystery ring on her finger when she'd been pulled from the pool.

"She'd been getting letters." Mr. Fournier's eyes fluttered open. "I'll never forgive myself for not going to the police first."

"What kind of letters?" The words flew out of my mouth before I could stop them. Would Truman consider an impromptu discussion with the distraught jeweler to be a form of questioning?

"Threatening ones. I opened one that arrived in the store's mail rather than her loft apartment upstairs. It read, 'I know what you're doing, and you won't get away with it.'" He brushed a new tear from the corner of his eye and swallowed. "Felicity convinced me not to go to the police. And now she's gone."

So someone else had known about whatever nefarious activities Felicity had been engaged in.

"That still doesn't explain the second ring," I pondered aloud.

"What ring?" Roger Fournier's eyes clouded over as he seemed to realize he'd said too much.

"It's nothing," I mumbled. I grabbed Rachel's arm and made a move to leave. "I'm sorry we bothered you, Mr. Fournier."

Rachel and I spilled out of the jewelry store.

"That was a dressing-down I never expected to receive." Rachel straightened her black tank top and shimmied down her green leather mini. The exquisite rainbow that had ushered us into the store was gone in an ephemeral vapor. The sky was a strange composition of granite clouds in the west, with a clear blue canvas in the east.

"Mourning will do that to you." I was worried we'd further confused and perturbed Roger Fournier in this delicate time.

A woman burst from the shop and gripped my arm. "Wait. I heard you ask about Felicity's other ring." The woman who stood before me was like the other piece of the puzzle to Felicity's striking good looks. She vaguely resembled Vivien Leigh, as her daughter had. Her nose was petite, and her eyes were a delicately shaped almond. Her hair was raven black, whether from a bottle or naturally grown.

"I'm Felicity's mother, Polly Fournier." The woman confirmed her identity and looked nervously back into the store. Her husband was nowhere to be seen.

"Felicity was seeing someone else besides her fiancé, Tanner." Her exquisite features, barely touched by middle age, seemed to cloud over. "I heard her arguing with a man in the loft one day when I came up during a break. He said he wouldn't leave his family for my daughter. Not just yet, that is."

"Not until what?" I stared intently at Mrs. Fournier.

"I couldn't hear that part. And I told the police after she was murdered too."

So Truman doesn't really tell me everything.

"Whoever he was, he was bad for my daughter. She was slipping up at her job, her head no longer in her work. She accidentally worked on a large pendant and reset it with a lab-created stone rather than the customer's original emerald." She glanced back through the glass store display. "I'd never seen Roger more furious. I was honestly afraid for Felicity." She seemed to have realized what she'd said, clapped a hand to her mouth, and hurried into the store.

"That was heavy." Rachel and I had hightailed it back to the Butterscotch Monster.

"Tell me about it." My mind couldn't make up whether Roger Fournier was a grieving father or had committed the murder of his own daughter.

I gripped the steering wheel as I carefully pulled out of my parallel parking spot. It had taken me nearly a year of driving the 1970s' boat of a station wagon to master parking between two cars end to end on the first try.

"If you grip that wheel any harder, it'll turn into a diamond itself." Rachel laid her lacquered nails on my arm. "We need to relax. All of this mulling over murder is bad for the psyche."

"But we can't escape it." I cut the engine. "First someone tried to kill Alma, then succeeded with Felicity. Then death almost came to our doorstep when someone shot poor Eric."

"And don't forget Glenn," Rachel added Alma's husband to the list. We sat in the car in contemplative silence.

"I'm so keyed up, I'm about to explode." I rubbed at the throbbing that had materialized at the back of my neck. "Thank goodness the only event we have left on deck is Eric and Piper's wedding."

Rachel nodded. "Which will be low-key." Eric and Piper had agreed to keep their big day, despite Eric still being on the mend. He'd attend his wedding while still using his wheelchair, and I'd moved the seating arrangements so the bride and groom could spend most of the wedding sitting at the center of the garden. Guests would have easy access to the couple to wish them well, but Eric could remain seated for the duration of the reception.

"And everything is done," Rachel added. "We just need to do our night-before prep work, wake up, and throw them a gorgeous wedding."

I nodded, a trickle of relief washing over me. "And Keith and Becca's wedding is still one hundred percent canceled." I felt the beginnings of a smile.

"I think you should take a break this afternoon, Mall." Rachel reached into the backseat and retrieved the large bag she'd been carrying around. "Go to the gym. I have an extra change of workout clothes in here. Take a yoga or spinning class or something. Sit in the sauna. Just work out all the stress and relax."

That's not a bad idea.

Half an hour later, I was ensconced on a bike at the sleekest gym in town, Bodies in Motion. The cavernous space had been repurposed from one of the vast warehouses that had been used to house glass from the town's factory a hundred years ago. The gym featured chic, loft-style exposed ductwork beneath high ceilings, and banks upon banks and rows upon rows of the best machines and exercise equipment, all overlooking the wide expanse of the Monongahela River. It was the gym I sent choosy guests to, a place to see and be seen. Rachel loved to come to classes at the gym, but I could never seem to find the time.

It was something I'd have to rectify. I realized I'd been neglecting my sanity by taking on more events to fill each weekend. Rachel was right; we did need to expand, and to do that we needed to hire another assistant. I no longer resisted the proposition and pedaled harder, excited to begin the hiring process. I could spend more time with Garrett and Summer, with my sister, and with my thoughts.

But my mind kept spiraling back to murder. I pedaled harder, and soon found myself dripping with sweat, my mind going numb. I quickly showered and dried off, happy to shed the clothes my sister had lent me, which didn't quite fit. The punishing workout had done some good, getting my blood flowing; the dark circles the week had wrought under my eyes had largely disappeared.

I peered into a retro-looking trophy case housed in the locker room on the way out. A stained and yellowed photograph that looked like it had been clipped from a newspaper featured a smiling woman. She seemed vaguely familiar. The caption read, "Local girl makes Olympic team." I puzzled at the woman's face but was soon distracted.

"I thought you cleaned Felicity's locker out last week." An attendee with a clipboard stood in the corner of the dressing room. Her hand rested on her hip, clad in the Bodies in Motion uniform of black leggings, tight magenta tank top complete with script logo, and an electric blue baseball cap. She also sported a decidedly annoyed look. The similarly clad woman she was castigating gave a weary shrug and continued to pull items out of the tiny metal locker.

"Call me crazy, but I know I got around to it."

"Well, it's not like a locker can just fill itself back up, can it?"

I squinted to see what the employees were arguing about, and failed to stifle my gasp.

There on the bench lay what appeared to be a vintage yet pristine copy of *Gone with the Wind*. The second woman poured out the contents of a tube sock, and a passel of large, vivid Kelly-green emeralds rained out onto the tile floor and ricocheted around like ping-pong balls. A heavy-looking ring, encircled with sparkling diamonds and more emeralds, lay next to the jewels. Next came a small, leather-bound book. The woman drew out a last item from the locker with shaking fingers. It was a conventional-looking key, tied to a red ribbon.

Alma was right. Felicity strangled her and stole her collection.

"I think you need to call the police."

CHAPTER NINETEEN

"There's just one problem." Truman tented his hands together and peered at me over his fingers. "I was there the first time Felicity's locker at the gym was emptied." He gestured toward the small collection of riches that had been stolen from Alma, now unceremoniously stacked on a wooden dressing room bench. "And none of that was in there."

"So what in the heck is going on?"

"Someone wanted us to think Felicity attacked Alma." Faith Hendricks shook her head, her milk-maid countenance aglow with theories. "They didn't figure we'd already gone through Felicity's locker the very day she was found in Becca and Keith's pool."

"So someone planted the items here after they strangled Alma, and also after Felicity died." Truman couldn't fault me for weighing in this time. I'd called him from the dressing room to alert him about Alma's purloined, and now found, collection. I decided to press my luck by asking another question. "Who would want to implicate a dead woman?"

Truman raised one bushy brow. "Unfortunately, your guess is as good as mine. Felicity led a double life of sorts. We're still piecing together the puzzle." He ran a hand over his weary, lined forehead. "Mrs. Fournier mentioned an incident when Felicity accidentally reset a large emerald pendant with a lab-created replica." He motioned to the tidy pile of large emeralds resting on the bench. "It now appears it was no accident. Felicity may have been dealing in counterfeit gems."

I gulped and studied the pair of shoes I'd borrowed from my sister. They were two sizes too big, and I kept my head down to examine them.

"What aren't you telling me, Mallory?"

"I happened to be at Fournier's Jewelry Store today." I tore my eyes from the running shoes and blinked up at Truman.

"You *happened* to be there?" A glint of anger flashed in his eyes, but he kept it contained.

I couldn't very well tell him I'd been corralled into the jewelry store by my sister in order to find out what engagement ring his son may or may not have bought for me.

"Mrs. Fournier told me her husband was so furious about the damage the incident would cause their store and reputation that she feared for Felicity."

A dawning look of understanding swept over Truman's face. I braced myself for a dressing-down that never came.

"Thank you, Mallory."

Faith caught his eye and gestured toward me. "Oh, very well." Truman accepted the digital camera Faith proffered and scrolled through a list of photographs. "We found this item in Felicity's Jaguar."

I peered at the digital photograph of a small wooden bead.

"I've seen this before." I closed my eyes and pictured the tiny item being rolled around and around as a worry stone. I opened my eyes to find Truman staring into them intently.

"Where?"

"I'm sorry. I can't quite remember."

Truman seemed to deflate against the bank of small metal lockers. "It's all right, Mallory. It'll come back to you."

Faith accepted the camera back and slipped it into her uniform pocket. She glanced at the gray plastic running watch on her wrist. "We'd better hurry. Felicity's funeral is beginning soon."

"You can't stop me." Becca glared at me in the gilt front hall mirror as she adjusted a rope of tiny pearls. She was dressed in appropriate garb for a funeral, at least, in a tailored Escada pinstriped black suit, the skirt hemmed in a pretty ruffle.

"But you weren't even friends with Felicity!"

"Frenemies is more like it, but that's an actual category of friend." Becca fluffed her hair, her black part more visible than ever. She'd been neglecting her meticulous touch-ups in the wake of her split from Keith. She still managed to pull the look off well, making the extra wide contrast in tones look daring and purposeful.

"And as I have no ride, I was hoping you would take me." Becca whirled around from the mirror and stared expectantly.

"No way, Jose." There was no chance I would aid and abet Becca in causing a scene at Felicity's funeral. Felicity had been found in Becca's pool, and there were many in town who thought Becca had murdered the woman. "It's not all about you, Becca."

"Fine. I'll call a cab." She retrieved her cell phone from her tiny striped clutch and pulled up a screen.

"Oh, just give me a second to change." If I went with Becca to Felicity's funeral, maybe I could keep her in check.

Five minutes later, I appeared back in the front hall in a black suit left over from my days as an attorney. It wasn't as jauntily cut as Becca's, but it had a pretty, feminine flared skirt, and it would be appropriate for a funeral.

"C'mon." We left the three kitties ensconced in my third-floor apartment, lest we trigger Piper's allergies. It probably didn't matter too much, though, as Piper spent her days either holed up in the honeymoon suite, tending to Eric so that he would be well enough for their upcoming wedding, or driving him to his doctor's appointments. Becca finally seemed resigned to her fate of being divorced from Eric and no longer engaged to Keith. She listlessly wandered around Thistle Park, sneaking Pickles from the third floor and taking him on long walks around the grounds, a leash attached to his collar. I wanted to suggest she consider moving back in with Jacqueline and Rhett but could also understand why a twenty-five-year-old woman wouldn't want to return to her parents' house. With each day Becca remained at the B and B, I had less heart to evict her.

We pulled away from Thistle Park side by side in the Butterscotch Monster and headed to the Methodist Church on the west side of town. I nodded my approval as Becca tied a subdued gray scarf over her hair and its trademark part, and donned a pair of large sunglasses, which occluded most of her face. At least she wasn't trying to outwardly steal the show at her rival's funeral.

The sad event was already underway when we slipped into the back of the church. Roger Fournier and his wife, Polly, leaned on each other in the front pew. Mr. Fournier wept openly, but his wife was a pillar of silent strength. I couldn't imagine burying a child, and my heart contracted in pain for them.

Unless Roger Fournier is Felicity's murderer, and his tears are tinged with guilt.

I recalled Polly's admission in front of her jewelry store about Roger Fournier's anger at his daughter, and Truman's reaction to that tidbit of information. But before I could truly ponder the information anew, Becca's nails dug into the flesh on my forearm.

"Ouch!" I extracted her fingers from my arm and sheepishly looked down. My outburst had caused several people to look our way at the back of the pews. But my exclamation had nothing on Becca's. She stared transfixed at a figure standing at the back of the church. The man in question wore a fedora that didn't quite cover his longish, iron-gray hair. He worked a small wooden bead between his fingers and looked up with tears coursing down his face.

"Dad? What are you doing here?"

I realized in a flash of cognition that the woman I'd seen Rhett embrace in the hospital parking lot had been none other than Felicity. I hadn't recognized her from the back. And Rhett had been handling the wooden worry stone the day Alma came home from the hospital.

Rhett was Felicity's lover.

"How could you?" Becca screeched her accusation toward the back of the church just as the minister took his place at the pulpit. I grabbed Becca by the elbow and hauled her outside, Truman and Faith hot on our heels.

"He's getting away." Truman narrowed his eyes as we all watched Rhett throw his body behind the wheel of his Lexus and peel away from the parking lot, kicking up pings of gravel in his wake. I held a now-weeping Becca, who had just realized her father had been having an affair with her childhood rival. My stomach did a sweeping movement of disgust, and I shared her horror.

"Let's get you back to the B and B." I steered Becca back to my station wagon, walked her in a daze to her room, and gently deposited her in bed. She seemed in a state of shock. I made her a cup of strong tea and brought Pickles to her. The big guy seemed to sense some seismic shift had occurred, and showered Becca's face with kitty Eskimo kisses. She numbly patted the Maine Coon and studiously ignored her cell phone, which was blowing up with texts and missed calls.

The next day was more of the same, with Becca barely consuming the chicken noodle soup and toast I brought to her bedside. I talked to Jacqueline and Samantha about whether we should intervene. But Becca didn't want to leave Thistle Park, so I let her stay in her room, working on her state of shock. To make matters worse, there was one person Becca was willing to reach out to, and he wouldn't even deign to take her calls.

"I messed up. It took losing my dad forever to realize I also lost the love of my life." Becca stared ahead as she pet Pickles. I braced myself for a soliloquy about how she regretted finally divorcing Eric. But Becca had a different idea. "I realize now I belong with Keith. And it's too late."

Truman dropped by to speak with Becca about her father's affair. He stopped to check in with me in the kitchen before he left. "That poor girl's a mess."

I poured Truman a cup of coffee and motioned for him to sit down. "She's been through a rough two weeks." Becca may have broken up my engagement to Keith what seemed like ages ago, but I wouldn't wish what had happened in the last fortnight on my worst enemy. "Have you arrested Rhett yet?"

Truman scowled and took a bite of the macadamia nut cookies I set before him. "The scoundrel absconded from Port Quincy. We have an all-points bulletin out for his arrest, but no one can find him. Jacqueline is no help either. She's glad the cheating joker is gone."

I dipped my own cookie into my scalding coffee and took a bite. I'd spent the morning finalizing the preparations for Eric and Piper's wedding, and welcomed the break to chat with Truman. "I wonder if Rhett tried to strangle Alma and stage it as a burglary."

"That's the working theory," Truman agreed. "Alma had always planned to bequeath her *Gone with the Wind* collection to Rhett. She suddenly changed her mind and gave it to Becca, and we think it was to punish Rhett for his affair with Felicity."

"And that's why Alma also changed her will to leave the rest of her property to Jacqueline instead of Rhett," I offered, recalling Becca's admission of that fact. "But why did Rhett kill Felicity?"

"Polly Fournier overheard her daughter arguing with a man in her apartment." Truman didn't know I'd already heard that from Polly herself. "It sounds like from the bits she heard, Rhett was planning on leaving Jacqueline after Becca married Keith and the big wedding was over. But that wasn't fast enough for Felicity."

"So she had to go," I whispered. A sickening knot of disgust formed in my stomach. I no longer wanted my cookie.

"We initially thought her murder might have something to do with her smuggling emeralds from Colombia." Truman didn't have any trouble finishing his. "She'd visit Eric and Piper in Bogota, buy emeralds on the black market, and place them in jars of peanut butter so she wouldn't have to declare them to customs. Then she'd sell them to buyers back here in the States, and upon delivery, she'd switch the emeralds out with lab-created fakes."

"And then sell the real ones again, earning twice the profit." It was a clever scheme.

"Eric had no idea," Truman said

"Except Felicity's father, who didn't quite buy that she'd accidentally switched out a created emerald for a real one." I took a sip of coffee. "And Tanner may not have known about Felicity's emerald swapping, but he did know about her affair with Rhett." That would explain his bizarre behavior after Felicity's body had been removed from the pool. Truman had the good graces to blush at the mention of Tanner. The young professor had been released from jail this morning, now that he was no longer accused or suspected of Felicity's or Eric's attempted murder.

"The ring on her finger must have been from Rhett," Truman agreed. "There are just two problems that still need to be resolved." He stared out the window at the copse of trees that hid the gazebo. He held up his index finger. "One: If Tanner didn't try to kill Eric, who did? And two, who planted Alma's collection and a copy of her house key in Felicity's gym locker after her death?"

I pondered those questions long after Truman left, as I put the finishing touches on what I hoped would be a beautiful day for Eric and Piper. My happiness at creating some joy for at least one couple was marred by my concern for Becca. A crazy plan began to formulate in my head to try to get Keith to at least return her calls.

CHAPTER TWENTY

"I wonder if impersonating a love letter is unethical." I glanced at my sister in the rearview mirror as we pulled away from the KFC drive-through.

"Who cares? This idea is brilliant." Rachel ripped the top off the bucket of chicken and delicately selected a drumstick. She bit into the meat and leaned back with a contented sigh.

"Um, leave some for Keith. If you eat too much, he'll know Becca wasn't behind this. She would never touch the stuff." I resisted selecting a delicious piece of chicken for myself lest I leave the steering wheel of my station wagon greasy.

"Fair point." Rachel finished her drumstick and placed the cardboard top back on the bucket. "But do you really think he'll believe Becca typed a love letter to him too?"

"She's pretty persnickety. I could see her choosing to print one out rather than write it by hand."

Rachel and I parked the station wagon on a cul-de-sac one over from Keith's McMansion and stole over to his property with stifled giggles and our bucket of fried chicken reconciliation. Thankfully, Keith's navy BMW was parked outside.

"We'll need to run to the trees behind that house." I pointed to Keith's neighbor. I hoped they didn't have some kind of fancy motion detectors on their property. I knew I'd sound insane if we were caught and had to give an explanation.

"Do you really think this'll work?" Rachel first pondered the bucket of KFC, then Keith's colossal Cubist house.

"I dated Keith for several years. And the way into his heart is paved with fried chicken."

We tiptoed up the front walk and deposited the chicken and the note we hoped Keith would believe was from Becca, respectfully begging for a second chance.

"One, two, three." I rang the bell, and Rachel and I booked it across Keith's manicured lawn, around the back of his neighbor's house, and into the woods, *Charlie's Angels* style. We made it out of the neighboring cul-de-sac without causing a fuss, and collapsed inside the station wagon with a gale of laughter.

"Let's just hope for Becca's sake that Keith takes the bait." I drove through downtown Port Quincy on our way home, and considered the events of the last few weeks as a stoplight grounded me in front of Fourier's Jewelry Store.

"There he is again!" Rachel hissed, and grabbed at my arm.

Garrett was just leaving the jewelry store, a small parcel tucked under his arm.

I gulped and willed the traffic light to change.

"Mallory." Garrett made his way over to the sidewalk and motioned for my sister to roll down the window. Because our wagon was from the 1970s, she actually could roll it down. "You two look like you're up to no good."

"You don't even know the half of it." Rachel giggled. She then gestured toward the small box in Garrett's hand and opened the passenger door. "I think I'll just walk home from here."

Oh no, oh no, oh no.

"Rachel, get back in the car."

But my sister was already on the sidewalk, sending me a big wink as she turned and headed in the direction of Thistle Park.

"What's going on?" Garrett slipped into the passenger seat just as the light changed, and I pulled through the intersection and parallel parked one street over.

"I'm not sure. Do you want to tell me?" My heart was pounding as I willed myself not to look at the tiny jewelry box. It seemed to contain virtual kryptonite, and every second in its presence ratcheted up my heart rate.

Garrett slid the top off the box and revealed a bed of velvet. A slim amethyst band nestled within.

"Do you think my mother will like this?" He held the ring up to the light. "It's Summer's birthstone. She has one for my birth month, and I thought it would make a nice belated–Mother's

Day gift. I had to do some sleuthing to figure out her ring size without her getting suspicious."

My fears dissolved into laughter, and I showered Garrett's face with kisses. He grinned in return, and pulled me in for a real scorcher.

"I hear the rumors around town too, Mallory." His hazel eyes grew soft and tender. "And while some day I'd love to make an honest woman of you, I want you to be an equal part of that decision." My heart beat with a different kind of excitement at his words. "I'll never pressure you. You'll know when I'm ready to take the next step, because it'll be when you are too." He grinned and pulled me closer. "I like things just the way they are."

"And I do too."

I dropped Garrett back at his car and found my sister halfway home to Thistle Park. I pulled the car over to the sidewalk, and Rachel hopped in. I drove away from the curb with what I was guessing was a dreamy smile on my face.

"Let's see it." She grabbed my left hand from the steering wheel, causing me to swerve wildly. Thankfully, no one was in the opposing lane.

"There's nothing to see!" I righted the boat of a station wagon and triumphantly waggled my naked and ringless finger in my sister's face.

"He didn't do it?" Rachel slunk back in the worn leather, utterly defeated and dejected.

"It was a grandmother's ring for Lorraine." I crowed out my answer and laughed until the tears ran down my cheeks. My sister crossed her arms in a pout over her chest as we pulled into the long drive in front of Thistle Park.

"Well, I'll be damned." I cut the engine behind Keith's navy BMW.

There he stood, my former fiancé of a year ago. He held the bucket of chicken under one arm and a bouquet of lush pink peonies under the other. He raised a bullhorn to his lips and took a steadying breath.

"Rebecca Scarlett Cunningham. Please give me another chance."

The sash of a second-floor window flew up, and Becca stuck her head out the window. "You came back!"

"I'd like nothing more than for you to be my wife." Keith echoed the same proposal I'd heard him deliver to Becca back in October, also not coincidentally the same line he'd once delivered to me. But the echo didn't bother me anymore, and I couldn't repress the grin spreading across my face.

"I'll love you till the day I die, Becca. You and your crazy cat."

Becca disappeared from the window, and sixty seconds later, the front door of the B and B ricocheted open. Becca ran down the stairs and threw herself into Keith's arms.

He planted a mad kiss on her lips, and when they surfaced for air, a wide smile broke out on Keith's face.

"You had me at fried chicken."

Ten minutes later, my newly ordained sister put her online-officiant credentials to good use. She married Keith and Becca out in the garden, with me and Pickles bearing witness. The bride wore jeans and carried the bouquet her groom had brought her. The vows were charmingly simple.

"Do you?" Rachel turned to Keith.

"I do." He wiped at the corners of his eyes and gave his bride a beatific smile. He seemed at peace standing in his khaki shorts and polo shirt, without the trappings of a big society wedding.

"Do you?" Rachel squinted against the low angle of the sun casting its last rays over the sea of crown vetch and clover in this largely untamed section at the garden's edge.

Becca paused, backlit from the sun, ethereal and lovely even in her casual garb. Keith took in a sharp breath.

"I do." Becca leapt into Keith's arms, and he spun her around and around. Pickles watched with contented interest, blinking his large citrine eyes.

The happy family of three sped off in Keith's BMW, where we'd placed a hastily drawn "Just Married" sign and tied cans of Pickles's cat food hanging down from the bumper.

I raised my hand to high-five my sister.

"All's well that ends well."

The next day dawned clear and bright. I was thrilled Piper and Eric's big day had arrived with no more murders, hiccups, or roadblocks. Eric felt well enough to attend his own nuptials, and even stood at the head of the aisle as he awaited his

bride. The wedding went off without a hitch, the
garden a vision in navy, cream, and silver, with the
flowers and foliage complementing the chosen
color scheme. Becca had grudgingly allowed Pickles to attend his former master's wedding, and the
pretty Maine Coon returned to Thistle Park for
the afternoon, this time clad in a kitty-cat tuxedo
for his second wedding in the span of a day.

Guests milled about the backyard and garden
paths after dining on salmon, gazpacho, and devil's
food cake. We'd decided not to feature the gazebo
in this backyard wedding; Eric's attempted murder
was still so fresh in all the guests' minds.

I gathered a bit of trash that had blown from a
guest's table near the edge of the garden and
placed it discreetly in a bag.

"Meow." A plaintive cry emanated from the
gazebo.

Pickles.

I now knew the distinctive cat's voice and
rushed to the scene of Eric's shooting. The sweet
kitty was caught on a spindle that had come loose
from the ornate gingerbread trim.

"Hold still, big guy." I worked at Pickles's collar
but couldn't get the sturdy leather to budge. "Just
a little longer, buddy." I extracted my keys from
the pocket of my dress and worked the threads of
the sharpest one against the thick collar. Pickles
wasn't in any dire trouble, but I could tell he was
getting uneasy with his collar holding him fast to
the spindle.

"There." The Fort Knox of a collar finally popped
off and rolled onto the floor of the gazebo. The

underside of the collar gleamed with fat green gems, a passel of priceless emeralds.

"Just what do you think you're doing?" Eric loomed in front of me at the entryway of the gazebo, gasping and grasping at his side.

CHAPTER TWENTY-ONE

"Give me the collar." Eric slid down a gazebo pillar and held his hand out. I took an instinctive step back and gave the big Maine Coon a pat. He ran off, hopefully acting as a cat Lassie to warn the others I may need some backup.

"Why were there emeralds sewn into Pickles's collar?" My voice sounded high and thin, and I willed myself to calm down.

"Because emeralds are the perfect vehicle to smuggle money out of Colombia." Eric sent me a nasty grin as he drew on some inner reserve of strength and struggled to stand. "Too bad Felicity never found out about this cache of beauties."

"You killed Felicity." It made sense. Felicity had traveled several times a year to visit Eric in Bogota. She dealt in counterfeit emeralds, and Eric must have been in on the ruse.

But he wasn't about to admit his guilt, even though he'd been caught.

"No, no, no." He shook his head and slid back down the pillar. Perhaps he hadn't been well enough to make it through his entire wedding after all. "Although I should have when I had the chance."

I winced at his words and edged closer to the gazebo railing. I felt my heart flutter up into my throat when Eric pulled out a gun.

Keep him talking.

"What did you and Felicity use the emeralds to smuggle?" I was genuinely curious, in addition to trying to prolong my life.

"Why, my excellent legal skills." Eric let out a maniacal laugh and attempted to clarify. "I take on immigration and asylum cases for fees that aren't exactly . . . ethical." He finished, "I have a perfect track record gaining asylum for each of my clients, but they have to beg, borrow, and steal to pay my price." He winced in pain. "To get the money out of Colombia and to my bank account here, we use emeralds. I'd clean my money by buying them in Colombia, and Felicity brought them back here. She was supposed to sell them, take her cut, and deposit the money into my account."

"But she swapped most of them out for lab emeralds, and kept the real stones to sell for herself. She was double dipping." I wondered what Truman would think of Eric's part in this plan. If I lived long enough to tell him about it. A thought skittered across my brain. "Did you try to kill Alma too?" It would make sense.

"That old bag and her husband knew something I was doing wasn't aboveboard, but they couldn't figure out exactly what." He spat out his words. "But that didn't stop them from blackmailing me into leaving Becca. I should have stood my ground."

"So you tried to kill Alma when you got back to Port Quincy in retaliation. Did you arrive earlier than I thought?"

Eric shook his head, as convincing an actor as I'd ever seen. "Wrong again, Mallory. I did pull a little prank on the witch right before we met at the Greasy Spoon." He went on when he saw the confusion on my face. "I painted the skull in the bathroom, and ruined the paint. But that was it."

I almost believed him.

"Then who tried to murder you in this gazebo?"

Eric shook his head, suddenly seeming exhausted. "I don't know. Tanner and I did fight before I got shot. He wanted to know what my business was with Felicity. He even accused me of having an affair with her. But then he left." He paused and frowned. "The only thing I recollect is that the person who shot me smelled of lemons."

He grasped his side and groaned. "It's too bad you had to meddle, Mallory. I can't just let you leave here and tell all my secrets to Truman, now can I?"

He made a final rally to aim the gun at me and promptly passed out.

Eric was carted away from his own wedding, first to the hospital on an ambulance stretcher, and several days later to the Port Quincy jail, when he was well enough to be booked and processed. He'd overdone it at his wedding, both when he'd been a cheerful groom celebrating his new marriage to Piper, and when he realized I'd cut off Pickles' collar in the gazebo and attempted to silence me forever.

"And to think we were congratulating ourselves on hosting a wedding for the only normal couple in the bunch." Rachel poured me a cup of coffee with shaking hands. I took a sip, grateful to be alive. Rachel and I were enjoying our breakfast on a wrought-iron table in the garden, drinking in the late-May sunshine and soft breeze.

"Hello, Dale." I sent a smile to the local gardener who tended to Thistle Park's blooms with skill and immense care.

"Sorry to hear about the wedding last night." Dale pushed a wheelbarrow over with several slim bushes resting inside.

Good news travels fast.

"We're all okay, and that's what matters." Rachel stood and peered into the wheelbarrow. "What are these?"

"Lemon verbena." Dale extracted a handkerchief from his back pocket and wiped at his brow. "The ambulance at the Mother's Day tea took out a host of plants, and I wanted something to fill in those beds."

I leaned down to take in the sweet, subtle lemony aroma of the plants.

Eric claimed his shooter smelled of lemons.

"It's Alma's scent, isn't it?" Rachel showed off her keen memory as she pulled back from the plants.

"Oh my God." My sister was right. Alma had announced to us the day she came home from the hospital that she wore the same scent as Scarlett O'Hara's mother.

"Yes, it is her scent. I've planted a whole host of lemon verbena at that ridiculous Tara of hers." Dale cracked a smile. "Although Alma plants a fair bit of her garden herself."

A panicked feeling raced over me. "Are you sure? Isn't she a little frail for that?"

"Oh no." Dale shook his head. "Why, Alma was an Olympic swimmer back in the 1950s. She's still as strong as an ox."

Strong enough to drown someone in a swimming pool.

"Rach, we have to go."

CHAPTER TWENTY-TWO

"We should wait for Truman." Rachel gestured toward Tara as I cut the engine.

"But he isn't answering his texts." It was a first, and I chastised myself for being surprised. He had a life too. Rachel and I waited for fifteen minutes in the Butterscotch Monster before we decided to see if Alma was even home. We rang the bell and got no answer.

"Let's check the back." I pressed on around the side of Tara and found myself staring at an immense pool.

"Scarlett O'Hara surely didn't have one of these." Rachel let out a low whistle.

Alma swam the length of the pool with long, powerful strokes. A prickle of recognition welled up in the back of my mind. I remembered the trophy case with the yellowed photograph touting a local girl making the U.S. team. The pretty young woman in the brittle photo had been Alma. The woman may have been frail when she tried to walk, but she was like a fish in the water.

Alma came up for air at one end of the pool and finally realized she had an audience. "Hello, girls. What brings you to Tara?"

I decided not to mince words. "You killed Felicity Fournier."

It fit. Even at the age of ninety, Alma was a skilled swimmer, strong enough to overpower Felicity in Becca and Keith's pool, especially if Felicity had been weighed down with the voluminous dress.

Alma blinked thrice, then let out a barking laugh. "Are you *insane?* I would never ruin a replica Scarlett O'Hara gown!" Alma splashed away as if, well, I'd just accused her of murder. When she'd reached the other end of the pool, she spoke again.

"I made it look like *she* tried to murder *me*. But I didn't kill her."

"You faked your own attack?" Rachel wore a genuinely puzzled look on her pretty face.

"I had to." Alma sighed and leaned on the ledge of the pool. "Felicity was badgering me morning, noon, and night to buy my collection. I didn't think she had the funds to make a proper offer, but I was wrong."

"Why not just get a restraining order against Felicity, like a normal person?" I couldn't keep the acid from my tone.

Alma gave a mirthless laugh. "I couldn't get a restraining order against Felicity when it came to my son Rhett."

"You planted your own collection in Felicity's locker after she died."

Alma nodded. "I didn't kill her, but I wasn't sorry she was gone. I thought it was the perfect opportunity, after I'd already faked my own attack, to finish the ruse and place my items in her locker."

"How did you fake an attempted murder on yourself?" Rachel stared at Alma in frank confusion.

"I just used a rope to make the neck marks, and took caffeine pills to speed up my heart. Something had to be done about Felicity. She was rubbing it in my face that she was going to marry Rhett, bide her time until I died, and end up with my collection anyway." Alma sniffed with disdain. "She even showed up here to flaunt the ring Rhett gave her!" She carefully climbed up the steps in the shallow end and exited the pool. "I'm no killer. I just wanted her out of the picture, that's all."

"So you were willing to frame an innocent woman to get your way." I was disgusted with Alma, even though I believed she hadn't killed Felicity. But she wasn't off the hook regarding Eric.

"And why did you try to kill Eric?"

Alma rolled her eyes and reached for a towel. "I'm telling you, I'm no killer. I didn't want him sniffing around my Becca, but I didn't shoot him."

"But his killer smelled of lemons." I gestured toward the lemon verbena growing all around the pool. "It's your signature scent."

A tiny detail wafted up from my subconscious, took flight, and nearly slipped away.

Lemons.

Someone else had grated up a tidy pile of lemon rind for us the day of the Mother's Day tea.

Wilkes whined somewhere inside the house.

"Does he hear us? I thought Wilkes was deaf." I turned to see the pretty Irish Setter exit a large doggy door to come join us at poolside.

"He is," Alma affirmed.

I realized who else had knowledge of Wilkes's disability. Someone who, in the heat of the moment, when her own fiancé had been shot, had once said the sweet dog couldn't even hear a gunshot.

"Who started the party without me?" Piper rounded the back of the house with a canister of something in her hands.

"Rachel, call 911."

"It's too late for that, Mallory." Piper pulled a gun from her pocket and trained it on my sister. "Drop the phone, Rachel."

My sister dutifully complied. Wilkes took one look at Piper and began a keening whine. He'd recognized Glenn's killer from a year ago. The sun was setting fast. It was hard to see at first, until some lights on a sensor clicked on. I wished they hadn't when I got a look at what was in Piper's other hand. It was a gasoline container. Piper held the plastic can like a designer purse, gorgeous as usual. With her old-timey film-star good looks, she could pass for a femme fatale. Literally.

"You ladies just don't know when to stop meddling." Piper grabbed Alma roughly by the arm and pushed her down onto a chaise longue. She took out a skein of rope from her trench and tied

Alma to the chair. With the threat of her gun, she repeated her actions with Rachel and me.

"I was just coming over to take care of Alma, but I see now I'll have to finish you all off." Her voice was cold, clear, and methodical. She whipped off the cover of the gasoline can and began sloshing the pungent liquid all over the bottom of Tara.

"You set The Duchess on fire." I struggled to loosen my hands from Piper's skilled ties, and only succeeded in giving my wrists a rope burn.

"I had to." Piper paused her dousing routine and gave a shrug. "Alma was bound to figure out someday that I'd killed Glenn. Plus, you'd been nosing around where you didn't belong too."

"You were willing to murder an entire room full of moviegoers?" Rachel's voice was disgusted and disbelieving all at once.

"Too many people knew too much," Piper reasoned.

"Why did you kill my poor husband?" Alma moaned from her chair, violently shivering in the now-cool air since she'd exited her heated pool.

"Glenn didn't mean to introduce me to Eric. It just so happened I met Eric the very day your husband paid him off to leave Becca. Glenn knew Eric was helping to provide asylum only to clients who could pay him a fortune, all while pretending to run a charitable organization for human rights. Glenn didn't want his dear, darling granddaughter mixed up in Eric's schemes. I was waiting to meet with Glenn to get some feedback on a paper for grad school and ran into Eric on his way out." A sick smile lit up her pretty face. "And the rest is history." Her face fell. "But later on, Glenn decided he didn't want his star student dating his former son-in-law. So he had to go."

Alma let out another wail and thrashed against the ropes holding her down.

"You impersonated Alma and told each vendor the theater gala was off."

"Very good, Mallory." Piper shrugged. "I didn't want Alma and Glenn's dream to come to fruition." She was on a roll. "And Felicity was getting too greedy. Eric found out she was replacing the emeralds he sent with her with lab replicas. I wanted Eric to get out of the gem smuggling business, move back here, and let me defend my dissertation and live a normal life."

Um, there's nothing normal about you, Piper.

"But Felicity wouldn't let Eric out of their deal. So she had to go too."

I realized then the woman Felicity had argued with in the Silver Bells dressing room had been Piper. Piper must have texted Felicity and summoned her to Becca's house under the guise of selling the Scarlett O'Hara wedding gown.

"And you tried to kill your own fiancé too."

Piper had grated a mountain of lemon peel for us the morning of the tea.

She nodded. "Very good, Mallory. I realized Eric might leave me for Becca. And he wasn't going to allow us to move back from Colombia. We had a deal. He'd get to work his scheme until I finished my dissertation. Then we'd move back to the U.S. and I'd get a position, and we'd be on the straight and narrow. But he reneged. So I stole Alma's stupid replica gun and shot him." Her wicked grin returned.

"And now it's time for you all to go." She struck a match and held it to the perimeter of the large white house. It quickly took hold, engulfing the whole back of the structure in flames.

Piper grunted as she pushed Alma's chaise into the water. The heavy metal chair, with Alma atop it, made a loud splash. It sank like a stone, and I gulped as I watched the tiny woman flail underwater, unable to break the surface. Next Rachel fell into the pool, and suffered a similar fate.

"Goodbye, Mallory." Piper pushed me into the pool. I gulped in water in a panic and kicked at the ropes tying me to the chaise. It was no use. My lungs filled with water. As my panicked brain screamed for oxygen, I recalled a laughing Becca three weeks ago, when Helene had toppled into the pool at Alma's hand.

Just stand up.

I struggled to grasp the edge of the pool and managed to right myself. I still stood doubled over because I was tied to the chaise, but I could just barely keep my head above surface. I pulled Rachel's chaise, then Alma's, to the stairs leading out of the pool, as they choked up lungs full of water. Piper stared in disbelief, right before Wilkes nudged her into the water. In the distance, sirens blared.

EPILOGUE

I felt lucky to be alive. Truman had finally checked his texts and came to the rescue. And three weeks later, I made good on my promise to Rachel to both expand our book of business and hire another assistant. On a warm June evening, I had enough time to go on a date with Garrett. We were catching a late-night screening of *The Wizard of Oz*.

We arrived at The Duchess theater just in time to purchase our tickets and grab a bucket of popcorn. Jacqueline waved from the ticket booth, the proud new owner of the business. Jacqueline planned on screening a colorful mix of old classics, art pieces, and current indie film hits. She'd sold out every showing her first month of helming The Duchess. She'd happily taken over because Alma was too busy with the community service projects she'd been sentenced to for faking her own assault. Rhett had slunk back to town a week after the local paper detailed Piper's arrest for Felicity's murder. He was no longer suspected for murder, and he tried to woo Jacqueline back, but she was firm in her decision to kick him out. Last I'd heard, he'd moved into Tara with Alma. The mother and son pair deserved each other.

Eric and Piper were safely tucked away, languishing together in the Port Quincy jail, sentenced to many years between them for their various schemes and crimes. The depth and dizzying web of mayhem they'd spun in their short time back in Port Quincy still baffled me as I reflected on the past two weeks. Piper's desperation to keep Eric had led her to murder Glenn a year ago, and her desperation to return to the States had driven her to murder Felicity and try to kill her fiancé. She was single-minded in her pursuit to get her way, at any cost, and I could sleep better at night with her behind bars.

I'd watched Pickles while Keith and Becca took an impromptu honeymoon in the Poconos after their quick nuptials in my kitchen. I was wistful as I drove the big Maine Coon back to his owners, and had nuzzled his head and his sweet, tufted ears as I rang their bell. Becca had flung open the lacquered door and received her cat, a dazzling newlywed smile lighting up her face. As I'd turned to go, a sleek Cadillac screeched to a stop in the circular drive. A figure exited the car and sprang up the walk.

"You ruined everything!" Helene quickened her pace, a menacing, white-hot look of anger boring into me.

I gulped and took a step back, putting a small topiary cone of a tree between us.

"Mother, I won't have you talking to my wife

that way." Keith materialized in the doorway and took Pickles from a shaking Becca's arms. He seemed to have thought Helene was blaming Becca, but I thought she'd directed her accusation at me. Becca sent Keith a look of tender affection, and I could practically see the steam rising from Helene's ears.

"But—"

"No exceptions. You can accept Becca as my wife, or I don't need you in my life." Keith sent Helene a pitying gaze, then shook his head as his mother gave a strangled yelp, tore down the path, and threw herself behind the wheel of her Cadillac. I'd restrained myself from giving Keith a high five, but instead gave Pickles another pat, inwardly cheering. Becca had mouthed a quick thanks and sent me off with a wink, and I left the newlyweds to start their new life together. The altercation with Helene had been a few weeks ago, and I'd been fortunate enough not to cross paths with her since.

June was shaping up to be serene and calm, my life settling back into mellow predictability.

I squeezed Garrett's hand as he ushered me down the red carpet to our seats. He leaned over for a tender kiss in the brief gap of time between the lights dimming and the start of movie previews. I felt cozy and safe, elated with the state of things just as they were, happy to be in Port Quincy and following my own yellow brick road.

RECIPES

Cherry Almond Cake

Ingredients:
1¾ cup flour
1 cup white sugar
½ cup cocoa
1 tsp. baking soda
¼ tsp. salt
¾ cup oil
1 12 ounce can cherry-flavored cola
1 tsp. almond extract

Directions:
Preheat oven to 350 degrees. Grease and flour a 9 x 9 pan. Sift together flour, sugar, cocoa, baking soda, and salt. Mix in oil, cherry-flavored cola, and almond extract. Bake in pan for 45 minutes, or until a toothpick or knife inserted in the center of the cake comes out clean.

Cherry Icing

Ingredients:
½ cup shortening
1 tsp. almond extract
3 cups powdered sugar
¼ cup cherry-flavored cola

Directions:
Beat shortening and almond extract together until light and fluffy. Add powdered sugar until mixed well. Slowly add cherry-flavored cola and beat for several minutes.

Pecan Cookies

¾ cup coconut oil
¾ cup brown sugar
2 tsp. vanilla
2 cups flour
1 cup finely chopped pecans

Directions:
   Grease a cookie sheet and preheat oven to 350 degrees. Beat coconut oil, brown sugar, and vanilla until smooth. Slowly add flour and pecans. Beat until smooth. Roll spoon-size portions of dough into balls and slightly flatten. Bake for fifteen minutes.

Connect with

Us

Visit us online at
KensingtonBooks.com
to read more from your favorite authors, see books
by series, view reading group guides, and more.

Join us on social media

for sneak peeks, chances to win books and prize packs,
and to share your thoughts with other readers.

facebook.com/kensingtonpublishing
twitter.com/kensingtonbooks

Tell us what you think!

To share your thoughts, submit a review,
or sign up for our eNewsletters, please visit:
KensingtonBooks.com/TellUs.

Romantic Suspense from
Lisa Jackson

Absolute Fear	0-8217-7936-2	$7.99US/$9.99CAN
Afraid to Die	1-4201-1850-1	$7.99US/$9.99CAN
Almost Dead	0-8217-7579-0	$7.99US/$10.99CAN
Born to Die	1-4201-0278-8	$7.99US/$9.99CAN
Chosen to Die	1-4201-0277-X	$7.99US/$10.99CAN
Cold Blooded	1-4201-2581-8	$7.99US/$8.99CAN
Deep Freeze	0-8217-7296-1	$7.99US/$10.99CAN
Devious	1-4201-0275-3	$7.99US/$9.99CAN
Fatal Burn	0-8217-7577-4	$7.99US/$10.99CAN
Final Scream	0-8217-7712-2	$7.99US/$10.99CAN
Hot Blooded	1-4201-0678-3	$7.99US/$9.49CAN
If She Only Knew	1-4201-3241-5	$7.99US/$9.99CAN
Left to Die	1-4201-0276-1	$7.99US/$10.99CAN
Lost Souls	0-8217-7938-9	$7.99US/$10.99CAN
Malice	0-8217-7940-0	$7.99US/$10.99CAN
The Morning After	1-4201-3370-5	$7.99US/$9.99CAN
The Night Before	1-4201-3371-3	$7.99US/$9.99CAN
Ready to Die	1-4201-1851-X	$7.99US/$9.99CAN
Running Scared	1-4201-0182-X	$7.99US/$10.99CAN
See How She Dies	1-4201-2584-2	$7.99US/$8.99CAN
Shiver	0-8217-7578-2	$7.99US/$10.99CAN
Tell Me	1-4201-1854-4	$7.99US/$9.99CAN
Twice Kissed	0-8217-7944-3	$7.99US/$9.99CAN
Unspoken	1-4201-0093-9	$7.99US/$9.99CAN
Whispers	1-4201-5158-4	$7.99US/$9.99CAN
Wicked Game	1-4201-0338-5	$7.99US/$9.99CAN
Wicked Lies	1-4201-0339-3	$7.99US/$9.99CAN
Without Mercy	1-4201-0274-5	$7.99US/$10.99CAN
You Don't Want to Know	1-4201-1853-6	$7.99US/$9.99CAN

Available Wherever Books Are Sold!
Visit our website at **www.kensingtonbooks.com**

Books by Bestselling Author
Fern Michaels

___The Jury	0-8217-7878-1	$6.99US/$9.99CAN
___Sweet Revenge	0-8217-7879-X	$6.99US/$9.99CAN
___Lethal Justice	0-8217-7880-3	$6.99US/$9.99CAN
___Free Fall	0-8217-7881-1	$6.99US/$9.99CAN
___Fool Me Once	0-8217-8071-9	$7.99US/$10.99CAN
___Vegas Rich	0-8217-8112-X	$7.99US/$10.99CAN
___Hide and Seek	1-4201-0184-6	$6.99US/$9.99CAN
___Hokus Pokus	1-4201-0185-4	$6.99US/$9.99CAN
___Fast Track	1-4201-0186-2	$6.99US/$9.99CAN
___Collateral Damage	1-4201-0187-0	$6.99US/$9.99CAN
___Final Justice	1-4201-0188-9	$6.99US/$9.99CAN
___Up Close and Personal	0-8217-7956-7	$7.99US/$9.99CAN
___Under the Radar	1-4201-0683-X	$6.99US/$9.99CAN
___Razor Sharp	1-4201-0684-8	$7.99US/$10.99CAN
___Yesterday	1-4201-1494-8	$5.99US/$6.99CAN
___Vanishing Act	1-4201-0685-6	$7.99US/$10.99CAN
___Sara's Song	1-4201-1493-X	$5.99US/$6.99CAN
___Deadly Deals	1-4201-0686-4	$7.99US/$10.99CAN
___Game Over	1-4201-0687-2	$7.99US/$10.99CAN
___Sins of Omission	1-4201-1153-1	$7.99US/$10.99CAN
___Sins of the Flesh	1-4201-1154-X	$7.99US/$10.99CAN
___Cross Roads	1-4201-1192-2	$7.99US/$10.99CAN

Available Wherever Books Are Sold!
Check out our website at **www.kensingtonbooks.com**